Blo

N.L. Hoffmann

Cover Design by Heather Senter at Book Cover Artistry

Blood Slaves

Copyright © 2014 by N.L. Hoffmann

Acknowledgments

I would like to thank everyone who supported me in my writing. Thank you Mom, Dad, Anna, Stefanie, Hannah, Aunt Wendy, Jessie, Ella, Deb, Sarah, Brittany, Krystal and Tiffany. Without you guys I would have chosen to stay hidden. Even though my work will eventually expand as I gain experience, it is because of you that I am starting somewhere.

Extra special thanks to Mom and Dad for inspiring my creativity. Without you guys I probably would have never tried. I love you both.

Thank you Aunt Wendy for having my back and encouraging me along. Love you.

My proofreader Alicia at AVC Proofreading.

Chapter One

It was a horrible way to die.

My breath left me as I laid there thinking the same words over and over again. I saw flashes of faces in front of me, none of them familiar, but then why would they be? This wasn't my life playing before me. I was trying to scream, but nothing would come out because of someone choking me in my vision. Right when things would go dim, the air would rush back into me, bringing me back to consciousness. With brutal intensity it would release, leaving nothing but a burning sensation in my throat and lungs while I gasp for air. Blinding pain from my limbs overrode the burning causing them to now feel like someone was taking needles to my legs and arms. I screamed only to hear laughter echo through my head from whoever was doing this to the victim.

It was impossible for me to even move. My only options were to wait it out and ride the pain because whenever I had a vision it held me hostage until I saw what was meant to be seen. It would end eventually and hopefully there would be no more suffering.

The pain was too much for me to bear and it began to feel like I was on fire, every nerve ending screaming for mercy as they set ablaze. The process repeated over and over again as the victim was continuously tortured in the vision I was having. The picture I was seeing would go dark, I was unable to breathe, and then I would be back again to feel pain.

"Blake!" Someone yelled. It wasn't as loud as the laughing, maybe I imagined it. Probably. It was unusual that someone could bring me out of a vision if the pain was a big part of the experience. Pain was like a drug and I craved it despite my desperation to prevent the feeling. Abruptly, the agony receded and pleasure rippled through my body as power filled it. I purred like a lover touched during foreplay.

Again! That was what the demon half of me was screaming. We had to have it again. The greedy bitch begged to have some more. Sure it was my half-self, but come on! Last thing I needed was to show the boss that the pain his niece suffered was actually a huge turn on for me. I couldn't help it, but he wouldn't understand that.

Then my whole body began to shake. Seizure? Odd, never had that happen before. I blinked several times, my vision coming into focus. My boss, Carter Roark's face appeared, looking concerned. Was there ever a different look from the man when it came to me? Hell no. Seemed like I was always in trouble, and he was always filled with worry. It was like a toddler taking her first steps, and he was afraid I would hurt myself. He always had this irrational fear that I would go out of control and kill myself.

My body shuddered as the final flow of energy disappeared. I felt good. More than good, but in my heart I felt guilt and sickness for even feeling sensations that were better meant for sex and not from someone else's pain. I was half demon which gave me the ability to experience visions of torture and death. Sometimes it was just flashes of potential violence, not always involving pain. Having visions was helpful when gathering information, but my demon's sick need for it was a problem for me. My vampire and demon were all about destruction. It took every ounce of me to prevent the crazy from coming out. I could destroy a whole city and still feel like I needed more to conquer. All I wanted to do was inflict pain while bathing in it, like a kid in a mud puddle. My two halves were like two different people having to share a single brain. One gets the left and the other gets the right. Almost like the light and dark devil thing.

"What did you see?" Carter demanded, his face filled with fear.

I tried to respond, but my throat was dry, so talking was out of the question until someone gave me water. As if reading my mind, Carter snapped his fingers. He accepted a glass of water from one of his agents and then handed it to me. He helped support my back off the floor, allowing me to gulp it down. While I drank it, I debated how much I should tell him. He was related to the girl I had visions of, so anything I had to tell him would probably cause a reaction opposite of winning the lottery. It was his niece, and she came up missing just a few hours ago. His sister thought she ran off with her boyfriend, but after realizing her purse and cell phone were still in her room, it became obvious there was foul play involved. Every once in a while a vampire got lucky and had a child. It was extremely rare, so if one goes missing it was big news.

There were a few theories on what could have happened, but I knew for sure what it was. She had been kidnapped by the Covert. The Covert was basically vampires gone rogue, but it was organized by someone who chose to deal with the criminal life. It was suspected he used to be someone high in society before something happened causing him to "act out." But of course that was only speculation. We lacked proof of any sort, other than the girls who would disappear and the bodies that would then reappear.

Their top income was a sex and blood combination. They kidnapped supernatural and human girls to sell them into slavery mainly for blood, but who was to say what really happened to them during that time. The customers were most often vampire. Essentially, they became a source of food for vampires who had an appetite for the unusual experience of holding someone against their will without having to hunt for the perfect victim. Hunting with their degree of violence was illegal under the vampire laws. It was actually illegal under human laws period without consent, but often there were ways around it. It could be overlooked in emergency situations. They had to take the time to clean up the memories to avoid the wrong type of exposure.

A lot of times these girls were victims of raves, where the outcome usually was death from so many vampires feeding off them. It was like a gang rape by fang and sex. Vampires associated their food with sex because of the amount of pleasure involved. The victim usually feels the pleasure if the vampire allows it. It all has to do with the vampire saliva. Glands release the appropriate amount of hormones needed to subdue the victim by overwhelming their senses. Like a predator attracting its prey. The ages of the victims varied, but usually the girls taken remained under the age of thirty.

It was an old business, and you would have thought they'd be caught by now. But that had a lot to do with the fact the girls were usually from the streets, where they wouldn't be missed. Some saw it as doing the humans a favor by cleaning up the criminals, whores and the homeless. Only now the Covert was going for ones that were important to society, women who would be missed. My only guess to why is whoever is behind the Covert was looking for a war.

Setting my glass down on the floor, I shook my head. It was sad to think it took something this drastic to raise a few eyebrows. I knew now this was going to be my case. Carter thought of me as his best agent, and no I am not full of myself. He seemed to rely on me a lot of times. I think that had to do with the fact he raised me like his own daughter. Of course, I was always willing to please him, I owed him a lot for the life he provided me. He had no one at all, so I tried to be there for him as much as possible, even though he liked to deny the need.

"The Covert has her." I responded finally.

Carter swore releasing me. I caught myself before my head slammed into the floor. One of the other agents, Ben Strayer, stifled back a laugh, avoiding my gaze. Time for a beat down. "Mister I am too big for my britches" was going to be at the suffering end of a prank if he didn't watch himself. I think he was long overdue. We were like brother and sister half the time, wrestling in the middle of the office area, which often led to Carter yelling at us, then making us sit on separate sides of the room. The whole time we would be making faces at each other. Carter knew, because he would yell at us to stop and slam his door to ignore the next tussle.

Another one of the agents, Luther Fryer, offered a hand so I could climb to my feet. I accepted his hand, tossing a glare in Ben's direction. He only grinned, making me want to punch him in the face. Taking a deep breath, we moved to follow Carter, who was already outside heading toward the car. Swearing, I jogged down the stairs from Lucy's room to catch up before Carter did something stupid. The man wasn't known to be reckless, but when it came to family, he went to extremes. It had a lot to do with his past. Anyone who knew his past was sure to avoid him. Now there was a direct attack which meant whoever is in charge of the Covert wants to cause Carter pain, to make him react without thinking.

Carter wasn't in the car. I saw he was over on the other side of the street looking over the edge of the hill. He was my boss, the one in charge of the SCD, Supernatural Crime Division within the FBI. I took a minute to admire the profile of the man who took care of me when my mother abandoned me. You would think he was seriously old, which he was, but not on the outside. To anyone who didn't know him he looked twenty-five, but in vampire years, he was over a thousand.

Carter knew I was coming up behind him, but he continued to stare out over the hill, watching how the moon reflected off the pond. When I came up beside him he just grunted, nothing on his face giving away what he was feeling. He looked like George Clooney, but younger. He probably could have been a real ladies man, but he never even bothered with them since his wife died nearly two hundred years ago. It was that incident that caused him to turn around his life. Secretly he blamed himself. What would a vampire be without the depressing self-blame attitude? Then I reminded myself about the pink loving bimbo at work. Apparently, he was okay with having her around. I did not want to know everything they did together.

"We have to find her." He said softly, shoving his hands into his pockets.

"I know." My heart clenched to see him so miserable. When my mother disappeared, Carter taught me everything. He taught me how to be the vampire part of me and helped with adjusting to the unknown changes that came with the demon half. We had been through a lot, so it pained me to not have an immediate solution for him. He deserved an easier life. Even with his change of lifestyle, the pain just kept on coming.

He abruptly turned to me with a fierce expression causing me to step back. "You have to go undercover."

Okay, wasn't expecting that. Old vampires were always so dramatic. I wanted to ask him how the hell he expected me to find the Covert? No one knew how to get in contact with them, let alone know who the leader is. "Okay…"

"We have been watching Nick Black for a while now. There are rumors about him having a pretty active social life. All which haven't been legal." He turned back out toward the pond. "I want you to find out as much as you can."

Sighing I stared at his profile. "Every vampire is into something illegal. I don't see the point in wasting time on him, Carter. We would know if one of the directors was being a bad boy."

He shrugged. "I would agree if it weren't for the dead girl found in his room three nights ago. Normally we would have let that go, but now under the circumstances, I can't help but wonder if there is more going on. This isn't the first time."

We started walking back to the car where he opened the door, letting me slide in first. I frowned, wishing I could pull my panties out of my crack, but not possible with everyone watching me. Looked like I had an uncomfortable ride ahead of me! Seriously, they needed to invent something that prevented wedgies. If not for situations like this, then for the nerds of the world that receive it on a daily basis from the oversized bully.

When he slid in and closed the door, he continued talking while watching Ben and Luther climb into the front of the car. Luther always drove. It was probably safer, since I couldn't imagine Ben being serious long enough to drive us to safety. Odds are he would see something shiny and go after it.

"He often hangs out at a club where the Covert recruits. One of his guards is suspected to be the go-to man when joining them. We are not sure if Nick knows this, but how a Director can be oblivious to such things has me wondering." His eyes darkened, fury once again sparking to life. "Normally I would say arrest the Guard, but I think it is best to go undercover and infiltrate the Covert. If you can get in, then we can shut the whole thing down."

Nodding, I listen carefully, making sure I got all the details. "Tomorrow Nick is holding a formal event at the headquarters. It is a masked event, so I guess I can plan for that." My anti-socialness was beginning to overwhelm me already just thinking about it.

The car pulled out onto the main road, merging into the night traffic. It was Saturday night, so a lot of the college kids from the local university were heading out to the clubs. Something I never experienced, but didn't really have the desire to. I liked kicking crime's ass more than being the university whore. Remembering I should be concentrating on my new assignment, I turned to Carter.

"So, even if I do get into this party, how do I get onto his Guard?" The only people he kept around him were the staff that took care of the cleaning and cooking, the rest were part of his Guard. The last time I heard him adding a new person was way before my life began. Everyone on the Guard was powerful. Usually powerful vampires led their own lives, but these guys were part of his line. His line meaning those he turned himself. A lot of them came from the army he led in wars.

Ben raised his hand. "Ooh! I know!"

Rolling my eyes I pointed at Ben as if we were on a game show or in a classroom. "Yes, Ben?"

He straightened, pulling the lapels of his coat straight. "We set up a situation where it seems as if Nick's life is in danger." He sounded an imaginary horn from his lips. "And then Blake to the rescue. We all know how Nick likes to recruit the best of the best for his cavalry."

I grinned. "So you will be one of the guys that attack Nick? And then I can beat your ass?" I asked, trying to sound hopeful.

Ben rolled his eyes, "Please, as if." He sounded like a damn valley girl. "Anyway, I am one of Carter's men. He would recognize me. I am like, famous." In a way that was probably true, since Ben came from a long line of European vampire royalty. When he became old enough, he instantly decided to rebel against his uncle's desire for him to take over in Europe as the head honcho for Germany's headquarters. Good ole' Ben ran off accepting a job from Carter.

Gazing out the window, I frowned thinking about how much more complicated my life was about to get. Undercover work was hard and something I tried to avoid. When Carter reached over for my hand I looked at him. His eyes were dark with sorrow. Damn it. I was sucked in.

"Who told you that Nick's guard is the go to man at the bar?" I asked him, laying my head back on the seat.

Ben peeked around the corner and waved a hand. "Me. I went to the werewolf alpha's club and saw him holding those white cards for the raves. I wouldn't have seen it if it weren't for him dropping the cards on the floor." He rolled his eyes. "What a douche. I never saw him before, so I can't really say who he is."

"And how do you know he is part of the Guard?" I asked skeptically. Ben's information was hardly ever reliable. He was good to have out in the field when it came to taking down a criminal, but any other time his information was lacking in some way.

He hesitated slightly and finally said, "Because I asked the bartender who he was and he told me it was one of Nick's guards."

Frowning, I thought about that. He probably had a lot of guards. If it were that easy, why don't we just question the guard that was spotted or just follow him to see if he can lead us to the Covert? I looked over at Carter who was staring down at the floor. It was because Carter didn't know if he could rely on Ben's intel. My fellow agent was known for making up things to make it look like he could get one up on another agent. It was really rare that Carter sent him out to do something without the aid of another agent. Still, we had only one lead, so someone had to follow it.

Carter wanted me to do it because he knew I wouldn't screw it up. Ben would probably go way overboard, costing his badge along with Carter's in the process. He was green despite his long history in law enforcement and as a vampire period. Sometimes that happened, but there was no denying that he was a good agent though, however, limited his skills were.

We were probably heading back to Headquarters where Carter would give me all the information he could think of on Lucy and the Covert. He would then probably give me Nick's file, making sure I knew everything about him. Unfortunately, most people were not familiar with his past and that included the SCD. Every vampire likely had a past, but some of them were worse than others. Carter's was full of blood, stuff he refused to tell me. It was something you kind of learned with vampires. Even being one, partially, myself, I end up getting frustrated because they want to be secretive. It just ends up getting shoved into the vampire's mind vault if he turned a new leaf. It was even rarer for anyone to get a glimpse after one reinvents themselves.

Streets of Lansing were not as attractive as the city would like to claim. Over the years, they did a lot of renovations by adding better walk ways, paying for stores to clean up the store fronts, and redoing the sewer systems so when it rains the flooding would minimize. Certain parts of the city were scarier than others, a lot of the crime happened on the North Side. Some say Waverly Road was the worst off because of the lower income taking cover there. Graffiti was on the walls of a lot of the closed down businesses. Even more everyday now that the economy was hurting businesses.

If I had to pick a favorite part of the city, I would say downtown with all of the small businesses and tall buildings. A lot of the government workers went for walks, especially at lunch time. The news was always out around the capital building, reporting on something stupid like smoking bans or the State once again trying to take benefits from their already income raped employees. It was harsh times and it wasn't all because of the supernatural. Humans did more damage to each other than we did to them. Yet, they couldn't realize that, so they continued to fear us.

Our headquarters was right downtown, off the right of the Treasury Department for the State. It was an older building, but we all learned to deal with it. All the other government workers did, so why couldn't we? The only thing I really hated about the building were the people who came in to make food down in the cafeteria area. They charged some ridiculous prices and the food was horrible! Sometimes I would sneak something up to my desk, thinking how good it smelled, take a taste of it and suddenly start gagging, wondering if I could get food poisoning. Carter and Luther would just stare at me speculating why I don't go down the road to one of the sub shops to get food instead of wasting my time. I had an answer. I was lazy. Pure and simple.

The building was short compared to the rest of the buildings. It had many windows that looked over the streets and a bridge next to it that crossed over the road to the other buildings. The dark brown bricks were ugly compared to the whiter, prettier concrete the other buildings were made of. The windows were square, several rows of them with nothing special to them. Home sweet home. I felt like I was at my job more than at home. All I seemed to live for was my job, even though I spent a lot of time in my office drawing stick figures. At home no one was there. At home meant I would be alone and I hated being alone. Carter offered me up a room in his house, but I refused. He needed his privacy and the dude needed to get laid. If I was there, he was less likely to get some.

I was right about when we got back he would be giving me folders of information. He piled them on me and gestured quietly for me to get to work. We worked mostly at night when everyone else went home. The creatures come out at the night and that was when most of the bad things happened. I wanted to be out in the field investigating something, not doing homework on some Director who would soon have me figured out. Since this was a Director, Carter needed to get the permission from the King. If he did that, the King of vampires would take over the investigation and that was one thing Carter did not want. This was a risk I did not want to take, but was willing to for the man who raised me.

Chapter Two

My office was in the far back corner of our floor, away from everyone and that was how I wanted it. Over in the other corner from me was Carter's office, but it was a regular room with an actual door. The rest of us had cubicles where we never saw the sun let alone the moon, unless we went out on an assignment. Which all of mine were now taken away, since Carter wanted my full attention on my undercover case. Damn him. I pictured the toddler version of me throwing herself to the floor, kicking and screaming. I was immature but mature enough not to actually do it in front of people.

It wasn't that I rather not help Carter, but going inside the Director of Michigan's home, pretending to be someone else wasn't my idea of fun. In each state there was a head vampire that was called the Director. He watched over the vampires in his region and made sure they followed all of the human and vampire laws. Looking over the Directors was a King. Each country had its own. The states we were lucky to have Declan Monroe and I say that sarcastically, because the man was a complete idiot. Sure he was one of the oldest vampires born way before Christ, but he only cared about himself. If it weren't for the few Directors that took the time to make sure the vampires were happy, everything would probably be out of control. So out of control it would be an everyday occurrence with something bloody happening. Like, going out to lunch having a normal conversation and your friend says casually, "Hey my neighbor lost his leg to a vampire bite the other day."

We did have our rogue vampires that chose not to follow the laws. It was why I had a job. The SCD controlled all of the supernatural population, which included the werewolves, shifters, pixies, fairies, and anything else you could think of. How did we hide so well? Easy, no one came out until it was dark. And those of us that did come out during the day, we could easily pass for human. Vampires were basically human if you ignored the sucking blood and the immortal life parts. And no, we aren't dead. Like anyone else, we have a soul.

I have the immortal and drinking blood part from the vampire side of me, but on top of that, I have visions that show me any conflict that happened in any one place. Also, I have the ability to appear and disappear from places, though it was still a work in progress. Usually, the only time it worked was when I was in a panic. My powers were slow to appear, but I was okay with that. The less I showed, the fewer questions I am asked from other agents. They don't take kindly to half-breeds. Everyone is all about the pure species. It is all the rage. Enter eye roll.

A knock on my cubical window made me jump. The undercover assignment occupied my thoughts more than I cared to allow it. Glancing over my shoulder, I saw someone that I truly disliked. It wasn't her snob attitude or her desire to make me feel worth no more than a slug. No, it was her over the top use of the color pink. I sometimes felt the urge to gouge my eyes out in order to save my sanity. Kristin Vaughn was a rich bitch that didn't deserve the attention of Carter. He deserved way better company, so I couldn't help but think he was only humoring the woman. She was a vampire, too, who was obsessed with everything Carter. She probably had some pink Carter fan wear. I bet if I went into her house there would be some sort of shrine. Maybe she even named her dildo after him, or carried one of those creepy hair dolls made from his hair. Briefly, I closed my eyes shuddering at the thought. *Enough of that Blake before you damage yourself mentally.*

Kristin flashed me a smile that was only meant to be on politicians. It was so bogus, I expected her to say she didn't sleep with that woman, or that man in her case, unless she switched teams. Her pink summer dress flowed around her tan legs. Flowers, yuck. My gaze met her blue eyes, only sparing a quick glance at her always perfect blond hair. She could have passed for one of those step-ford wives. *Where are the damn cookies?* My demon snarled, thinking she was freaking hilarious.

That was a thing with me. It felt like the vampire and demon in me were two different beings. Each always wanted different things, so it constantly felt like I was at war with myself. My demon was always ready to jump into a situation as long as blood was involved. Where my vampire figured we better watch out so no one cuts our fucking head off. Sure, they were opposites, which often complicated things for me. Often I would go against the demon and follow my vampire instincts. My vampire thought about stuff in a sensible way. The demon was tired of being controlled, and it only seemed to worsen as I got older.

"Can I help you?" I asked, spinning my chair enough to face her.

She swirled in to take a seat in one of my visitor chairs, her perfume nearly made me gag, forcing me to hold my breath. "Carter says I am to dress you for a ball so I brought you some dresses to try on." She looked me up and down, barely disguising her dislike of my look. What was wrong with jeans and a T-shirt that said, "You can't see me because I'm a ninja?"

"I think I can manage on my own." I snorted, turning back around to my case file on Nick. I looked at his picture admiring the rock star good looks he had. Seriously, he was drool worthy for sure. His dark brown hair was all disheveled, dark brown eyes that probably could melt any girls heart without a single word from his oh so desirably plump lips. I did one of those girly sighs. Nick Black was good enough to eat. I felt my fangs slide out, as if they wanted to sink into some big juicy donut. Oh yeah, Nick's juicy donut, but the one that attracted me the most was his second, the Deputy Director, Eli. He was super yummy. But before I could go over his assets, Kristin cleared her throat.

"Follow me."

"I'm good, thanks, I don't like pink." I replied, flipping through some more photos. Man, he had a nice ass too. Examining the photo of him about to enter a car, I hardly noticed Kristin coming up behind me. Abruptly, the file was gone causing my demon to growl with annoyance. Demons are sex crazed beasts and here she was stealing my eye candy.

"Does Carter know you are drooling over your targets?" She asked, placing small pale hands on her hips.

Raising an eyebrow, I looked at her. "Does Carter know you drool over him?" I plucked a tissue out of a box on my desk. "Here you might need this for later."

Her face turned a flaming red, and the hatred I knew she disguised so well began to leak out in her expression as she hissed like a wild animal. "We must get to work."

Throwing up my hands, I stood up pushing back my chair. "Fine!" Taking a glance at my watch, I scowled. "It is only two and the party isn't until eight."

She clucked her tongue at me, her blue eyes flashing with annoyance. "Dear, it is going to take that long to make you look approachable." Her gaze slid up and down taking in my clothes and hair. "Gods, I should have come in earlier, this is barely going to be enough time."

I ignored the insult and followed her out, mocking the way she walked the entire time. Immature I know, but the woman pissed me off. I couldn't help myself, some people just bring out the worst in me. It would be lying to deny that most of the time my thoughts were erratic and very immature.

Clenching the chair, it took all my strength not to rip off Kristin's face and that was me being nice about it. When she tore off the wax around my eye brows, I fought instinct. It was bad enough she took it to my legs and my girl part down south. Who was going to see that? Wasn't there a gentler way? Oh, yeah there was, but Kristin said she really didn't feel like coming out every other day making sure I wasn't showing any stubble. Like I needed a babysitter. Please.

I had no idea what she did to my hair, but the dark brown curly locks she made were shiny and perfect. My hair was never perfect. Usually something was causing it to look as if it was trying to run away from the rest of my head, but now I looked like Eva Mendez, excluding the perfect bronze skin. I was white, almost shockingly but there was no way I would be going for a spray tan. Knowing my luck that would go completely wrong and I would be orange. Kristen's reaction would put my demon in overdrive.

When she came out of the locker room with my evening dress I almost ran, but suddenly Ben was there blocking the doorway with a smug look on his dorky face. Was it sad they could already guess my reaction?

Unquestionably.

Slumping over, I went back over to where she was and snatched the hanger away. *At least it wasn't pink*, I thought, walking back to the bathrooms in just my underwear and bra.

By the time I was completely ready it was seven o'clock. Kristin had been right about how long it would take. Nothing about me looked like the old Blake. The vanilla scented perfume was kind of nice, though, not too strong. Examining the new me in the locker room mirror, I ignored Ben's cat calls and looks of lust, things I didn't. He was good looking in his own way measuring up to Dane Cook, but tonight I looked like I deserved better.

Kristin had picked out something that was way more expensive than I would have chosen for myself. There was no doubt I looked good in it. My figure was amazing and never once had I realized it, until now. The dress was pure white and strapless, it pushed up my boobs more, making them larger than they already were. She did my hair up, leaving curls down to touch past my shoulders. My makeup was done in smoky eye colors. I would totally have sex with myself.

"Not bad, Kristin." I murmured, doing a girly twirl in front of the mirror.

Kristin just rolled her eyes, grabbed her purse. Suddenly, she stopped. "Forgot this." She handed me a mask that was all white with silver beads around it. "It is a masked party." Then she disappeared before I could thank her, not that I would. It would probably inflate that already big head of hers.

The Michigan vampire headquarters was larger than I thought, currently housing Nick and his guard. If something happened to Nick, the position would go to his second in command and then so on. For the last four hundred years Nick had been in control, bringing Michigan up to be the most desirable state for vampires to live. According to his file, he was about fifteen hundred years old with a horrible history. He had been a killer, who suddenly went clean when he took over the

Director position. Vampire rehab or something. And yes, they did have those.

He was probably one of the most feared vampires, next to Carter. They might as well have worked together. Nick's file wasn't as detailed as I would have liked it to be. Most of the information was merely based on rumors than fact. Hopefully getting more details on his past would be easy, to understand the man behind the political mask. From what I understood, he knew how to play the system, most of that ability coming from his criminal history. Sad that skills used in the criminal world worked really well in the political one.

My gaze went over the stylish mansion, noting the very detailed molding around the top of the building, it was engraved with what looked to be vines. The place was all white with huge steps that led up to big wooden double doors. Now when I thought about it, the place looked like a mini White House, it was just missing the fountain in the front.

People were already going inside, dressed in their tuxes and dresses, and masks on their faces. No one even admired the house like I did, it was beautiful and a big part of vampire history. The grounds were covered in flowers and a large section of it was roses, they have always been part of the Director's house. It was in memory of one of the vampires that was killed during the early nineteen hundreds. Apparently, the town she lived in found out she was a vampire, so the men decided to take it into their own hands and burn her house down, then burned her on a cross. People said that she was the secret lover of Nick's and that was why he insisted on roses. Apparently, he had chosen to be gone that night after promising to be there, but that was all rumor. The vampire world was filled with them so no one, not even the SCD, could be completely sure they had the right facts.

Handing my keys over to a man that was parking the guest cars, I ignored his eyes on me. I was in too much of awe looking at the mansion to care, when under usual circumstances I would have snapped at him to take a picture. Carter's house wasn't nearly as big, but then again, he didn't have to house about twenty vampires.

The doors opened for me by a bulky guard exposing a huge lobby with antique chairs lining the walls, where people would normally have to wait to meet with the Director. A few stood in the hallway talking while holding their glasses of wine, all acting as if they were important people. No one acknowledged me, so I stepped through, my heels clicking on the marble. Over to the right was the ballroom area, where it became louder with music and people talking. My gaze traveled over the few who danced and then over to the groups of men talking business, laughing by throwing their heads back and slapping each other on the arms like they just heard the best thing ever. Some were women gathered, giggling about who knew what, probably spreading rumors to ruin another's reputation. I felt out of my element. At that second, I wanted to run.

Before I could, I caught a scent that surprised me. Werewolf. It was rare for werewolves to mix with vampires, usually fights broke out and people died. Recently it had become part of Nick's mission to get all the races to work together peacefully, his first step was using his best friend, the alpha of the Michigan pack. Unlike the vampires, the werewolves didn't have a King or a mega alpha. Each state was considered a pack and each alpha was part of one big council. I thought that sounded better, then they could all take votes when a problem came up. Sadly, vampires were all about control and Declan, the king of vampires, liked having it.

Moving through the crowd, I followed the scent, enjoying the mixture of the wolf smell and his cologne. Werewolves had the best blood at least that was my preferred type to drink. There were four others around him, somewhere. Three were probably his personal body guards and the other his date. Not sure if he married yet, at the last update for our division he was dating, but not exclusively. It was unusual for werewolves to stick to one person and if they did, it was usually their chosen mate. Yeah, I didn't believe in that mate shit either, but so many did, just like fairy tales.

Bumping into him I swore out loud. Quickly, I turned away feeling like a fool, and then tried to think of the best direction to get away from him. I had been too busy enjoying his scent that I failed to tell my brain to stop before plowing into him. *Idiot!* My vampire screamed. I never stopped embarrassing myself and obviously my vampire half was all about going unnoticed by those around us.

Someone grabbed my arm, jerking me to a stop, so I turned around to apologize for bumping into them, but came face to face with the alpha himself, Michael Bishop. "Shit."

He busted out laughing, his dark brown eyes lighting up. The alpha's face was covered with a mask like everyone else's, but it didn't cover up the strong jaw, or the stubble coating his face as if he forgot to shave. I knew that wasn't the case, werewolves grew hair fast and that included the women. I would have hated to shave three times a day.

This werewolf didn't need to shave, I loved the five o'clock shadow. His dark brown hair was fabulous and if Kristin hadn't already done a wonderful job on my hair, I would have been jealous.

"Where are you going?" He asked, pulling me up against him, hands moving down to grip my ass.

I gasped, shocked over his forwardness. It wasn't news that werewolves were so up front, but I didn't think they would attempt to get it on in a crowd. My mouth just hung open in shock while my brain yelled at it to shut. "Stop acting like a fool," it cried. But I couldn't, what was I supposed to do? I never had this happen to me before.

When I didn't respond, he took my hands into his and smiled down at me, eyes searching mine with the eagerness of a virgin boy. "Dance with me." Leaning forward he smelled me, growling deeply, sending vibrations all the way down to my core. It would be lying if I said it crept me out. It totally turned me on. "You smell wonderful."

Laughing nervously, I said, "New perfume."

"I doubt it. Something underneath the vanilla I smell on your skin." His lips brushed over my neck and I shuddered, my defenses melting instantly. "It's you."

Smiling, I pulled back, slapping his chest with one hand. I was totally flirting now. "I bet you say that to all the girls."

He shrugged before spinning me in a circle. "Not really. It surprisingly takes very little to convince them to join my bed."

"I won't be joining your bed." I said, trying to ignore the heated sensation I got when his hand went onto my back and nearly to my ass again.

Michael chuckled. "I figured as much. For now, anyway." When I went to object, he pulled me even tighter to him. I felt my body responding, moving into him. He groaned. "Your body says differently."

Breathless, I shook my head insisting, "I'm good."

Again he laughed throwing his head back at my attempt to not be into him. He went to say something, but a tall man came up alongside of us. "May I cut in?"

Growling, Michael's eyes flashed showing the wolf inside. The man stepped back with a grin on his face. "Hey, forgive me, Michael, but Nick wants to see you. Why let the lovely lady stand by herself if I can take your place, however temporary?"

Smooth, I thought. Michael nodded, gave me one last look before pinching my ass making me jump with a yelp. Grinning, he hurried through the crowd to find Nick. I stared after him in disbelief. The nerve! Suddenly, I had my back bone, too late to stand up to the werewolf, though. Man, I was such a slut. Not really. Last time I was with anyone was… well, we won't think about that, because it was an awful long time. I could probably put virgins to shame.   The man taking Michael's place smiled down at me as we started to dance again. I didn't recognize the music, but obviously he did, because he started humming to it. "Lovely music. I was pleased when Nick brought in this group to play tonight."

Trying to place him, I went through the files in my brain. None of the known guards matched up to him, so it only left the second in command, Eli Dexter. The one I thought was way better looking than Nick. He had always been second in command to Nick, even in the military. Even beyond that when Nick had his own kingdom. He was famous for collecting information without being caught, a spy among vampires. Aging vampires will gain powers as they get older and Eli seemed to have a lot of them, all of which are undocumented. He was someone I didn't want as an enemy. Eli was also quite a ladies man, most of the information in his file went over how he bed women high in the royal food chain. Even some queens, when it was probably wise to keep his distance. Another fault in vampires, they always considered themselves the cream of the crop.

"You don't have to dance with me," I said, trying to pull away. He held firm, continuing to smile, if not more because he was amused by my attempt to escape.

"Don't I, Blake? You are here for a reason and I want to know why." While his eyes darkened at the possible threat of me, his smile continued to hold on his face.

Sighing dramatically, I rolled my eyes, pretending his knowing my identity didn't bother me. "I was bored."

He laughed, "Hardly."

Shrugging, I looked up at him. "What do you want me to say? Hey, I got fired from my job and now I need a way in?" I was beginning to panic. Carter should have realized someone would recognize me. Now what? Play along is what. Trying to keep my heart under control, I continued to keep eye contact with him, coaxing my pulse to slow down to normal so he wouldn't notice.

"Carter wouldn't fire you."

Shrugging, I nodded slightly. "True, but Declan would. When you piss off the King, he goes for the jugular, Carter can hardly argue." Frowning, I looked away, trying to pretend the situation was upsetting me, but didn't want him to see.

After a few seconds of silence, he sighed. "I believe you. It is unfortunate, however, Nick isn't looking for anyone new for his guard so it is probably best if you leave before anyone is alerted of your presence. You aren't exactly liked among our people."

I nodded. "Figures, but Nick isn't the only big dude here."

He grinned. "Big dude."

Grinning back, I allowed him to twirl me. "Any suggestions?" I asked when he bent me backwards, his eyes focused on my breasts.

Opening his mouth to respond, he suddenly straightened, pulling me up with him. His gaze went distant and then he took off without another word. Wondering if the boys were in action for our plan tonight, I hurried after him, cursing the heels Kristin put me in. My legs felt like they were one step away from breaking, either from a fall or just stepping wrong.

Eli hurried around a corner, ignoring people's stares as he passed them. The guard saw what was happening, two blocked the entrance of the room before I could escape. This would take some maneuvering, I decided. Finding the gap between them I dived through, summersaulting like a badass ninja. Looking back, they both stared at me in surprise, but neither moved because the crowd got closer. They had no choice but to leave me for someone else to catch, but the other guards were too busy trying to close off the other entrances.

My heels clicked against the marble floor and when I went around a corner, I nearly fell on my face. Growling, I tossed off the shoes, ignoring the cry of outrage from the receiving victim. Yelling and what sounded like flesh hitting flesh came from the end of the hall inside an office area. When I got to the door it opened up to another room that I soon recognized as a meeting area or a court room. It was huge, but not as big as the ball room. This held a panel where judges were supposed to sit. In front were two tables with three chairs in front of each, the marble floor matched what was in the front lobby, reflecting the chandeliers that hung from the tall ceiling.

When I heard more yelling, I turned to find a group of men at the end of the room, preparing for a fight. Nick was in the middle of a fight between three other vampires, each looking like they wouldn't be much for him to handle. On the floor were his two guards and Eli, passed out or injured. Where was Michael? Hurrying over, one of the bad guys turned to face me, his fangs out and his eyes black from rage. This didn't look like something Carter set up. He held up his sword ready to take me down with it. Vampires didn't fight with guns, only swords or katanas. At least that's the way it was supposed to be, but sometimes when you went into a fight ready with a sword, you came face to face with a gun. I had neither of those, but I did have a stake and knives. Lifting my skirt, I took out a wooden stake and held it ready to attack. The rogue only sneered before charging me, fangs out, ready to tear into skin when they had the chance.

Quickly, I ducked his first attempt to cut off my head with his sword. He screamed in fury, taking another shot which I managed to dodge, but barely. I kicked out, hitting him in the face and he flew back losing his sword. With vampire speed he was up and running at me again. Before I could move, his body slammed into mine taking the breath out of my lungs. He had me down on my back, grinning like a school boy who was about to get some action. Oh, this was too easy. "Got me down on the floor, now what do you want to do? I have an idea, but I bet it's not what you're thinking." I swung up my arm, coming back down to stab him in the back. His whole body went up in ash, covering me. Young vampires went up in dust. The older they are, the longer they took to go to ash. Bile rose in my throat when I tasted some in my mouth. Spitting it out, I climbed to my feet just in time to be hit by another rogue.

This one smelled horrible, like dried, old blood which came off of him in waves, smelling of rot and death. His fangs were yellow and dripping with spit. Rabid vampires, how nice. I dodged his swinging fist to only meet him with my own in his stomach. He groaned bending over, but moved fast enough to avoid a kick to the face from me. "What did you do, take a bite out of a dog? Is that why you are foaming at the mouth?" I asked, moving out of the way when he tried to tackle me.

I glanced over at Nick who was holding his own. He managed to pick up a stray sword, now meeting his opponent's with ease. The metal clashed as each expertly moved into the proper footings. The rogue he was fighting was old, someone who probably hadn't been a rogue his entire vampire life. The others I had taken on were young but strong.

Nearly getting my head kicked off, I jumped back into a fast flip, my foot hitting him in the face. He fell to the ground and I raced over to straddle him to place my hands on his head. I twisted, hearing a sickly snap of his neck and then the ripping of skin as I tore it from his shoulders. His body went to ash.

Scrambling up, I went to save the day for Nick, but he flashed me a warning glance telling me to stay off his territory. So, I just watched as he swung his sword skillfully, his movements graceful. As if realizing I was there, the rogue made one mistake of giving me a sideways glance. That's when Nick swung, the blade going through the rogue's neck. His mouth fell open in surprise, his sword clattering to the ground, and he soon to follow. He wouldn't be turning to ash right away. I never understood why the older ones tend to stay whole long but my guess was that it had something to do with the vampire species.

The story of vampires came from a Demigod who wanted to create his own race. Only his own race was what killed him in the end. The race happened to be vampires. He created us in hopes to destroy everything his father made in the world. It all backfired on him because all he cared about was conquering and proving his father he was better. Since then, some of us developed a conscience and all we have ever wanted to do was belong. Most of the supernatural creatures were created by a Demigod. All of them tried to play God one too many times and paid for it in the end.

Nick leaned against his sword, the tip down in the only carpet of the room. It used to hold a display of pictures showing each Director in the US, but over half of them were knocked down and broken, parts scattered around the room.

He was truly handsome. Hot even. Nick was a rock star look alike. His dark brown hair was disheveled, like he just rolled out of bed a few minutes ago. When his blue eyes focused on me I stood straighter, daring him to say something offensive. I don't know why his look caused me to feel suddenly insecure.

Running footsteps came into the room and he looked past me to make eye contact with them before saying, "Seize her."

Chapter Three

Nick motioned for me to take a seat in one of the plush leather chairs in his office. I debated on doing just that when he made the decision for me. "Don't make one of my men force you," He said in a low voice.

I slid down into the chair, already forming plans on what I would do if I needed to get out of the chair to attack. He saw me assessing the situation and chuckled, leaning against the desk, palms braced along the edge.

This wasn't supposed to happen. I was now in the Director's custody. And for what? I had no fucking clue. My eyes avoided his for a while as I took in the room finding that it was all male. The walls were plain white with pictures of far off places like Ireland. One wall was a large book case filled with books that had to do with history of our people, legends, laws and anything else you could think of. When I came back around I looked at the giant desk once more noticing opened files, a laptop that was shut, and a cell phone.

"Was this a planned attack?" He asked, his voice startling me.

I just shook my head. When he became frustrated, he tore off his mask, tossing it onto his desk, looking elegant as he did it. "You invade my home and for what reasons, Blake?"

Why was everyone so convinced I was on the attack here? I was minding my own business and here I played Good Samaritan to help a single man against three rogues. Did I get thanks? Hell no. Who cares if there had been a planned attack in place by me? Luther probably called back the whole thing when they realized some rogues snuck into the house to do it for him unknowingly.

"Answer me!" He bellowed.

Whoa, angry vampire. "I didn't invade your home. Why you would even think that is beyond me, my Liege."

A flicker of surprise appeared in his hard gaze. "You are half demon." Like that explained anything.

Shrugging, I gave him a look that said, "And your point?"

He growled. "And you are Sara's daughter!"

I raised my hand like a kid in school. "I still don't get it."

"Do you know what your mother has done in the past?" He snarled. The man could still look beautiful when he was pissed off, but still I had no idea what my mom had to do with me. When I didn't respond, he started pacing the room. "Just tell me why you are here."

Sighing loudly, I slouched in my chair. "Declan had me fired from the SCD. I came here to see if any of the big wigs are looking for some extra guards."

He turned to look at me skeptically. "I appreciate your assistance with the rogues in the meeting room, but I am not in need of additional guards."

"I didn't say you." I know that was childish, but why should I make him think I came only for him? He wasn't the only important person out there.

Glaring, he started up his pacing again. "This ball is no place for job searching. I am sympathetic to your losing your job, but this is not the right time."

The office door opened and Eli strolled in looking like he hadn't been unconscious. His mask was gone, so it allowed me to look over him appreciatively. The man had gorgeous reddish brown hair and now it was arranged carefully to hide the fact he just came out of a fight. His bow tie, now undone, hung loosely around his neck. "I think you should reconsider, Nick. Lucifer's daughter would be a brilliant move on our part. If my opinion matters, I think she should be your Guardian."

Nick's head snapped in my direction. "Lucifer's daughter?" He asked in astonishment.

Okay, so not even I knew that part. Suddenly uncomfortable, I stood up. "Okay, I don't want to be the feature of today's freak show, so I'm leaving." Turning, I went to the door, but Nick was suddenly in front of me blocking the exit with his arms out. I blinked several times at him when I stopped. "I can go, Nick. I know my rights."

Eli chuckled. "As a vampire, you have no rights when it comes to the Director."

Anger flaring, I turned to him, watching as he stepped back in surprise. I wondered what he saw. "I will not be held captive!" Turning back to Nick I glared, pointing at him. "I saved your ass, rich boy!"

Nick grinned, turning on the charm. "That's why you can't leave, I need you."

The way he said it suddenly had my stomach flipping uneasily. What was with the change of heart? He acted so cold and superior to me minutes before and now he was trying to add me to his employee roster. My head said to go with it, I needed it, but my anger was sparking to life, a flame that couldn't be controlled. "Just a second ago you were all set for sending me to the dungeon, what changed your mind?"

You are a secret weapon. They want to use you.

Looking around, I tried to find the source of the voice. Nick looked at me confused, trying to figure out what I was looking for, but I ignored him. Going insane, I was going insane.

Hardly, love, this is your father.

I stiffened. "In my head?"

Nick frowned. "Pardon me?"

Lucifer laughed, the sound filling my head. *Best not to talk out loud or they will think you're crazy, daughter.*

"Don't call me that, I don't even know you." I growled, sensing Eli coming up behind me slowly, as if he was afraid to startle the dangerous animal. Okay, so I just went from intruder, to awesome, to let's approach carefully so we don't become dinner.

Speak in your head child or I might have to save you from the white padded room.

Deciding to ignore him, I visualized a wall appearing around my mind hoping to block him out, then focused back on the two men who were probably already on the phone with the closest psych hospital. "Did you need me for anything else, because I'd like to go home?" My anxiety rising, I shifted uncomfortably as they stared. Eli was now in front of me, both men unsure of what their next move should be. Shit, they thought I was nuts.

Nick cleared his throat. "I want to offer you a position on my guard, Blake."

Mr. Predictable at your service. My eyebrows raised in mock surprise. "And why would I want to be part of your guard? Bossed around like the rest of the little people? Thanks, but no thanks." Moving forward, both men stiffened in response. They looked from each other as if debating what they should do. Seriously, why were they acting this way? "What the hell is your problem?" I snapped.

Eli pointed to his eyes. "Your eyes are red."

"What?" I stomped over to a door that probably opened to a bathroom. When I realized I was right, I kicked the door all the way open, still barefooted. Looking in the mirror, I nearly fainted that it was actually true. "Shit."

"The demon in you." I jumped when Eli appeared, looking fascinated.

Spooked, I hurried past him going straight to the door. Had to get out of here. My eyes never glowed before. First my father decides to pop in for a mental visit and now my eyes were red like I was being possessed?

"Wait! I will make you my top guard, not the captain, but my personal guard. My Guardian." The eagerness in his face was priceless, but I couldn't bask in the ambience, because I was freaked out.

I wanted to scream "Leave me alone," but I didn't. Instead, I slump my shoulders looking at him. He had moved over to the window near the bathroom, hands shoved in his pockets. God he was hot. Man, my emotions were all over the place. Rage to horny, come on Blake! "What is so special about this position?"

Astonishment flickered on his face. "Well, you would be guarding the Director with a place to stay, here in the house. You will be paid well."

Debating on making him grovel some more, I smiled big, showing my teeth. "Good."

Score one for team awesome, aka me. Everything was going according to plan, now what? I had no idea. He didn't seem like the type that would be running an underground blood slave business. It kind of made me wonder if Carter ever did meet Nick before, because well, if he saw what I saw, then he would know Nick couldn't be part of something so horrible. Then again, Carter wouldn't view Nick as a big cake waiting for me to take a swan dive in either. I shuddered, thinking about it.

Nick treated me like shit before, but once he realized the treasure I was, he instantly pounced. Now to some that would sound kind of suspicious, like maybe I had juicy blood that would sell high on the black market. When I thought about it, that really did sound suspicious, but I had to plow ahead because it was my job and Carter would have it no other way.

*

Eli dropped me off at my apartment telling me they would pay for the remaining part of the lease, including putting my things in storage at the end of it. As Nick's personal guard I had to have my room next to his inside the mini white house. Lovely. I prayed that I didn't need to stay undercover that long.

I hoped they were going to give me a decent room, because I was not a fan of small spaces. If it was like a closet, I would protest and sleep somewhere else. Like maybe his office. Yeah, that was big and his chair did look really comfortable. I pictured other things that would be comfortable in his chair. Shutting down my brain from the thoughts, I shoved another pair of jeans in my duffel bag. Quickly, I reached under my bed grabbing my katana. The blade whispered as I pulled it out, so I could see the engravings on it again. It was probably the only thing my mother ever gave me before she disappeared. I didn't know what the words meant and was kind of afraid to ask anyone. She wasn't the best person in the world. A vampire with witch blood wasn't something people took lightly. She was a practicing dark witch who was later turned into a vampire. One that had been turned against her will.

Some wondered how the hell I came into the world as a half demon, vampire, witch combination. Well, the witch and vampire were obvious. Daddy dearest decided to strike up a deal with my mom back in the day, which I had no idea that it was Lucifer. He said if she would have his child he would tell her the location of the man who attacked her. At least that is how I think it went. There were rumors and several of them, just one happened to be the most heard of. Sara had a reputation that made a lot of people fear her. What she had done to the man that attacked her was horrifying, something you wouldn't suspect from someone like her. I saw pictures of end results, the man was mummified. Usually a vampire will go to ash when he was killed, but this didn't happen. He was still alive and had no way to die. It was like she placed a curse on him.

Refocusing on the current take, I then pulled out my long sword that strapped to my back under my clothes. Quickly, I grabbed a change of clothes choosing a plain black shirt, bra, panties, and a pair of flared jeans, then picked out some boots. Dressing quickly after strapping on my sword, I grabbed more weapons that I hid inside my closet. It was a hole that opened with an eye scanner. I was high tech, but only because Carter funded it. Girls like me could never afford that fancy kind of stuff. It had been a gift from Carter, because he was sick of seeing my weapons lying out in the open. I wasn't careless, but where else could they go? Shoved under my bed in a box? Hell no, they deserved better than that.

Deciding I should probably call Carter, I took my cell phone off my night stand hitting speed dial. After a couple of rings, he answered. "Hey boss, letting you know I am in."

Carter sighed in relief. "Good, I was worried when Luther told me those rogues made an appearance."

I explained to him what happened and then said, "Oh, and seems my father is trying to contact me."

"What?" Carter sounded as shocked as I felt.

When I told him that it was a mental phone call he chuckled. "Interesting. I wonder why after all this time he chooses to contact you now?"

I shrugged and then realized he couldn't see me. "I really don't know, but I blocked him out. Having a demon in my head is really disturbing."

"Blake, you do realize you are half demon?"

Sticking out my tongue and glad he couldn't see me I said, "Right. Anyway, I have to move into the house since I am his personal guard now. Contact may not be much."

"That is fine. Luther will make contact later."

After hanging up with him, I hurried to finish packing. After having my own place it was going to be hard living somewhere else. I zipped up my duffel bag after shoving some toiletries inside. Hearing a knock at the door, I slung it over my shoulder, strapped on my katana and went to open it. Eli stood waiting. I said, "Let's go Jeeves!"

Eli seemed more relaxed around me because he just laughed at my Jeeves comment, with an eye roll. So we might actually get along. I wasn't sure at first, because he seemed protective and serious about everything. That probably had to do with the fact of not knowing my intentions. Apparently I was more of a threat than I thought, but really didn't know why. This required some thinking about and asking Carter a ton of questions later.

The ride started off pretty quiet. I looked outside at the city not admiring a single thing. Lansing wasn't special, but what city really is? I was more of a country girl that thought things like nature was worth looking at and not run down houses. Summer was on its way out and the fall on its way in, some days it was cool and others it was hot. People crowded the downtown streets, crossing the roads as if no cars were coming. They didn't think twice about the risk they took without following mom's number one rule of look both ways.

Glancing over at Eli, I watched as he focused on the road ahead. He was driving faster than he should have, but the cops were out somewhere else, obviously. He drove me in his personal vehicle, which was a sleek black BMW that had me drooling from the moment I saw it. My car was a mustang, one of the new ones. I loved it, but looking at Eli's car I was afraid I may have to cheat on it for something more beautiful. My hand went over the leather seat I was in. Smooth like butter.

"Having fun?"

Startled from my thoughts, I looked up at Eli, who flashed me a grin. My heart stuttered a beat, crazed over how gorgeous he was. Looking away, I forced a smile. "I want a car like this." I opened the glove box, examining the contents.

Eli cleared his throat. "Umm, that's private."

Shrugging, I continued to dig through his stuff. "You should only keep important paperwork in here." I took out a handgun, examined it, and then dropped it on the floor.

"Hey, that's loaded!" Eli cried out.

I didn't want to face yet another attraction to a man, so what better way than to annoy the crap out of one before he decides to get too close? Frowning, I found some candy. I held up one of the peppermints and raised an eyebrow. It looked old and somewhat melted. "Saving it for later?"

Exasperated, he snatched it away. "I didn't know it was back there."

Nodding and doing a slight shrug at the same time, I continued to paw through the box. It was small, but there was a lot of crap, like a junk drawer you found in a hoarder's house.

"Do you even have a registration or insurance in here?"

"Of course."

I raised an eye brow at him. "Are you sure?"

"Yes! Now please get out of there."

Heaving a dramatic sigh, I shoved everything back in including the gun, then slammed it shut. Plopping down, I rested my head back. "I am hungry, we should stop somewhere."

Eli shook his head. "Nick asked me to bring you straight back, your duties will begin immediately."

Sitting up I looked at him. "For real? Can't I start in the morning?" My stomach growled noisily, my cheeks burned from embarrassment.

This time it was Eli's turn to sigh. He slowed the car down in front of a drive thru. I glanced up in surprise, but sat back like a good girl before I ruined my opportunity to eat. When he rolled down the window I unbuckled, practically jumping into his lap to give my order. He gasped in surprise, making me wonder if I smashed his bits, but couldn't care less at the moment. I was starving, man!

When the lady in the speaker asked me if I was finished ordering I looked over at Eli, who just shook his head. "That will be it!" She ran through the order, which could probably feed a family of five. My stomach grumbled thinking about the burgers and fries. Oh yeah, dinner was going to be good. I was a junk food eater. After eating this, I would have to see if there was any bagged blood at the mansion. Part of my hunger might have been for that, but anything would do for now, before I ended up gnawing on something of Eli's.

I blushed remembering I was still on Eli's lap. He just smiled in response, not even trying to touch me out of respect. My body was screaming for contact, aware of his closeness all of a sudden. "I guess I should get off you."

"If you wish." He continued to smile when I looked at him with a jolt. Slowly crawling back, I inched into my seat, heart pounding and loins harassing me for the tease. Have to clear my brain. Carter wouldn't be happy if I was getting it on with the enemy. I couldn't help but glance in his direction when he went to accept my food. I could totally dream about it though.

Eli parked so I could eat. Shoveling in the food, I offered him a cheeseburger with a questioning look. He nodded, obviously now hungry because I was moaning with happiness as I ate. When he took a bite of the burger, his eyes rolled back as if he just tasted heaven. I grinned at him. "Never had a burger?"

He took another bite. "Not in a long time. Nick tends to eat at expensive places or have big dinners. Burgers are never on the menu. Especially, fast food burgers." Flashing a smile, he took another bite. "Fabulous."

Nodding in agreement, I shoved some fries into my mouth. "So, does Nick get attacked a lot? With him being the Director I would assume there has been a lot of assassination attempts." I chatted with a full mouth.

Shaking his head, Eli swallowed his own food. "No, but it has been happening more and more. We haven't been able to figure out why. Someone has been trying to stage certain things to make him look guilty of crimes." When I looked at him in a way that said continue, he went on. "Someone put a dead woman in his bed about three days ago. We were totally surprised. Of course, we had to have the King's people handle it. Nick is the Director, using any of our men would compromise a case, especially when most of them would act to protect him." He rolled his burger wrapper into a ball, then sat back in his seat to get comfortable. "Then tonight was the rogue attack."

Frowning, I smashed down the food bag since I was finished. "Who was the girl?" I asked.

Eli took the bag from me, put the car in gear, and then slowed next to a trash bin to toss it in. "A girl that has been missing for a while. It was suspected the Covert took her, but then again any missing female is automatically assumed to be taken by them." He shrugged. "But in this case it has to be true with all the bites on her body, and she was branded."

Startled, I looked up. "Branded?"

He nodded. "The Covert symbol was on her inner thigh. Seems like they brand their girls for publicity reasons and ownership." Eli's face kept going from in the light to in the shadows as the car went down the road. It was hard to see his expression with the light changing so much.

Who would want to frame Nick for Covert kidnappings? The Covert themselves? They did take a girl who was of high importance and that could only mean war, but someone was trying hard enough to point in Nick's direction for the blame. I didn't really understand that part, unless Nick was lying because he got caught red handed with a girl. Wouldn't surprise me since vampires were notorious liars.

Neither of us said anything on the way back to the Mansion. When I saw the White House of doom, my heart began to beat faster with anxiety. I was afraid to be in this house. Nick was the Director of the State, which meant he was only one level beneath the King. Messing with people who are of importance was risky. Carter probably didn't get the King's permission to investigate. That could be a whole lot of trouble for him, but that happens when things like this become personal, and I should have known it would have with Carter when he told me his niece was suspected to be missing. The victim's family often jumps to extremes to save them. Helping Carter was probably the best thing I could do for him now. So I would stick it out until I found her. If she was even alive.

Climbing out of the car, I went to the trunk as Eli popped it open. He grabbed my duffel bag, while I took a case full of my personal weapons. His hand was at my elbow guiding me up the steps. Two guards stood frozen, not even making eye contact when we approached, but one eventually moved when we were close enough, so he could open the doors.

The mansion was quiet, so the party had already ended. People were inside cleaning up the food and any other mess that had been created. Eli took my weapons case and pointed at a door near the end of the hallway. Nick's office. "He is almost certainly waiting for you. We are a little late, so I am sure he is pretty pissed off." He grinned. "I will put this up in your room."

Watching him climb up a marble stair case I felt disappointment from him leaving me. Sure he was the Director's second, but man he was every bit worth the few seconds I watched him walk up the steps. He still had on the tux, but no longer the loosened bow tie hanging around his neck. He looked like someone who was relaxing after a long day at work.

Someone cleared their throat and my gaze zoomed in that direction. Nick was standing half out the door with an expecting expression on his face. Hurrying over, I went to meet him and followed him inside the office. Michael was sitting in one of the chairs, one leg crossed over his knee. He turned to look at me, a wolfish smile on his face. Oh no. I felt like a deer in the woods being hunted. Squaring my shoulders, I hurried over to the other chair to stand. Nick went behind his desk, now dressed in a pair of black dress pants and a white button up shirt. He motioned for me to take a seat.

I sat down, clutching the arm rests for dear life. So many men! How was I going to survive? I felt like a fourteen year old boy trying to lose his virginity. Only I was without the nude magazine and lotion. This was probably the worst job assignment ever. It was like being inside the Playboy mansion, only it was the Playgirl version. How does one cope with that? They couldn't. I was doomed to fall into temptation. My hormones were raging, trying to get the rest of my body in gear by forcing me to seduce one of these guys. Only none of them seemed to get the response out of me like Eli. Michael maybe. He was like taking a taste of the forbidden fruit with him being a werewolf and all.

From the corner of my eye, I saw Michael's nostrils flare and then a smile come to his face. Shit, he could smell how much I wanted him. I bet even Nick could, but if he gave any indication there was none in his expression. Trying not to squirm, I avoiding his gaze when he tried to catch mine.

"I am pleased you accepted my offer, Blake." Nick smiled warmly, hands clasping together on the desk. With his rock star hair it was hard to take him seriously, but one glance at his eyes, you could tell he was all about business.

Eli came into the room taking a seat in the chair next to the window. He gave me a bright smile before crossing his arms and focusing on Nick. Oh triple damn. I was in deep shit.

Happens to the best of us, love.

Oh, not you again. I mentally cried. Wrong timing!

Seems you let your guard down when you're ready to jump a man's bones! A deep laugh echoed through my head.

Bastard.

Oh come on, love. Daddy is here now.

Took you long enough, where the hell you been? No pun intended.

Again Lucifer laughed, his voice awfully deep, like scary deep. *It is against our law to contact our children before the age of twenty-five.*

"Blake?"

Coming back to Earth, I looked around finding the three men staring at me with puzzled expressions. "Sorry, continue."

But they all kept staring at me. Nick frowned. "We asked if you needed any special equipment."

"Oh." I forced a smile, feeling sort of out of it. "Uhm, I can't think of anything right now. I am kind of tired. Actually, I need some blood." I stood up, wiping my clammy hands on my jeans. All of the men watched me as if they could sense something was wrong.

Instead of commenting, Nick motioned Eli to go get some blood. Then he looked over at me. "We aren't finished. Eli will get some blood for you, right now we have to go over the dress code." When I took a seat, he nodded and continued. "We all wear black here. And everyone wears this." He opened his hand, dropping a silver ring on the top of the desk. I leaned forward grabbing it. There was a ruby in the middle with the letter 'm' around it. A ring for the Director's guard.

"Nice." I said, slipping it on my right hand ring finger. Perfect fit. I wonder how much it would go for at the pawn shop. Oh, I could sell it on the down low to another vampire.

"This one is different from the others. The rest have a smaller stone and their engraving says Michigan House Guards. Yours says Guardian." Nick leaned back in his chair, hands behind his head as he watched me. "Don't lose it. Last thing we need is someone running around the city pretending to be a house guard." He shuddered as if picturing the results of it.

I nodded, turning to look at Eli when he came up alongside of me. My skin heated with awareness, but I pretended not to notice. Taking the bagged blood, I slapped it onto my fangs feeling a rush of relief as my body began to feel normal. Maybe I was just low on blood and that would explain my crazy behavior. When I finished that one, I tore off the bag and accepted another one he handed to me. When our hands brushed, my insides warmed. Quickly I stood up becoming nervous with all of the attention. "Umm, is it okay if I just head to bed?"

Hesitating, Nick nodded. "Eli, if you would, take Blake to her room."

"No!" I said sharply. Everyone once again turned to look at me, Eli looked even more confused than the other two.

"Blake, you don't even know where your room is." Nick pointed out.

"I- why don't you take me then?"

"I have a meeting with Michael." The look he gave me was one he would give a pain in the ass child. I half expected him to tell me to go to my room without dinner, something Carter said to me almost every night when I was younger. Of course, he would come back into my room an hour later with a tray of food.

Giving in, I nodded. Not good. Something was wrong with me. When we left the office I looked at Eli nervously, not sure how to act. Well, my body wanted to react one way, but my brain was yelling fuck no! Not in a way that he was disgusting, but to say it was a bad move right now. Have to keep my head in the game.

Eli didn't say anything as we headed up the stairs. The steps spiraled around until it came to the balcony, where there was a line of rooms, which I assumed were for the guards who lived in the house. Taking another set of steps we came to the third level, which revealed only four doors. One at the far end of the hall, one center, then another two towards the other end of the hall. He led me to the other end of the hall, where he opened the door revealing a huge room.

The bed was massive, white sheets, white curtains and white carpet. I almost felt like I would dirty the place just from looking at it. I looked down at the carpet, debating on if I should go in. The walls were all white with nothing on them, as if they had been freshly painted. The dressers were even white! "Holy shit, why is it all white?"

He smirked, taking my elbow to lead me in. Tingles shot up my arm and down to my core. Pulling away from him, I tried to pretend it was because I wanted to look out the window, but he realized what I was doing, so he grabbed my arm, a questioning look on his handsome face. "What's going on?"

"Nothing." I said, dragging the word out, as I pulled my arm away to head to a doorway on the far side of the room.

Eli scowled, moving so fast he was in front of the door before I could escape into the bathroom. Damn it was huge! A tub in the center of the room with steps going around it, two sinks on one wall and the toilet on the other side. Strange set up, but it was awesome.

"Something is wrong. You don't want me around or touching you."

"Really it's nothing." I insisted.

"So, if I were to touch you," he grabbed my arm again, "you won't pull away?"

Going stiff, I tried to pretend it didn't bother me, but it was hard to do considering the urge to jump his bones was growing by the second. Oh my god, I couldn't take it anymore! "You need to back off, I don't even know you." I said softly.

He paused, then released me. "You're right." Quickly he turned on his heel, leaving me in my room to think about why he hesitated. Like he wanted to tell me something.

Chapter Four

The sun was peeking through the curtains as it was going down for the day. Vampires stuck to the nightlife, because the sun took a lot of energy. Our bodies having to constantly repair ourselves forced us to drink more blood. There was more science involved than I cared to think about and it was never my area in school. Well, school was never my area, period. My alarm didn't even go off, so why was I even awake?

Yawning, I stretched like a cat, while trying to blink away the sleep from my eyes. Then I saw him, an unfamiliar man was sitting in the corner of the room, in a chair. Immediately my defenses were up, and I had a knife in my hand from under my pillow. The man was around my age, tan skin, brown hair, and a goatee. His green eyes stared into mine, something about them familiar. "Who the hell are you?" I demanded, not liking the idea of being naked under the covers with a strange guy in my room. Was this the part where I screamed "rape!"

"Do you always sleep with knives under your pillows?" He asked with a British accent.

Raising my eyebrows, I pointed my knife at him. "Well, you are a fine example of why I do. Who the hell sneaks into a vampire house and sits waiting, watching someone sleep? Are you that fucking disturbed?"

He only smiled, lifting a hand with his index finger tucked in. A tea cup appeared, steam coming from it. Tea, it smelled like tea. My nostrils flared taking in more of his scent. Sulfur. "Demon?" When he nodded, I rolled my eyes. "Figures, only you guys would be tempted to go into a damn war zone." Wrapping a sheet around me with one hand, I watched him. "I didn't summon you, so go away." I did a shooing motion with my knife hand.

The demon chuckled, his green eyes bright, filled with amusement. Then it hit me. "Shit."

When he nodded, I tensed for action. "Lucifer is what most call me, but you may call me father, dad, or daddy, but I would prefer dad or father. Daddy just sounds plain weird when you refer to me." He shrugged before setting down his tea on the dresser. It disappeared when his hand left the handle.

"I'd rather not. I don't want you here anyway, so leave." My voice low enough to sound threatening, or so I hoped.

Lucifer raised his eyebrows. "I figured you would be difficult, but you must know that things are changing dramatically for you. Haven't you felt different?" When I didn't answer, he took that as admission. "I need to show you how to handle the new powers. We can't have demon spawn running around killing people, or the big man upstairs will be set on punishing me for even longer than eternity, if that is even possible." He chuckled. "You are big news down in the underworld. It's not like I make it a habit to sleep with women on Earth and then hope they have my child."

"Swimmers gone on strike?" I asked.

He chuckled again, shaking his head. "You have your mother's twisted sense of humor."

Frowning, I said, "Well, I'd rather not be compared to her."

"Why is that?" He asked, bending a leg over one knee and clasping his hands together in his lap. His suit looked expensive, fitting his form perfectly like it was just made for him. I wondered if that was even his real form, demons sometimes took on different forms to make their victim feel more at ease.

"She left me is why." I replied. "You know how kids are, I have abandonment issues.

Lucifer sighed. "There is a lot you don't know and not having all the answers gives you no right to judge. She didn't leave you so you can quit acting like a baby. She is with me in hell and has to remain there."

"Why?"

He straightened. "Shouldn't you be passed the stage where you keep asking why? It is for me to know and for you to not find out." He rose. "Be ready tonight after your work is over." Then he was gone.

Waiting a few seconds to make sure he was gone for sure, I wrapped the sheet around me some more and dragged it across the floor, as I made my way to the bathroom. The robe was hanging on the back of the door, so I snatched it putting it on over the sheet. The sheet dropped to the floor, and then I kicked it to the side, not worrying about cleaning up the mess I was making now.

So mom was in hell for some unknown reason. I didn't know if that meant I should forgive her for leaving me behind or not. Things weren't making sense, but when did they ever? My life was filled with unexplained things, I just had to learn how to accept it and move on. My birthday was over a month ago, so why was Lucifer just now showing up? True, things were feeling different and that included my hormones. I thought they were already bad, but it was becoming almost too much to keep away from guys. Like a cat in heat, I wanted to rub my ass on every passing man.

Blowing out an irritated breath, I went to my duffel bag to pull out a pair of black leather pants and a silk red camisole. This was news that had to be relayed to Carter, in case I was compromising the case with personal problems. Of course the bastard had to come at the worst time. He couldn't hold off on having a family reunion until after the case was over? Carter was too invested in the case, so even if I was to lose a limb, he would expect me to get to the bottom of it.

Slipping on my panties, I heard someone coming up the hall. Hurriedly, I went to the door and locked it. Then there was a knock. "Blake?"

Nick.

"Uh, yeah?" I stumbled over to my pants, nearly falling on my face, but managed to get them and slip them on with a quick zip. When I heard the door handle moving, I shook my head in disbelief. Seriously? Was he trying to come into my room? Slipping on the camisole, I went over to the door to unlock and open it.

Standing with a tray of food was Nick looking like he had been up for more than an hour. He wore a pair of black slacks and another button up white shirt that was rolled up at the sleeves exposing well-muscled forearms. "Breakfast?" He asked.

"I can see we have no boundaries here in this house," I muttered. Eggs, bacon, toast and pancakes, yum. Grabbing the food, I took it to set on the dresser. Snatching a piece of bacon, I went to the mirrored dresser to examine my wild hair. Sure enough, it looked horrible. My brush was still on the dresser from using it after my shower yesterday morning, so I dragged it through my hair, opting to put it up in a ponytail. I didn't feel like messing with it, so lazy day it would be. I grabbed my katana sitting on the other dresser, strapped it on. Swearing because I forgot my other sword, I motioned for Nick to turn around. Moving fast in case Nick decided to take a peek, I strapped that on and slipped the camisole back on. "You can turn around."

He watched me with an amused expression on his handsome face, as I dug through my case of weapons. I found my wrist sheaths that held small knives. Grabbing my boots, I checked the toes and heels to make sure the knives were working in those and then slipped them on. Complete in arming myself, I felt my body relax with the familiarity of them and grinned. "What is on the agenda today?"

"You have a lot to put on." He said, leaning against the dresser after snagging a piece of bacon to eat as he examined me from head to toe. Staying silent, he chose to ignore my question.

Nodding, I went to the tray to chow down, accepting that he was the type to play mind games. The pancakes were fantastic! They were all covered in fruit and syrup. Ooh! There was sausage on the plate too. Dancing in place I hurriedly ate, moaning every time I tasted something different. With a full mouth I said, "This is fantastic."

He chuckled. "I will tell the chef your compliments." Brushing off his hands, he headed toward the door. "When you are finished with your breakfast just leave the tray there. Someone will get it. Then meet me in my office, it is time for you to meet your team. You have a lot of catching up to do, so no minute to waste."

Team? Watching him leave, I shoveled some more sausage in my mouth. So now I had a team? That was interesting. For once I can boss people around and make them suffer like I always have to. This was going to be fun. I hated always being the one getting told what to do and then my uncontrollable need to rebel even though I knew I would end up getting punished. Eager to see who would be working under me, I finished up the last of the pancakes and then hurried out of the room.

The house was pretty busy for people just waking up. Already all of the chairs in the lobby were full with people who were eager to see Nick. I noticed some of them were human, but the majority were vampires and I knew that because they stared hungrily at the humans. All were dressed in suits looking tense as if they were auditioning or interviewing for a job. Nick was a hard ass so the nervousness was warranted.

"Nick is looking for a new accountant because he fired the last one."

Jumping, I looked behind me to find Eli starting down the steps, only inches away. Once he made it to the bottom I followed him, keeping my mouth shut. He was probably super pissed at me, but what could I do really? My job was what was important. Love later. Not that I couldn't find it later since vampires lived for a long time. Unless someone went "Off with her head!" as an axe came down over my neck. Considering my luck, it all really wouldn't surprise me. Knowing that was possibly in my future should have detoured me from causing so much trouble.

Eli glanced down at his watch frowning. "I have to go begin the interviews." He mumbled, moving away from me.

Relieved we were avoiding the elephant in the room, I followed, but at a much slower pace. Everyone in the lobby looked over at me probably wondering who I was, since the guard mostly consisted of males. Most female vampires kept to themselves when it came to employment. A lot of them liked to keep their independence and owned their own place of business or played the stock market enough to live without working much.

My hand settled on the top of my katana as I sauntered behind Eli, my ponytail bobbing back and forth. From the office door I could already see people inside standing and waiting. They wore similar clothing which looked more like a uniform. I wondered if my red camisole would get me in trouble, but Nick didn't say anything to me when he glanced up.

There were four people waiting. One was a female with super short black hair that was spiked with electric blue tips. Her skin was even paler than mine, but all I could really see was her face and neck, since she wore a long sleeved shirt. Next to her was a really tall man that was bulky like a wrestler. I bet two hundred dollars he was approached for wrestling as a career. Probably had the name Tallman Vamporilla or something. The dude was huge! His hair was a shocking red color, the length reaching his shoulders. When his gaze met mine I saw nothing but green flames. Was he full vampire? The scent was off about him, but figuring out what was making my nose work overtime. Deciding I would find out later, I went to the next person who was still taller but only half the size as Vamporilla. He was Asian from the looks of it. His muscles were glistening with sweat, probably coming in from a work out. I had to see what the workout room looked like.

Then last, but not least, was a blond haired vampire who looked bored. He examined his nails, rubbed them on his shirt. He glanced up at me, but that was all he did before going back to examining his nails. Nice. It didn't look like I was going to get much of a team, but what was the saying? Don't judge a book by its cover? If they proved to be spectacular I would never judge another person by their appearance again.

Nick was seated behind his desk reading a file. Looking up he smiled, waving for me to come stand next to him. I did like a good girl, but hopped up on the edge of the desk to sit. That earned me a raised eyebrow from Nick, but I didn't comment.

"This is your team. Even though you will be with me most of the time, there may be tasks I send you on. These four are yours to command. Becoming part of your team is like a promotion for them." He explained, as he sat back in his chair. Reaching in front of him, he tossed a file in my direction. "My first task for you is to find out who left the girl in my room. I know you will have to be around me most times when I go out in public, but use these four to do some legwork in the meantime." His dark gaze then swung to the four in front of him. "You are to follow every order she gives. Do you understand?" They all nodded, giving him the respect I wish they gave me when I first came in.

Pleased he said, "Now for introductions." He nodded to the tall guy to start.

Clearing his throat, tall guy didn't change his position of spread out feet and hands behind his back. His fiery gaze met mine. "My name is Mitch O'Rourke. Been serving Nick since 1787. I am half vampire and half werewolf."

"Ah that explains it. I knew you smelled funny." I said, shaking my head. I should have realized the combination. Had I taken time to break it all down, figuring it out should have been simple, but I had a five second attention span.

"Smell funny?" He asked, somewhat unsure on if he was able to ask me, but pissed enough to suffer any consequences for doing so.

Nodding, I said, "Yeah, when I came in here I knew you weren't full vamp, so I was trying to figure out the other half of you."

Black haired girl rolled her eyes. "He is sensitive. All men are."

Mitch glared at her. "You weren't spoken to."

I hurried up off the desk to get between them before something happened. "No, it is fine. It is okay if you guys talk when you aren't spoken to. Unless I am giving a briefing and anything else important. Right now this is me trying to get to know you. I want you guys feeling comfortable around me, not walking on egg shells."

"This is the guard, ma'am. Everything is based on orders." Mitch replied.

Getting toe to toe with him I looked up into his face having no problem showing my authority. "You work under me, which means what I say goes and that includes on how freely you are to speak around me. Are we clear?" The steel in my voice surprised him, but he quickly recovered his face going free of any emotion. He nodded, straightening his back and moving his gaze over my head to stare at the wall behind me.

I went back to my spot at Nick's desk, earning a smile from him. "You may go." He said, nodding to short hair girl.

"My name is Charity Williams. I have been with Nicky-"

"Hold up." I said, putting up a finger. "Nicky?"

Nick sighed loudly, as if I was proving myself a pain in the ass already. "Nicky, yes. She is my sister by marriage, will you now allow her to continue?"

Shrugging, I nodded for Charity to move on. Charity just flashed a smile, making her already childlike features more childlike. "Now I think you know how I became part of the guard. I can tell you stuff like what pisses him off more than anything. Or that he watches the Princess Diaries at least once a month."

"Holy shit! You watch the Princess Diaries?" I gasped, looking at him in exaggerated shock.

His face was red with either embarrassment or anger. When his whole body began to shake and his fist clenched, I went for the latter. "Charity, this is hardly appropriate." He snapped.

Leaping off the desk again, I went to Charity's side, putting my arm around her shoulders. "Now, now, Nick, is this how you treat your sister and now my favorite person in the whole wide world?"

Shaking his head in disbelief, he leaned forward to run both hands through his hair in frustration. "Please continue before I turn one of you to ash." He growled.

Both Charity and I grinned at each other. It was almost scary to find that Nick had no sense of humor. He was constantly getting angry with everyone over small things. The dude seemed to get easily embarrassed or maybe it was the lack of respect from Charity? He didn't want everyone to see that someone could actually treat him as an equal.

Taking my seat back at the desk, I looked at the Asian guy raising my eyebrows. "I am Chad Chung." He said. What surprised me was how he spoke in an American accent. Almost like some kind of surfer dude and when it isn't something you expect, it always takes your brain two seconds longer to register what he said.

"How old are you?" I asked curiously.

Chad frowned, trying not to let the question bother him too much. "I rather not say."

When I raised my eyebrows in challenge, he turned to Nick for help. "Are you fucking kidding me?" I leapt off the desk again, stomping up to Chad. Okay, so this was probably the wrong way to go with people on your team, but it pissed me off that he looked to Nick for help. I was the boss and they would all get that in their heads. If they didn't, well I couldn't trust them. "You answer my damn question." I snarled like I was a drill sergeant in the military.

"I think it is inappropriate to ask one's age, Blake." Nick said from behind me.

Looking over my shoulder at him I glared. "I asked a question and I expect a response, Nick. How else will they learn to respect me? It doesn't matter if I asked which way his dick pointed, I want a damn answer."

Charity tried to hold back her laughter and when it was proving to be difficult, so she turned around to get a hold of herself. Nick shook his head, scowling. My guess was the introductions were not going according to plan. He waved at Chad, surrendering. "As I said, you are to do as she says."

Defeated, Chad's shoulder slumped. "I am only ten in vampire years."

My mouth fell open in horror. "Are you kidding me? I thought you gave me the best of the best? I wasn't expecting some kind of rookie that barely has his training wheels removed."

"Blake, Chad is the best at what he does. Show her, boy." Nick sat back in his chair, steepling his fingers as he waited.

Charity ran to the back of the room to retrieve a duffel bag, reminding me of a kid who just saw the presents under the Christmas tree. I watched her with a 'what the hell' look as she unzipped it and dropped it in front of Chad. He climbed inside, sat down and then leaned forward. Charity pulled the zipper around and then threw up her hands. "Tada!"

I looked at Nick. "Nice trick, but does he have the strength and skills to hold against a master vampire?"

Master vampires were very old vampires who often develop special abilities. Under usual circumstances a ten year old vampire would be down within seconds because they wouldn't be able to hold up against a thousand year old vamp. With me it was a little different because of my demon blood. I had more strength than your typical vampire. Plus, special abilities for the win! Nick probably had his own powers, but I didn't know what they were. Neither did the FBI, which probably wasn't a good thing, unless he didn't need to use them that often.

"He can. What you probably cannot detect in his blood is the shifter. He changes to tiger form," he explained. That was another reason why purebloods didn't like mixed bloods. Somewhere in our genetics our two halves force us to be stronger. But to have a mixed blood child was rare, so for me to have two on my team made me really special. I rubbed my hands together greedily.

Chad was let out by Charity and I pat his head. "Nice."

Nick shook his head. "They are not pets!"

I grinned. "I have always wanted a pet tiger." Crawling away, Chad looked at me as if I was a nut. "I don't have to feed him raw meat or anything, do I? A scratching post? What about one of those laser lights? I have always wanted a cat so I could do that. " I sighed dreamily, staring up at the ceiling.

"Blake!" Nick stood up. "He needs to be treated like any other vampire, so stop being a complete ass." Leaning forward with his palms faced down on the desk he glowered at me. "Let's get the final introduction out of the way before I ring your neck."

Charity grinned. "Isn't he Mr. Sunshine?"

The blond vampire straightened after realizing he was up for his introduction. "I'm Reed Velrosa. Been working for Nick about three hundred years now. My father used to be his best friend, so naturally I became part of his guard, like my dad."

"Good. Now take this folder, go to the conference room in the basement." Nick said, snatching his phone to make a phone call.

I high fived Charity as we exited the room. Mitch led the way down the hall further where it was a little darker. The lights were dimmer, forcing my eyes to adjust, finding shapes of objects around us. We went around the corner that led to an elevator. Once we all piled on, Reed hit the basement button. After a stomach dropping experience, the elevator doors opened revealing another hallway where the floor was made of industrial tile and cement for walls.

About four doors down the door opened and Eli stepped out. He motioned us to go inside, but put a hand up for me to wait. When the others went inside he said, "Thirty minutes and Nick has to go to a meeting with Declan."

I groaned. "Declan?"

Eli nodded. "You will have to go with him. Naturally I go, but obviously he needs you now, so make this quick." Then he took off, not saying another word to me. I wasn't sure if I should feel hurt or not. I only knew the man about a day now so what the hell was my problem? I wasn't the kind of girl who pined after a man. Not that he looked like your typical man, I would totally take a bite out of him. Pushing my perverted thoughts away I decided now wasn't the time to analyze the situation. There were more important things to do, like finding Lucy.

Inside everyone was seated around a long table, whispering like kids in a classroom. The lights were bright but dim enough to not overdo it on a vampire's vision. There was a marker board to my right side and a desk with pens and paper scattered everywhere. I handed each of them some of the items, then sat down to look through the folder finding information on the missing girl. She was human, which was no good. Last thing we needed was a human panic attack. Usually the authorities would come around, then human protests would be set up around vampire hang outs, but most of the time there were the crazy religious people who believed in them. What the hell did they know?

Didn't they realize vampires weren't real? Gosh.

What humans can't understand, they fear. The girl had only been nineteen, which made the situation even worse, if that were possible. She was probably a college student and relied on her parent's money to get by. How were you supposed to disguise the bites so humans didn't know they were from vampires?

The human authorities didn't know about the Covert because it was a vampire dirty secret and a big part of our history, unfortunately. We didn't need to panic the human population with the truth about our existence and up until recently neither did the Covert. Apparently, they changed their mind. Flipping through more information on the girl I stopped to read who the parents were. "Shit."

"My sentiments exactly," Mitch said, obviously reading the same thing. "How the hell are we supposed to cover up the Deputy Mayor's daughter?"

Frowning, I went through the folder, completely examining everything. "Simple. She has been reported missing for over a year. We can dispose of her body, but this will require some drastic measures." As vampires we did what we had to do in order to survive. Our kind was more animalistic than we cared to admit. One human death could mean the end of a vampire race so care had to be taken. If the Covert kept targeting celebrity children we were in deep shit. Obviously, it had been going on for a while. How long had Declan known? If he knew people who mattered the most were disappearing at the hands of the Covert, shouldn't he have launched a full investigation? You would think. But then Declan was not your idea of a good King. How he managed to be in charge for nearly two hundred years was beyond me. The man was lucky to get that position and for him to be in control so long was by far a miracle. He killed the previous King when his guard should have been there to protect him, but considering how sadistic some were, they could have been easily paid off.

"I can only imagine how many of these girls have gone missing. What other important women are out there?" Charity asked, viewing the crime pictures. "I heard men have been missing also. More of them than before."

Mitch shrugged. "We need to find out how they decide which ones to grab." He looked over at Charity. "I've heard about the men, but it has to happen so infrequently that it goes unnoticed.

Chad nodded in agreement. "Male or female, we have to get to the bottom of this before the humans get wind of our kind."

"We should hang out at some of the clubs. There has to be a way in to one of those raves by club connection. Where else do you find the freaks?" I asked. Then I thought about the Internet. There was probably a website or forum for this type of thing. Heaviness set in my stomach as I thought about it. I didn't even want to think about the possibilities.

"Good idea," Reed said in response to my club idea. "I think we should start out with the club that holds the best clientele. The vampires that buy the victims have to have some kind of money, right?" We all nodded in agreement, but that didn't eliminate that many vampires considering most of them have been alive for long time.

"We should hit The Beast," Reed nodded as if he finally made up his mind.

Standing up I looked up at the clock. "Sounds good. So about midnight we will head out over there. Please wear street clothing so you can fit into the club scene, we can't look like the guard, obviously."

Mitch grinned. *"We,"* he motioned to the four of them, "look like the guard. You are the one looking like a rainbow."

Looking down at my red camisole, I stuck out my tongue. "Whatever, just do it. We meet in the lobby. Now I have to go play body shield with Nick."

Chapter Five

Deciding at the last minute I should probably look the part, I ran up the two flights of stairs to my room. My tray was already gone, bed was made and the floor was cleaned up from my clothes that I had left lying around. I pawed through my duffel bag finding a small black t-shirt to wear. Finding a bra, I tore off my camisole, slipped on the bra and then the shirt, hoping that I wouldn't be late for Nick's meeting. When I turned around, I squeaked in surprise to find Michael watching me from the doorway. My god the man was a pervert!

"Uh, you could have knocked," I said.

Michael grinned, leaning on the door frame as he crossed his arms over his wide chest. "But the door was open. Free viewing."

Blowing a strand of hair from my face, I glared. "No one comes up here but Nick," I said. "He is busy downstairs and I am in a hurry."

"So, you were okay with Nick walking in on you?" He asked with raised eyebrows, trying to poke at me.

Exasperated, I shook my head. "Nevermind. I have somewhere to be and this conversation is boring me."

Moving like a wolf stalking his prey, he got in front of me, his chest nearly knocking me back. "I came here to talk."

Checking my weapons again, I shrugged trying to make it seem like his abrupt behavior wasn't bothering me. "So talk."

Amused, he nodded. "I want you, Blake."

"Great! This was an awesome conversation, and unfortunately I am not interested."

Surprised, he chuckled. "Right, but your body says otherwise. I can smell how much you want me right now."

Stupid werewolf nose. Why did I have to be Miss Obvious in all of this? I just continued to go through my stuff, finding my knives I could stick inside my boot next to my leg, so I could feel less awkward in his presence. I then went to the mirror to check my hair, took the ponytail out and redid it. Still ignoring him, I went into the bathroom to grab some mints the cleaning person left behind. There was some in the room, too, but I wanted to get out of his view. Like that worked. He took that as an invitation. How? I have no idea, but the alpha wolf followed me in and closed the door.

Panic reared its ugly head because now I felt like a caged animal, which wasn't a good thing for two reasons. One, I hated feeling trapped, it was like being in a coffin and despite it being a complete myth, the whole idea of being in one scared the shit out of me. Two, alpha boy was putting himself in danger by locking himself in a room with what some may consider a wild animal. But the last was probably canceled out, since he was basically a wild animal because of his wolf.

"Bathrooms usually mean privacy," I said, backing up as he stalked toward me.

He only grinned, pressing me against the wall, his breath on my face. "Tell me you don't want my cock inside of you."

When I went to respond he pressed himself against me, letting me know someone was really happy to see me. I swallowed thickly, looking up at him. This was bad. My body was already heating up with anticipation. Down Demon! Down! Oh no, she didn't want to listen. Sex meant power to her. Little slut. Why didn't my vampire just tie the bitch up?

Putting my hands on his chest I tried to push him away, but he ran his hands up my sides causing me to sigh as heat pooled low in my belly. His thumbs brushed over my nipples and I trembled, ready to give into what he was offering.

"Blake?"

Eli! The spell broken, I pushed Michael out of the way ignoring his shocked cry as I went passed him. Squealing as he nearly caught hold of me again, I hurried to the door before he could stop me. When I looked behind me, he was still in the same spot, eyes lit up with the possible chase. "This isn't over." He growled, sending a ripple of fear mixed with sexual need up my spine.

Oh gods. Throwing open the door I ran out of the bathroom right into Eli's arms. The air went out of him as he grabbed me in shock. He went to say something, but stiffened when

Michael came out adjusting his tie as he if just finished getting dressed. What a jerk-face. "We will continue this later, Blake." He left the room quickly.

"Stupid wolves!" I hissed angrily, moving away from Eli. My reaction was a little late, but that was okay because Eli wouldn't know that "Thinks he can pee on me to mark his territory." Annoyed, I smoothed out my shirt unable to stop thinking about Michael touching me. I shivered, unable to help the ripple effect the thoughts.

Eli stood there watching me with what looked like jealousy. When he saw me staring at him, the emotion melted away, and he was blank faced leaving no evidence of what he was feeling. "Michael usually gets what he wants."

I started laughing. "Yeah, and it doesn't help my demon half decided it was a good time to let him have it. I barely have any control. Fuck. I should ask Lucifer about this."

"Lucifer?" Eli asked.

Nodding, I looked at the bedside table. Five minutes to be in Nick's office. "We better get down there before Nick decides to send someone after me. The man is really impatient. I think I pissed him off this morning."

Laughing, Eli caught up with me in the hallway. "He likes you, though, that is what counts."

"If you say so. I think the man is at war with himself, unsure if he should lock me in a cage or kill me." I hurried down the steps with Eli following me. A meeting with Declan, this ought to be fun. He didn't know I was undercover. He knew who I was too. Hopefully he didn't blow my cover, or shit will hit the fan.

*

We were meeting Declan at his hotel and that was pretty weird considering he rarely met with anyone because of his fear of being assassinated. If he did agree to meet with you was always on his terms or be punished. The man was a freaking immortal Hitler. If it wasn't against the laws he probably would resort to killing us and torture. Shit, wait, he does do that. Silly me, how could I forget how much of a sadistic bastard he was?

I looked around outside the hotel, listening to anything that may be out of the ordinary. It wasn't that far from headquarters, since both were right downtown. It was within walking distance, maybe a mile and a half. I didn't smell anything threatening just a mixture of the factory two miles away with a faint odor of vampire somewhere, but too far to be threatening.

The placement of the hotel was ridiculous. It was right in the middle of the city and you had to park on a ramp. You basically had to go through a maze just to get to it. We were greeted by an average sized vampire with light brown hair once we made it to the door. His hair was brushed in a Boy Scout style, and he probably never changed it once since his younger years. Whenever that was. I wasn't old enough to really tell vampire ages yet. That came about a hundred years later or so.

This little vampire was Ormond Zietal. Declan's man slave. And yeah you could take that any way you wanted, because Declan probably done it with this man. Lover, friend, or slave. Take your pick. I don't judge people, but Declan was on the top of my list to not picture doing something naughty. Seriously, the guy made me vomit a little just looking at him. You couldn't tell him that, though. He thought of himself as a god. No one could possibly resist someone as old and powerful as he. I snorted at my thoughts, earning an agitated expression from Declan's boy toy.

"Mr. Declan is waiting in his suite for you, Nicholas." Ormond said, leading the way to the elevators.

"Please, call me Nick." Nick said, looking completely at ease.

Everyone in the lobby stared at me. The girl with a giant katana strapped to her waist. I might as well have been waving a red flag at a bull, but no one said anything. Just stared, almost making me feel self-conscious, but I couldn't let that get to me now. My main worries should be Nick and the possible exposure because of Declan. Besides, they probably saw a lot of weird things with Declan being a guest.

Eli stayed alongside of me and whispered. "The man thinks he is better than us."

Nodding I smiled. "Oh yeah, I know. I have met him before, little creep."

The ride in the elevator was quiet as we went up. The doors opened up to the floor of the suite without having to stop for anyone else to get on from other floors. Down the hall we could hear some classical music playing, Declan was obviously in that direction. We continued to follow Ormond. The suite door opened and a waiter exited. I saw the two pin prick marks on his neck and he seemed a little dazed. Looked like Declan got hungry and made sure to erase the guy's memory, because he was hardly able to walk straight. Not only that, he didn't even look at us as we stopped to wait for him to move past. He was going to be a zombie until he made it downstairs.

Ormond frowned, obviously not pleased with the idea of Declan sucking on another man's neck. His body became rigid as he entered the room. I could smell blood in the air when we crossed the threshold, my fangs threatening to come out as the vampire wanted her own blood. Declan was seated on a couch with a robe around him. It was plainly obvious he was nude underneath. One arm was propped up on the back of the couch and the other hand holding a wine glass. If I was to describe him, I could best compare him to the actor Daniel Craig when it came to the looks department.

"Welcome, Nicholas and Eli." He took a sip of wine his gaze sweeping over us and then froze. "Blake Noble?"

Nick nodded, gesturing toward me. "This is my new personal guard, my Guardian."

Studying me, Declan leaned forward to set his glass on the coffee table in front of him. He was debating on how to respond to my presence. My heart pounded as seconds ticked by waiting for him to blow my cover. "She will make a very good one for you, Nicholas." He said finally. My body relaxed all over. I thought my heart would burst from my chest in panic. Carter really should have told Declan. This could have been a horrible meeting because of all the ends not being tied up.

Declan gestured toward the loveseat across from him. "Please, sit."

Eli and Nick sat down while I took a stand behind them, ready for any possible action. With a slight smile Declan looked amused. "I have brought you here to discuss the recent situation of the Deputy Mayor's daughter found in your room. He hasn't been notified yet, but the body has been taken care of. If anyone is to approach you, the story is that you know nothing about it."

Nick nodded his head. "Yes, sire."

"Good. Though, I have my doubts that you are not responsible for killing this girl." Declan said with a serious expression.

"Sire, there is proof on her body that the Covert is responsible. The brand is there." Nick pointed out.

"Which could easily be duplicated by you. Anyone can create that damn brand." He said, waving off the idea like it was a fly.

"Seriously, Nick, can you honestly blame me for suspecting, considering your past?"

Stiffening, I felt the tension rising in the air. Nick's jaw muscles jumped and I could see the anger taking hold of his body. "That is long in the past." He growled, trying to control his emotions.

Declan shrugged. "Jack the Ripper is hardly that long ago."

Oh my gods. I couldn't believe what I just heard. Even shock registered on Eli's face, but he quickly covered it with a blank face. People suspected he was a vampire, but Nick? That would have been my last guess. How could a homicidal maniac become cured? Well, I guess that was a dumb question considering most of the older vampires had murdered people in the past.

Smiling, Declan looked to me and Eli. "Didn't know that did you? Did you know his wife was his first victim?"

"I thought she died by fire?" Eli said, trying to correct Declan.

"No, that was another woman, the secret lover." Declan motioned for Ormond to come sit by him. When the man did, he started playing with his hair, looking eerily calm while doing it. Ormond's eyes fluttered closed as he sat to enjoy it. He looked like a doll compared to Declan. So pale, almost porcelain like.

Nick stood up. "Is this why you brought me here? To accuse me of murdering this girl?"

Throwing back his head, Declan laughed loudly. "Oh no, I am just warning you. If another incident occurs like this one inside your home, you will be brought to justice. Death is the penalty, of course."

"Of course." Nick all but spat. "I can promise you I had nothing to do with this girl's death."

"Promises, promises, Nick, you said the exact same thing back then." And when Nick tried to object, Declan said, "Dismissed."

When we were back in the car everyone was silent. I couldn't get over the Jack the Ripper thing. Horrible things happened to those women. A lot of it I wouldn't have suspected Nick to do. Yet, he had basically admitted to everything in front of us. How many people knew of his past? Probably most of the old vampires, but that may not even be true if the SCD records held nothing about it. I didn't know if I could stand to be so close to him at the moment. I would probably have nightmares after finding this information out. And what Declan had said made sense. How could we not know that Nick wasn't the one responsible for this? His past was an indication he could be that horrifying.

I felt his eyes on me, so I shifted uncomfortably. He sighed loudly before saying, "I feel like I need to explain to you about my past." He said to me and Eli.

Eli cleared his throat. "If you want." But what he meant was, "You bet you better tell us!"

Nick chuckled. "Not if I want. I have to explain, otherwise, you will always wonder about me." He gazed out the window for a few seconds clasping his hands together. "I didn't do the mutilation to the women. My partner did. The cuts to the throat covered up the fang marks and that is the gist of what I did. Sometimes I drained them dry. I will also admit that I may have slept with a few of them." He shrugged. "I wasn't at my best then, obviously."

I patted his shoulder awkwardly. "I guess that makes it better, since you didn't gut them and stuff. But I still think we should Nick proof the house and remove all sharp objects."

He rolled his eyes at me and looked out the window again. "You have a way of making a man feel better, Blake." He chuckled.

Eli glanced at me from the rearview mirror, his dark eyes meeting mine. "Did you get a chance to look over the folder?" He asked me, changing the subject.

Nodding, I said, "We have some ideas that we can go over tonight when I get back."

Nick took out his cell phone, scrolled through some contacts. "Good, the sooner we can figure this out the better. Last thing we need is the news getting a hold of this information."

*

By the time we got back to the house it was nearly time for me to get ready for the club. Hurrying up the steps, I went through my duffel bag only to end up disappointed. Dumb ass me forgot to bring some clothes to go out in. Angry, I threw my hands up in the air swearing up a storm.

"Problems?"

Eli stood at the door holding a bag. "What is that?" I asked, walking over.

He watched me, then at the last minute before I could grab it, he pulled the bag back. "I will let you have this if I can go tonight."

"Go where?" I asked innocently.

The look he gave me made me laugh. "Seriously, I know you guys plan on going to the clubs. I want to help you find out what the hell is going on and why someone is trying to frame Nick for murders."

"Fine." I reached past him, snatching the bag. Looking inside, I found a corset with red lace and leather pants. Raising my eyebrow, I stared at him.

His face reddened with embarrassment. "I had Charity pick it out earlier today after your meeting. I kind of figured you came unprepared for nights out." What he meant was, he thought I was a lost cause when it came to fashion just like Kristin did.

After I thanked him, I watched him walk down the hall and then wiped away my drool on the way to take a shower. The shower relaxed my entire body as the hot water beat over my back. Tonight I was hoping someone had some kind of information about the Covert. For the vampires to let this go for so many years was ridiculous. The number of people had to be staggering and to think some of them were ones that no one even remembered. Usually those who lived on the streets were already forgotten. Here the Covert was making money on the lives of innocents. Rape, drained of blood and who knows what the hell else had been done to them.

Rinsing the shampoo from my hair, I turned my thoughts to my SCD job. To be honest, I was enjoying the personal guard more than my agent job. I wouldn't tell that to Carter, though, because he probably would ask me if someone messed with my head, like changed my memories. That was impossible on other vampires, unless the master vampire was one of the first to be born. There was only one vampire left from the first ones, and no one even knew where he was. The first vampires were called Ancients, and I found the name amusing because it wasn't a word I would use to describe a superior being.

My shower went a little faster than I wanted, but the team was probably already downstairs waiting for me. Then there was Eli, who was coming and my heart couldn't help but beat faster in excitement or was that fear? At this point, I wasn't sure if I was happy about that or not since nothing good could come from us hanging around each other. His presence would be distracting enough. But he wanted to help, so why not let him? Nick was supposed to be a suspect, but I had the gut feeling he wasn't. The man may have had a past but who doesn't? My life hadn't been as long as his, but I was almost positive that soon I would begin to regret events in my life just like anyone else.

Remarkably, the corset fit perfectly, squeezing me all in the right areas. Had I not been used to wearing them, I would be walking stiffly and probably not survive the night. Charity guessed my size pretty well, so that only helped. I left my hair down, allowing the curls to go natural. I had those loose cork screw type that most people wish they had and me wishing I never had them. Sometimes they were such a pain in the ass to control, I thought about chopping off all my hair, but most of the time I would straighten them out to show them who was actually in control.

Spritzing on some perfume, I went back into the bedroom to load up on weapons again. I put on my leather sheaths for my wrists, knives in my boots, and the blade down my back. I had a shorter version than the one I usually used. The corset revealed too much of my back for me to wear the one I preferred, but there was no way I was going without any weapons. Maybe one day I would actually use a gun, but so far I hadn't run into a situation where a sword couldn't take care of business.

Downstairs everyone was waiting, like I thought. Charity had chosen similar clothes to mine, but she had no color on hers, they were completely black. Mitch, Reed and Chad all wore jeans and regular T-shirts that were tight enough to expose the lines of their chests. We all looked fantastic. Looking around I was trying to find Eli, when he appeared at the top of the first set of stairs. My mouth dropped open. Charity came over and pushed up on my chin, offering her assistance so I didn't make a fool of myself.

Eli looked amazing. Of course, I always saw him in suits and nothing else. Not that I knew him long enough to see him in anything else. But from the look of Charity's expression, it was rare to see him without his professionalism. For the club outing he wore a pair of faded blue jeans and a white button up shirt that was open at the top and sleeves rolled up to his elbows, exposing muscled forearms. His skin was smooth and tan, providing amazing contrast with his shirt. Hairless chest, whoa baby. It took every ounce of strength I had not to jump and have my way with him. Even his hair was styled differently. The scent of his cologne filled my nose making my brain go foggy and causing my hormones to rage like girls at a boy band concert.

"Shit, Blake, do you need a napkin?" Reed asked, laughing.

Mitch and Chad rolled their eyes and started to lead the way. "I'm driving!" Mitch called out before anyone else could.

Did everyone have a fabulous car? My hand hovered over the exterior of Mitch's Mercedes. Nick must pay really well for them to afford expensive things like cars. "To the Bat mobile!" I cried, hurrying to the car.

"We have to take two vehicles." Reed said, heading over toward a red truck. Chad caught up with him. "See you guys up there."

Charity called shot gun, but I suspected that was done on purpose. Before she climbed in, she gave me a thumbs up, raising her eye brows. In response I just rolled my eyes at her attempt to force Eli and me together.

*

The Beast was a club that no one outside of the supernatural would recognize. To people outside of the supernatural world it looked like an abandoned warehouse. It even had the graffiti and broken windows. The actual club was underground and the main hangout for Supernaturals, and from experience, not the good kinds.

We all walked to a black door that was guarded by a burly werewolf. He looked at us with zero emotion on his face. "Names?" He asked, looking down at his clipboard.

Mitch said, "We are friends with Alex."

Alex? Whoever that was helped us get into the club. We followed Mitch, who seemed like he knew more about the club than the rest of us, his stiff demeanor completely disappearing. Obviously we knew who the player was, because he winked and slapped girls' asses as he went by, heading to the stairs where a line started to get to the main floor. Eli smashed into the back of me. "Sorry, people behind me." He whispered. Not that I was complaining. Again his cologne overflowed my senses.

"What the hell is holding up the line?" Someone asked from the back.

"Shut the fuck up back there!" A man in the front yelled, which I assumed was one of the bouncers. Or maybe not. People were assholes these days.

Eventually we made it to the front of the line where another bulky guy was, but he was a vampire. He opened the doorway for us to go in. "Table fourteen." He instructed.

"Weird, we are assigned tables." I mumbled to Charity.

She nodded in agreement. "I think it is to keep seating space available for everyone. If each table is assigned to someone, they have a spot to go back to."

Kind of made sense, but I wasn't going to put too much thinking into that. We went over to a table with a card on it labeled with our number. A waitress came over immediately, dressed in netting everything. There was just a black patch covering up the important bits. Reed just stared as if he never seen a woman up close before. Mitch jabbed his elbow into him. "Get in already." He growled, annoyed.

Everyone ordered their drinks and looked around the club, checking out anything that stood out. The music thumped and the lights flashed along with the beat of it. There was a variety of races around. Pixies, fairies, werewolves, vampires and even elves, which were rare enough in themselves.

Reed climbed over the table and hopped off. "I am going to go investigate." He grinned.

Chad rolled his eyes. "In other words, he is going to go find himself a female."

Mitch climbed out himself. "Sounds like a good plan to me."

"Make sure you actually do some work out there!" I yelled.

"That translates to no boning until you get some information we need!" Charity called out after me.

Eli shook his head. "Come, let's dance." He took my hand leading me out to the dance floor.

"I think I should look around some and I think we can do that best by splitting up." I hedged, looking around while he dragged me out to the dance floor. I needed an escape plan and fast. This was exactly what I was trying to avoid, but the man was stubborn.

"In a little while. For now, dance with me." Eli was an excellent dancer, his body moving, without missing a beat. Sometimes I caught myself just standing there and staring, when my brain would suddenly come online and say "Hey get moving before you look like a dumbass." Which from the expression on Eli's face, it was already too late.

When the music slowed some people cheered, because they could get close to their partner. Before I could make my escape, Eli tugged me toward him, knocking the breath from my lungs when I slammed into his chest. When I moved stiffly with him, he chuckled. "You are so fighting this." He said, lips next to my ear.

Shivering, I shook my head. "I don't know what you are talking about."

"Don't you? This attraction and you can't deny it because your body tells different."

"That's the demon. She'll boink anything." I replied, pulling back enough to look at his face, but quickly averted my eyes.

He didn't seem to like my answer, so I just pulled away. "Let's split up." I hurried in another direction, feeling a twinge of guilt at the same time. We couldn't do what we wanted. There were bigger things to accomplish, like finding Lucy, Carter's niece.

Someone grabbed my arm, spinning me around and into them and I gasped, realizing I was now in the arms of a werewolf. Fuck! Michael. He flashed me a wolfish grin as his hand slid down my back over my ass, until his fingers could get a good grip. "Fancy seeing you here." He growled, lowering his head to nibble on my neck.

Sighing, I rolled my eyes. "For some reason, I suspect this isn't a coincidence."

When I tried to pull away, his hands gripped my ass tighter to prevent me from moving. "Even though I love the idea of following you, I didn't. I own this place." He said, allowing one hand to gesture around the club.

"Well, that is great." I said with less enthusiasm than he wanted. I patted his chest. "But I have to go now. Eli and I have a date." I lied.

I tried turning away from him, but he held on. "I know you aren't on a date. I heard you telling him that you needed to separate."

Laughing uneasily, I looked around me for an escape. "Yeah, that was a joke. You know, har har."

He went to say something else when Eli appeared. "I came back for my date." Grinning, he put out his hand, waiting for mine. Michael released me, his eyes blazing with fury.

"Does Nick know you are dating his Guardian?" He asked.

Eli's face turned cold, eyes almost black. "We are adults here. Neither of us need permission to date." It was then I felt a release of power from him, it rolled out in waves stunning Michael and me. It was hard to breathe, my hand squeezed Eli's. Just as fast as it appeared, the power was gone.

Shocked, Michael straightened, rolling his shoulders to show he could handle anything. "Seems I learn something new about you, Eli. Does Nick know he is hiding one of the Ancients?"

My head snapped around to stare at Eli. The missing Ancient was Eli? Michael grinned. "I guess not. Considered yourself warned." He turned, disappearing in the crowd.

Giving me an apologetic look, Eli pulled me into him. "Not the way I wanted you to find out." He said, beginning to dance with me slowly, even though the song was now fast paced.

"I don't get it. Why would you hide?" I asked.

He smiled shyly, looking around. "Because I do not want to be Vampire King."

Making an 'o' with my mouth, I allowed him to pull me even closer to him, parts of our bodies matching up in all the right places. "If people find out, what happens?"

Eli shrugged. "Either they will try to kill me or try to force me into the position of the King. I like where I am because I have an almost uncomplicated life." He smiled looking down at me.

Right then I wasn't sure what to do. I knew a big secret that could impact the vampire race heavily. Michael now knew, which meant Nick would soon know. My gaze met Eli's, they were like a direct tunnel into his soul. He looked incredibly lonely and I never noticed it until now. Sliding a hand behind his head, I drew his mouth to mine. He kissed softly at first, body still stiff as if he was waiting for me to run. When I met him with more force he relaxed, wrapping his arms around my waist, rolling his body into mine so that my knees became weak. My tongue touched his, then grazed one of his fangs drawing blood. He moaned loudly sucking on my tongue, fingers kneading into my back. Warmth wrapped around me, binding me closer to him. I realized it was his power releasing coiling, warm tendrils around me.

"I don't mean to interrupt, but I found this." Reed appeared next to us, not even bothering to comment on what we were doing.

Growling, Eli pulled away from me. I was still dazed, my body slumped against his, but he held onto me as if he was afraid to let go. He took the card into his fingers and frowned. Seeing his expression, I looked down and immediately my mind cleared. It was a business card, plain white with just an address on it. "Where did you find it?" I asked.

Reed nodded toward the other side of the club. "Restroom. Figured we could see what we find there. This was inside one of the stalls, like someone dropped it pulling their pants down." He wiggled his eye brows.

"That's disgusting, Reed." I flipped the card over and saw the words, "More bites, more fun." Shoving it in my back pocket, I grabbed Eli's hand heading toward our table where the other three were waiting. "We're going to check this out."

*

The address wasn't that far away from the club. It was on a side street where one lone house stood, glowing luminously with all the lights on inside. There were no cars around, which I thought was pretty weird considering there was supposed to be a party going on inside.

We debated on our next step now that we finally had a lead. People who were invited probably arrived on foot because too many cars would be like placing a neon sign on the house with the giant words, 'party.' Unless it was a small party. Leaning forward between the two front seats, I drummed my fingers on the passenger seat. "Mitch, you and I will go in."

Eli protested, "No, I think I should go."

"No offense, Eli, but everyone knows you are the second to Nick. Having the Deputy Director show up will only cause everyone to flee, and we will still be in the same spot, only now they will know we are closer to discovering them than before." I squeezed his knee to show I wasn't trying to be a bitch. His hand slid over mine, the warmth sending tingles up my arm.

Mitch and I prepared to get out, but Eli grabbed my arm to stop me. I went to snap at him when he pointed out the window where someone was coming up the walkway. Imagine my surprise when I saw that it was Ben. "No fucking way!" I hissed. Seriously, Ben? Grabbing the door handle, I leapt out of the car before Eli could stop me and was on Ben within seconds, holding the sword from my back at his throat. He stared at me with surprise, eyes wide and mouth gaping open.

"B-Blake." He choked. Noticing he was doing something behind his back, I yanked on his arm causing him to drop whatever he had in his hand. Eli appeared next to me, so he bent down to pick up what ended up being a cell phone.

"He texted a group of numbers." Eli showed me the screen of the phone. On it was the word, "run."

Giving Ben a fangy smile, I pulled him an inch from my face. "You're so dead." I dragged him across the street while around twelve vampires ran from different exits of the house. I pointed behind me for my team to run after them. Everyone, including Eli, ran after the vampires, disappearing behind the house where most of them took off. "I can't believe you would betray Carter like this."

Ben glared at me, trying to shake me off like he was a trapped animal, but my grip only tightened around his shirt. "I didn't know his niece would be grabbed. I am only in it for the raves until my own girl gets captured. All I need is for her to understand that true love has no bounds. We were meant to be together." His gaze went far off, dreaming about whoever this poor girl was.

I shook him hard to get his attention. Where the hell was the Ben I knew? The one who always joked around with me? Despite how much of a pain in the ass he was I enjoyed his company. "Who is the girl you wanted captured?" I asked trying to refocus on the potential capture of another victim.

That's when my whole body went cold as I realized what was happening. This had been a trap. He smiled. "You."

Chapter Six

"She's breathing, but I can't get her to wake up."

The voice was distant, but I recognized it as Eli's. Darkness wrapped around me, the pressure of it nearly suffocating. My body floated, though not going in any specific direction, since I couldn't tell which was the right way or the wrong way. It felt like I was in the middle of nothingness, that I just existed in nothing but dark space that was neither hot nor cold. If they would just shut up I could actually get some sleep. Whatever this was, it was peaceful and numb. I liked not having to feel anything.

"At least her pulse is steady." Came Charity's voice. "But she should be awake by now."

"We don't know what was in the needle." Mitch's voice was fading.

"Crap-" but the voice disappeared and I could hear no more.

*

Bright light this time, too blinding to see beyond my eye lids. The darkness was better, at least there was no pain there, so where had it gone? This light was hot, too bright to look into, like my eyes were slowly frying from being too close to the sun. Trying to get away from it, I ran in what I thought was the opposite direction, but the pain only continued, white hot racing through every part of me. My brain screamed for me to find an escape before we finally disappeared completely.

"Blake."

The white cleared revealing a dark figure in the distance, but the sound of his voice made it seem like he was right next me. "Who are you?" I demanded, relieved as some of the pain was dying away.

"Daddy dearest." Came the reply. "You can fight this off. Think of hot lava flowing through your veins and the poison will burn away, since you are only halfblooded you can fight this off."

"Easy for you to say. You aren't the one boiling alive from the inside!"

His face appeared in front of my vision. "If you don't, you will die. Ben added salt to the serum, which is deadly to demons."

The white hot pain returned and I probably screamed, but couldn't hear with the sounds of my blood boiling in my veins. I kept trying to focus on lava like Lucifer told me to, but it was too hard to concentrate past the pain. All I could think about was a flood of water filling me to put out the fire. Someone just needed to throw me into the damn ocean. Then I realized, the pain was slowly easing away as coolness inched its way through me, disappearing until it fizzled out.

*

"Fuck! What the hell is coming out of her skin?" Reed cried, jumping back to only slam into something that made a loud noise. My eyes blinked open just in time to see him fall flat on his ass. Not vampire smooth either.

Eli was at my side, his hand hovering over my arm, afraid to touch me. "Steam or something is coming out of your pores." He said lines forming around his eyes and mouth from concern.

I laughed, choking on a puff of steam that came from my mouth. "Wow, must have put the fire out."

Letting Eli help me sit up, I looked around realizing I was in the mansion, but not in my room. Reed and Charity were next to the bed, Eli next to me. "Where am I?"

"Eli wanted you to stay in his room." Charity replied.

Raising an eyebrow, I looked at him. "Because I had to watch you and work at the same time. It has been two days, Blake."

Hurrying out of bed I stopped, recognizing I was completely naked. My mouth fell open, while staring accusingly at Eli. His hands went up in defense. "Charity did that, not me." He said hurriedly, before I could make it over to strangle him.

Charity grinned. "He was afraid you would ring his neck. Looks like he was right, poor guy." She came over helping me wrap the sheet around my body. Reed was looking in the other direction to give me some privacy. "Oh look, Reed is being a gentleman."

Reed shook his head, his expression hidden from the rest of us. "Kind of, I looked long enough to see the butterfly tattoo on her hip. And damn is it hot!" He pretended to fan himself with one hand.

Eli growled. "Leave, Reed, before I snap your neck."

Grinning, Reed snuck another look before zooming out, when Eli stood up ready to go caveman on him. Rolling my eyes, I walked out of Eli's room to go down the hall to mine. I went to my duffel bag on the floor to find it completely empty. Charity followed me into the room, and then walking to the closet. "Everything is in here now. I figured it was time you officially moved in."

When she opened the closet I frowned, confused. "These aren't mine."

"No, but they are now." Nick's voice carried in from the hall. After about two seconds he was in the room, dressed in black slacks again, but with a navy blue button up shirt. "Good to see you are awake, I missed my Guardian."

Rolling my eyes, I went through the clothes thinking they were all exactly what I would wear. Further down the rack were dresses and anything else I would need to attend formal dinners or parties. Not that I planned on wearing them. Ever. "Thanks." I said, feeling a little disturbed by the acts of kindness. Or maybe that was my pride. I hated when people bought me things that I felt I could easily get for myself.

Charity pushed Eli and Nick out. "She wants to get cleaned up, and you're making it stuffy in here." She said slamming the door in their faces. She then went to the bathroom where I heard the shower start up seconds later. "Go ahead and get in, I will pick out some clothes for you. You should probably take it easy today because we have no idea what was in that needle. Eli sent it out to get it examined but that could be days." She told me, coming out of the bathroom. "All we could smell was salt and considering you are part demon, I imagine it was what caused all this mess."

"Where is Ben?"

"He escaped. Eli went after him, but the little bastard disappeared. Stupid mother-"

I hurried into the shower in time to not hear her finish the name calling. I debated on how I would contact Carter. It was important he knew that Ben had betrayed everyone and maybe then he could track him down if I couldn't. None of it made sense. All this time he was the enemy? After years of service? It didn't explain why he would waste so much time just to do what? Capture me?

After my shower, I dressed quickly, thankful that Charity left to do whatever it was she had to do. Nick was busy in his office with someone that came in to see him and Eli was in there with him, which gave me the perfect opportunity to escape.

My car was in the underground parking garage where the rest of the vehicles were. Once I made it out on the road, I flipped open my sun visor revealing the roof of the car underneath. With some digging I found the secret compartment that hid my company cell phone. Carter answered after the first ring, his voice a comfort to me.

"Where have you been? Luther tried contact, but you never checked your phone." He sounded pissed off, but obviously had no idea what happened to me.

"Ben betrayed us. He attacked me, Carter. We found him trying to go into one of those raves, but the whole thing had been a set up to get me."

Carter was silent for what seemed like a long time. "That explains why he hasn't shown up for work. I figured his father forced him back overseas, which wouldn't be the first time."

"Unless he was lying even then, Carter. He is part of the Covert somehow, either as a buyer or even the one who has been leading it." I sighed, putting my car in park when I came to a grocery store about ten miles from the mansion. "He poisoned me."

Growling, Carter said, "Luther will find him, and he will be punished accordingly." In vampire language that meant he would be put to death. "I will send Luther to help you look at the rave location. Be there in a half hour."

The phone call ended pretty quickly after that. I had to assume he wanted to get Ben taken care of as soon as he could. Putting the car back in drive, I went in the direction of the rave house from two nights ago.

Two nights. I couldn't believe I went through two nights, missing the chance to investigate the house sooner. Who knew what had already been removed from there. So much of the evidence could have been ruined. We were lucky it hadn't already been burned down by now. That would have been the fastest way to eliminate everything.

Inside the house was still lit up, but I doubt any of the vampires that were inside we concerned with the electric bill. Hopefully no one returned to do any cleanup. Past evidence usually ended up burned but the house seemed completely intact. But then again, rogues failed to think of the consequences when they were constantly high on human blood. Rogues usually drugged up their victims to feel the effects through the blood. Eventually they just went crazy, their minds unable to heal the damage fast enough at the rate of their blood consumption. Even the supernatural can be as dumb as a human addicted to a drug that would eat you from the inside out.

Climbing out of the car I unsnapped the top of my katana, my hand resting over it as I climbed up the broken walkway. This was one of the worst parts of Lansing. A lot of what you saw happen around the city was drug related, and that even meant the murders. In these areas people watched knowing that you were an outsider, ready to take you out before you could tell anyone anything.

Somewhere in the distance someone yelled and then a child screamed as if in pain. Across the lawn, made of mostly dirt, were three houses that looked completely identical. Each had about five people sitting on the porches, watching me climb up the steps to the rave house.

"Hey! You can't go in there." Someone called out from the side of the house.

I looked around the corner and glared at the man standing there. His pants were riding low, exposing some pin striped boxer shorts. He wore a sweatshirt with some kind of designer logo on the front of it. His ball cap was twisted to the side and in his hands was a gun. Did they have people watch the house? My fangs slid out and I watched his eyes go wide, his hand wavering for a second before suddenly straightening with a fearless front.

"I can go in here. It is you that needs to get the hell out of here before something bad happens." I threatened, hand ready on my katana. He probably would be able to get off a shot, but I would miss the bullet with plenty of time to take him down with one swipe of the katana. Everyone around would do one of two things, come help him with guns blazing or take off running. I voted for the latter.

The guy looked at me, slowly blinking as if he was on something, and then pushed out his chin, moving his gun in a sideways gesture that screamed thug. "I have to watch this house and you are on private property, bitch." The entire time he was talking, he danced in one spot, one hand pulling at his jeans to keep them up, rocks crunching under his feet. If he tried to run he wouldn't last two steps without tripping on his own pants. I didn't see how this could benefit the tough guy routine at all.

Sighing loudly, I pulled out my katana. "Seriously, dude, you are nothing but a weak human. I am vampire, which means I can rip your throat out before you can even think about pulling the trigger."

"Blake, stop playing with the boy and just kill him." A voice said, coming from another direction.

I grinned, realizing it was Luther. "I would, but you know the saying and me having to do the opposite. Quit playing with your food and all. What fun is that?"

Luther grinned, flashing his own fang. The guy suddenly got nervous, swinging his gun back from me to Luther. He was beginning to panic. I could taste it in the air and my own heart began to beat with anticipation of a hunt. With amazing speed, Luther was suddenly in front of the guy holding his head in a way to expose his neck. "I haven't eaten yet today. I think you'll do."

The guy began to struggle, trying to call out for help. "You're just making it more fun by wiggling around." I said to the guy.

Smelling the tears in the air, I put the katana back in its sheath and watched as Luther said something to the man. With zombie like movements, the guy went back over to the house behind the one we were at. Luther looked over at me and grinned. "I love being vampire." It was rare that he even tried to have fun, so all I could do was smile in response.

I pushed in the already open door of the house. "Making him do what you want with your vampire powers is less fun than all the other choices." The smell of blood and death immediately hit me, making the vampire inside of me rear its head and the demon rub her hands in anticipation. I closed my eyes briefly trying to see if I could sense anything in the house. Bracing myself for the impact, the images began to flood me. Before the visions took over completely, someone wrapped their arms around me to stop the fall that was about to happen.

The pain was the first thing that hit me. It was a full body burning sensation that my demon converted into her personal snack. She sucked it in, enjoying the stark fear, panic and extreme pain the girl had experienced. Faces swarmed into my vision, some distorted, but one wasn't. I could only make out one feature, silvered eyes. His fangs briefly came into view before he bit down like a snake. I screamed when pain laced through me, but then moaned when it turned into something that felt so good my whole body hummed from it.

My vision flickered now to a different room in the house. Hands were tied up above my head and I could feel the ache in my arms from being in one position for too long. It was barely a twinge compared to the new sensations around my breasts. At first tender and then sharp pains as fangs sank into my skin. My head felt weird as if I was drugged, unable to really focus on the activity around me.

The ceiling swam in circles when I came out of my visions. I expected to see Luther standing above me, but it was Eli instead, holding my head in his lap, hands running through my hair. I scrambled forward, immediately regretting it when my head swam, nearly throwing me off balance. Eli held me to him when he came closer, whispering soothing words as if I was a wild animal.

When the spinning stopped I pushed him off, getting to my feet. "What the hell are you doing here? Where's-" I was cut off when I saw Luther knocked out cold on the floor of the house. "Oh my gods, what did you do to him?"

"He had you." Eli said, confusion in his face.

Snarling with rage, I went to Luther tapping the side of his face lightly with my hand, but his head just rocked back and forth. Knocked out cold for sure. I looked up to glare at Eli. "He didn't have me. He was helping me while I went through that damn vision."

Pushing to my feet, I paced the hall wondering if I should wait for Luther to come to before I headed up the steps. Looking over at Eli, I pulled on his suit coat until he took it off for me, and then I bent down, shoving it under Luther's head. "He better not be in pain when he wakes up." I said through clenched teeth, as I turned to head toward what I assumed was the living room.

Eli caught up with me. "What visions?"

Spinning around I poked him in the chest with my finger. "Exactly. We don't know enough about each other to even think about being this far in a relationship. Stop fucking worrying about me. I don't need someone following me everywhere. He's my friend and wanted to help me."

I looked around the living room finding an old couch with springs sprouting out of it. Some parts of it covered with duct tape that didn't help much in keeping it together. On the floor in front of it was an old blanket with blood all over it from two nights before. Blood was on the walls, splattered wildly all over as if someone took a paint brush and went crazy.

Moving toward some steps on my left, I went up closing my eyes to smell and hear everything. Still only blood and death. As I neared the top I smelled rot. The smell led me to the far back room where a body laid. The face was gone, bite marks all over his body, hair covered in dried blood. Why would his face be gone? All you could see was the actual face bones, pieces of skin and muscle still attached. My stomach rolled violently, so I looked away.

Shuddering, I swallowed back the bile that tried to force its way up. I turned to leave the room, nearly running into Eli who still tried to offer me comfort. I pushed him out of the way to investigate the other rooms. There were three others, not including the bathroom and it took all I had not to turn around and leave the house.

The next room I came to nearly made me gag again. The walls were covered in human remains as if they exploded. Lying on the floor was an old mattress where it looked like a body had once been. There would be no way to identify this person unless there was some sort of DNA or dental record.

Moving to the next room, I went inside finding no bodies, but torn clothing. One vision slammed into me letting me see the horror of several vampires feeding on a single person. "Blood slaves, all of them. How can someone do this to people? How can they live with themselves?"

Eli was following me closely, seeing almost everything I was aside from the visions. The next room was where the girl had been tied from my vision. She was alive! Hurrying over I lifted her head, but it rolled to the side. Barely alive. "Call Nick. We need someone here, she is still alive." I said.

Pulling out his cell phone, Eli pressed speed dial for Nick. After a few rings Nick answered. Ignoring the rest of the phone call I went for the rope around the girl's wrist. She was completely naked with bites all over her body. Her legs were tied off to the side, bruises lining the inside of her thighs around the bites and not. Shaking my head in disgust, I let her slump over my shoulder as I bent to lay her down on a torn mattress. I then went to her legs to finish untying them. She groaned, her head falling to the side, eyes closed. The girl couldn't have been any more than twenty, looking like she probably attended a college. Her nails were done professionally, she looked like someone of importance. Swearing, I looked around for something to cover her, but there wasn't anything.

Hearing someone coming up the steps, I shot up in time to see Luther turn the corner into the room. He looked pissed. When his eyes found Eli he went to move toward him, but I was in between them before he could take another step. "You don't want to go after him, he's a lot stronger than he looks."

Luther only rolled his eyes in response. "You forget one of my abilities is to sense a vampire's power level."

I went to tell him what the truth was, but Eli put his hand on my shoulder and shook his head. He still didn't want people to know, despite what happened at the club with Michael. Rolling my own eyes, I turned back to the girl who was still breathing shallowly.

Eli hung up his phone and shoved it in his pants pocket. "They should be here in about five minutes. Where's my jacket?" Remembering he took it off downstairs, he ran down bringing it back up just as fast with his vampire speed. He went to the girl covering her, trying to give some kind of dignity. He had respect for humans and he cared about them, which was something you rarely saw in vampires. Guilt overwhelmed me for yelling at him when he tried to protect me from Luther, who he thought was a bad guy. Turning away, my gaze met Luther's. He saw. He saw the developing feelings there. Carter will probably find out soon then, which will only ruin my chances in solving the mystery on his niece. It would probably be a day before he called me back.

*

Back at the mansion I decided it was high time I found out where the workout room was. I changed into a pair of yoga pants and a halter top, glad to be out of the clothes I wore to the house. I felt like death was crawling all over me, but I could hold out for a shower until I burned some of my anger off.

Charity joined up with me when I made it downstairs, showing me the way. It was just going to be a regular workout slash watch the hunky guards sweat. Girl stuff, you know? I needed to keep busy until the victims' identities were figured out. I wanted to know if any of them were Lucy, because that was my main goal, finding her. Some of the victims would have to be identified by dental records, and others we just had to hope there was something in the databases of the police departments.

Those images would be forever burned in my mind. I felt sorry for the girl who would have to live through the memory of the torture she endured. I didn't think she was human, but then again, all I could smell was something sweet, which usually indicated some kind of fey. The Fey were something vampires liked to get a hold of, because of the amount of power in the blood. She would be staying down in the medical room of the lower level until they could get more information from her. I wanted to know her name, but she hadn't woken up since the last the time I found her breathing.

The workout room was past the ballroom, down another hallway. Inside the mansion it looked a lot bigger than the outside, housing tons of rooms and so many other facilities. The room that was our destination was huge and my mouth couldn't help but hang open in awe. There hung a few punching bags, some weight machines, sparring mats, walls covered in different types of weapons, and even bleachers for those that just wanted to watch. It smelled of sweat and blood. Over in the far corner one of the cleaning people were cleaning a blood covered mat. I would hate to have that job, but I guess someone had to do it.

Charity grabbed my hand. "Come on, I have someone for you to meet. The only other girl on the guard."

Following after her like best friends in school, I spotted a girl lifting weights. She was tall with an athlete's build, square shoulders and tapered body. Her blond hair was up in a ponytail and her body covered in sweat as she lifted. Vampires could lift a lot of weight with our strength, but it always proved useful to stay in shape. We could run far and fast, but we could run faster and further if we trained for it.

The girl got off the weight bench, dried off her hands on a towel and reached out a hand to me. "Hi, I am Beth Sanders." She flashed me a brilliant smile.

"Hi, Blake Noble." I took her hand, mine much smaller in hers.

She nodded. "We all know who you are. The half demon vampire that got the Guardian position before any of us." When I stiffened, she waved it off. "No big deal to me, because protecting Nick is a tough job. I rather avoid Nick as much as possible. It is like catering to a spoiled child of a rich family."

"Agreed." Charity and I both said at the same time. We all laughed, heading over to the sparring mats where two male vampires were fighting hand to hand.

The small, black haired vampire was avoiding contact easily with the other, much bigger vampire. Even though the bigger one was graceful considering his size, he still couldn't catch the smaller one. Beth cheered, causing the bigger one to lose concentration long enough to receive a slash across the abdomen. He glared at Beth and then at the smaller guy for catching him off guard. Big vampire guy healed instantly, leaving him fresh again. Still the mat was dotted with his blood, leaving evidence behind that the smaller guy got one up on him.

Charity leaned over toward me pointing first to the small guy. "That is Derek Hollins. He is from Italy and very good at hand to hand combat." She grinned then pointing to goliath. "That is Mark Bathory."

The last name sounded familiar and then it hit me. "Is that-"

She nodded. "Yes, he is related to that woman."

My mouth formed an "o" and she busted out laughing. "Don't worry, he isn't crazy. In fact, he is an excellent lay."

Beth rolled her eyes. "Don't let her fool you, she's is in love with the bastard."

Blushing, Charity stared at Mark. "She hates him, because he is a jerk to everyone but me." I could almost hear her sigh with adoration. I stuck my finger in my mouth making gagging noises and she laughed, pushing me playfully. "He is well hung, seriously it is like-"

"La, la, la!" I sang, putting my hands over my ears. That was way too much information, especially since I didn't find him the least bit attractive. In fact, now that I knew who he was related to, his creepy factor went up about twenty notches.

We all started laughing. "Blake!"

Turning, I spotted Nick at the doorway of the gym and he looked pissed. "Uh oh." Charity sang.

"Yeah really." I grumbled, jogging over in his direction, regretting that I might miss working out the anger I felt boiling underneath.

*

By the time I reached the doorway he was already gone and entering his office when I went around the corner. I stepped over the threshold of his personal space, only to stop suddenly, my heart going in full out panic mode. "Shit." I swore.

Nick waved his hand and the door slammed behind me. Well, that answered one of his powers questions. Telekinesis. He looked extremely angry, his power swirling around the room, causing pictures to sway on the walls. My first thought was to run like a frightened rabbit. Find a hole somewhere, maybe under a bed, but that wouldn't save me from this. My gaze skittered to the center of the room where Carter sat.

Spinning on my heel, I tried opening the door, but it wouldn't budge. I then put my full weight into it, both hands wrapped around the door knob, trying to calm down enough to think up fire. Nick sighed loudly. "Give it up, the door won't be opening."

"Come, Blake, this is hardly mature." Carter said. I could swear there was some form of humor in the tone of his voice.

Giving up, I turned to face the crowd. "So, what's up?" I asked casually as if I wasn't trying to escape two seconds ago.

Pointing to one of the chairs, Nick walked around his desk to cross his arms, dark eyes poking holes right through me. So what would my excuse be? Before I could even think of something he spoke to me. "I wasn't expecting this, Blake. I trusted you and for me to not see through this… it just amazes me."

I didn't say anything, so he continued. "Someone brought it to my attention that you are an agent for the SCD. I took it upon myself to see if this was true and it so happens that you are in a way working for the agency as a contractor."

Carter nodded. "She comes highly recommended, too. One of the best assassins the government could hire."

Assassin? Are you kidding me?

Nick turned around to bring out a folder. "I need to see in writing that I am your only employer, unless hired by the government on an occasional contract and that you are not an agent with the agency."

I stiffened, trying to hide all my reactions. "You want me to sign a contract?"

He shrugged. "Yes, this was drawn up by Declan and Carter. Under vampire law it isn't appropriate for a Guardian to be working for a

Director and the FBI, mainly because of the conflict of interests. Politics and everything." He watched me carefully, gauging my reaction. When he handed me a folder and a pen, I scanned the long paragraphs, frowning. Down at the bottom it said, "If employee has been found in violation of contract then such crime is punishable by death."

Looking up at Carter, I asked, "So you helped draw this up?"

He slowly nodded. "It is for the best."

Anger swelled in me. This meant I wasn't working for the agency anymore. That would be the only reason why Carter would allow the form to even be drawn up. Carter stood, buttoning up his suit coat. "Just sign the paper, Blake. I must go now, Nick, always good to see you."

"Same, Carter."

Hearing the door click shut behind him was the final straw. He just walked away from me, despite being the only family I knew. Why would he do something like this? It didn't make sense and I wanted to find out why. For now, I would sign the damn paper. So I did.

Nick took the folder back, obviously pleased that I just signed my life away to the devil. "I knew it wasn't true. Declan likes to make up stories and well, from my past experience Carter hasn't always been trustworthy. He and Declan were always in cahoots with each other." He folded his arms across his chest. "I told him you wouldn't betray me and this just shows I was right."

When I didn't say anything he moved toward me, stopping about a foot away, lifted my chin so my gaze met his. "Don't even doubt me when I say I trust you. I know we haven't known each other long, but I do know making you my Guardian has been my best decision in years. And for allowing me to do this, to prove you are one of my worthy soldiers, I would like to take you to dinner."

Shifting uncomfortably I shook my head. "No, that is okay. I need to be alone right now, actually. What I saw at that house was horrible and I need to come to terms with it." For Carter to blind side me like this was the ultimate betrayal. "If I need a day to myself be willing to accept the request and that is all the pay back I need."

I stood up preparing to leave the room, but Nick's voice stopped me. "Make that two paid days off. Like I said, I do appreciate the sacrifice."

Nodding once, I hurried out of the room.

*

After getting dressed into a pair of jeans and a plain black shirt, I went to my car to get the cell phone. First I dialed Carter, but there was no answer. When I dialed Luther he picked up after about two rings.

"You shouldn't be calling me." He said softly into the phone.

Grimacing, I clenched my fist. "What the hell is going on?"

"Carter decided this."

"Why though? I thought Carter..." my voice trailed off, my heart dropping.

Luther sighed. "Don't call me again, Blake. It's for the best. For both of us."

Let down, I was confused more than ever. Rage filled me and all I could think about was hiding in a dark hole to die. Feeling my skin prickle, I ignored it. I was just too furious. Beads of sweat traveled down the side of my face, over my lips, and down my neck, as I continued to think about how the only father I ever had, turned his back on me. I had to get to the bottom of this. Why people I knew most of my life would suddenly betray me, didn't make any sense.

The driver side door flew off and I jumped in my seat with surprise. Eli's face appeared, he was trying to talk, but all I could hear was this noise that sounded like a train. Blinking several times, I didn't move until something pulled me forward.

"Holy shit!" Someone cried out.

Confused, I looked around finding a crowd staring behind me. When I looked behind me, I nearly screamed. My car was on fire! I leapt up prepared to save it, but Eli grabbed my arms. "Don't, it is long gone now."

"What the hell happened? Someone try to kill me?" I asked bewildered.

Mitch came up beside me, shaking his head, the reflection of the fire flicking in his gaze. "No, you did this."

Hissing like I cat, I launched myself at him, only to be pulled back by Eli. "I did not!"

"Uh, yeah you did." Reed said, coming up alongside Mitch. He made an explosion gesture with his hands. "You made it go boom."

Nick came out of the elevator across the garage, looking around, trying to search for the reason of the commotion. Flanking him were two guards I never saw before. That was my job. Here I was posing a risk even to him. Lucifer really needed to get on the ball with my training before I killed someone unintentionally.

Eli wrapped his arms around me, trying to offer comfort. The heat from my body was disappearing replaced with chills. When Nick made it over to me he smiled. "Looks like we struck gold." Meaning me.

Chapter Seven

Pacing on the mats that were now laid out across the whole gym, I scowled up at the ceiling as if that was where he would drop from. "Come on you bastard! Aren't you demon enough to show up when I call you?"

Eli started laughing. "I hardly think that is the way you summon a demon."

Shooting him my best death stare, I stuck my tongue out. "I see your lips moving." I said, making mouth moving gestures with my hand.

"I believe you need chalk and some other stuff like that." He said more seriously.

Shrugging, I continued to pace. I was worked up. Pissed off worked up. Fighting would help burn away all the energy. Glancing over at Eli I smiled. Something else would really work too. Eli sensing the change in my mood met my gaze with awareness. Instantly he was moving toward me. Our attraction to each other was undeniable and I was ready to let it all hang out.

"Please, let's not continue that thought." Someone growled from across the room.

Jumping, I spun around to see Lucifer sitting in an elegant chair that wasn't there before. Again he held a cup of tea, but in the other hand was a cigar. He was in black slacks, loafers, and a button up shirt with a tie hanging loosely around his neck. Something was on his face and when I went to get a closer look my eyes went wide when I realized it was a lipstick mark. "Interrupt something?" I asked, placing my hands on my hips.

Lucifer look daggers at me, tossing his cup of tea so it disappeared. "Something, indeed. My dear daughter you have the worst timing. Your mother was about to-"

Hands flying up in a defensive gesture, I took one step back. "Hold it there. I do not want the mental image."

Shrugging indifferently he stood up, the chair then disappearing. He took a handkerchief from his pants pocket and wiped away the lipstick on his neck and face. "Well, let's get this over with. We don't need you setting something else on fire."

My mouth fell open. He saw that? How much did he see in my life? Everything? Even when I had to go to the bathroom? Looking over at Eli, images of possible sessions of screwing popped into my head. Even those? Seeing the direction of my thoughts Lucifer smiled, but didn't deny it. My whole body reddened. Eli shook his head, moving over to the wall of the gym, where he slid down to take a seat on the floor. It didn't even faze him with the possibility of getting his expensive suit dirty. We could fix that with taking it off. My hormones revved up picturing him without a shirt on. If I could just snap my fingers and pop the coat off- "Shit!"

Eli leapt up startled. He looked down at his bare chest. Then he glared at Lucifer, who was already putting his hands up in his own defense. He pointed at me. "She did it."

Scolding me with a shake of his finger and raised eyebrows, Eli's lips twitched. "Control yourself. We don't need naked men on the streets every time you think about them without clothes on."

My mouth opened to say, "Why would I think about other men naked?" when I stopped myself. Did I really mean that? Closing my eyes briefly, I pushed the thoughts from my head and focused my attention on Lucifer. "So I can do the magician act like you?"

Nodding slowly, Lucifer shoved his hands into his pockets as if contemplating how much he should tell me. Making a decision, he turned to face me. "Within limits. His clothes are probably thrown somewhere in this house. You can only make stuff disappear within short distances." He explained. He snapped his fingers and he was wearing something different. It was weird staring at a demon who looked so normal in a pair of jeans, t-shirt and biker boots. "I got your mother with this look." He grinned evilly. "She says she likes my-"

I plugged my ears and closed my eyes. "Please stop!"

When I pulled away my fingers I heard nothing. Lucifer wasn't making a sound, yet his lips were moving. He grinned, did a small wave of his hand. "Good, looks like your powers are coming all at once, but all are highly emotion driven. We need to train you not to do it because your mad, scared, or," he glanced over at Eli and his half nakedness, "horny." His lips twitched with amusement. "This will work on any demon as well, but none can break it like I can. You are my daughter, so I have full control over the powers my body gave you. Only sometimes those powers can disappear and never return. There isn't anything to say what really happens."

"Okay, so how can I control it before I set someone on fire?"

A key appeared in the air in front of me. I rolled my eyes. "For real? We can do without the graphic presentation. The key means what?"

Lucifer sighed loudly, coming up to me to snatch the key from the air. "This is what your mother made you. She did a spell on it that is to help dampen the emotion side effect, for now. This should work until you are more in control of your powers. " When he turned around the key disappeared and then reappeared around my neck.

"Spooky." Eli whispered.

"You're telling me. We're screwed if all demons can do this stuff." I said, shaking my hands out. "Okay, first lesson, Father."

Lucifer glanced over his shoulder a pleased expression on his face, but when he realized my comment was out of mockery he rolled his eyes. "First lesson is appearing and reappearing."

I waved it off. "Been there, done that. Let's do something fun."

He sighed dramatically. "You know how to do it when you're scared. You need to use it in defense when you call on it." When I went to say something he held up a finger, telling me to be quiet. He closed his eyes, took a deep breath, and then opened one eye waiting for me to follow. So I did. My shoulders relaxed, I took a deep breath. Waited. Nothing.

"Doesn't work." I said.

Eli chuckled. "Give it time."

Shaking his head, Lucifer smashed out his cigar on the wall. The ash and butt disappeared. "Look, you need to learn how to relax. Take a deep breath, imagine nothing, and then think about being in another place."

"That takes too long. How is that supposed to help me in the middle of a fight?" I demanded.

Again Lucifer shook his head. "You did not get this attitude from me. I know when to shut up if I want to learn something." He tilted his head as if listening to something. He grinned. "Your mother just admitted to giving you her stubbornness."

"Okay, if we are going to do this, mom has to stay out of it. I am not ready to get into that bowl of doom." When he went to object, I shook my head. "You want a part of my life then get to work."

Lucifer shook his head. "Children these days, so ungrateful."

Eli suggested I take a meditation pose, so I plopped down and crossed my legs. "Humm."

Rolling his eyes, Lucifer glared at Eli accusingly. "See what you started?" He looked at me when I opened one eye to see what his expression was. "You do not need to hum. Now, do it the way that I told you to do it."

Closing my eyes, I took several deep breaths. Forgot what I was doing. "Wait, what was I supposed to try to do?"

Shaking his head in disgust, Lucifer ran his fingers through his hair. When he was done he looked like a mad scientist. He growled. "Eli, you must leave, you are too distracting!"

Eli grinned. "Glad to know."

Tapping his biker boot impatiently, he crossed his arms over his chest. "Go over there and sit."

Obeying, Eli went to the wall, still grinning like a fool. Apparently he had some doubts and liked the idea of being distracting to me. Finally Lucifer glanced back at me. "We are teleporting, basically. Think of a place, go there."

Deciding to take it seriously, I closed my eyes, thinking about a location. But every time I thought of one it was too far away. Growling, I puffed out a breath of air attempting to think of my room in the house, only the image disappeared and was immediately replaced with Carter's house. We had some unsolved issues obviously. Maybe when that was done, I could see why he let me go from the SCD. Why he put me in a position that forced me to change my life and possibly end it if I didn't follow the contract? It was all really hard to deal with when someone who raised you was the father you never had. Despite Lucifer being readily available now, he wasn't when I was younger. Carter would always be the one who popped in my head if I thought about a dad.

After a few long minutes of realizing nothing was happening, I opened my eyes and nearly shit myself. Not for real, but you know what I mean. Nevermind. Anyway, I was sitting in Carter's living room. Thank god he wasn't around, or else I would be in a whole lot of trouble. Climbing to my feet, I looked around at the large living room. He had a granite fire place and it was probably my favorite place of the house. Tapping a foot, I wondered why the hell he would have the fireplace lit if he wasn't home.

It was then I smelled it. Death. Hurrying through the living room, I went into the hallway that led to the kitchen and the bedrooms. The house was in the middle of nowhere, seriously. He lived on three hundred acres of land he bought when he was married. The woods were almost too tightly compacted to the house, only giving enough room for the porch, shed, and the circle driveway, in case he needed to turn around. The driveway was nearly two miles long and during the winter it was hell to travel.

The scent of blood led me through the kitchen to one of the bathrooms. There lying on the floor in just a towel was Carter. Shaking in fear that he may be dead, I bent down feeling for a pulse and found none. He was gone. Blood pooled under his head, and it was then I realized his neck was cut from the rest of his body. The cut had been so smoothly done that it didn't even slide away.

Who did it? Declan? Why would he do it this when he was King? Maybe it had been the Covert. I didn't get it. Anger rose causing my whole body to shake. I felt my skin prickling again and I screamed, furious at whoever did it. I would kill them and it wouldn't be a quick death.

"Breathe, child."

Turning, I found Lucifer behind me. His gaze fell on the body behind me. He grimaced, moving around me so he could bend down. "Quick death, he felt no pain."

"No shit, Sherlock. I could figure that out for myself." Only I hadn't yet, because I was too angry to think straight. Suffering the vision would give clues.

As if reading my expression Lucifer grabbed a hold of me, even though flames licked my skin. "Don't do the vision. I can tell you right now there is no information. Whoever it was came up from behind."

Shoving him away from me, I allowed the vision to come at me with a rush, not caring about the painful crash as it exploded into my head. Only, it lasted a second. It was just like Lucifer said. It came from behind, all Carter saw was the flash of a black mask. Coward. The killer couldn't even face him without a damn mask on!

"I am sorry." Lucifer said. My first thought was to tell him to go to hell, even though it was a waste of effort, since he came from there. But what made me really stop was that he did look sad for me.

Needing someone, I hugged him feeling his body tense with shock. After a few seconds, his arms went around me offering immediate comfort. Then I pulled away, looking away from him. "Don't expect that to happen again."

He chuckled. "I figured that out myself."

Looking down at Carter one more time I thought about the mansion gym.

*

When I got back into the gym, Lucifer was already there and had apparently told Eli about what happened. Eli's smile fell from his face and he immediately came to me, his arms open. I accepted him, burying my head into his chest, his warmth rolling over me as the power he released offered comfort.

"Ah, an Ancient." Lucifer looked far away as he contemplated that. "Thought they were all dead. They even damned someone to hell for lying when he said there was one alive." He shrugged.

My eyebrows rose. Demons knew about the Ancients? Of course they did. A Demigod creating their own race would be news on other realms. Frowning, I looked at him, remembering he made it back first. "What did you do, take a detour?"

"Oh, you mean, how I came back so fast?" He only smiled and shrugged. "What is important is you can do long distance and that is more than we thought possible. I believe you have more demon in you than expected. Your mom must be hiding some." He smiled, tilting his head again as if listening. "Lessons tomorrow, I must go."

Before I could respond, he was already gone. It was then one struggling tear made its way down my cheek. Eli searched my face, anger burning in his eyes. He wiped away a tear with his thumb. "We will catch whoever did it." He promised.

Nodding, I said, "I don't know why I should even care if he didn't want me anymore."

Eli put his hands on my shoulders and leaned back to get a good look at my face. "He raised you and you saw him as a father. That is all that matters." I didn't know if it was a good thing or a bad one that Eli knew Carter raised me. Nick wouldn't be happy at all and we'd go back to that trust problem we had earlier. Without Carter around, who knew how that would end up.

"We have to tell Nick. I want to be primary on his investigation." I started toward the door ready to take on the job when it dawned on me. "I can't. Because he is SCD, the FBI and the Vampire King's people are going to be investigating."

He took my hand and started me forward again. How could a man be here for me like this when we knew each other for such a short time? And why me? There were much more powerful women for him. Someone who was in a leading role. Not someone like me, who got herself kicked out of the SCD and guarded the Director like some kind of accomplishment lacking fool.

Eli led me into Nick's office, where we found him reading through one of the big books from the book case. He looked up when he heard us come in. "Yes?"

When I tried to explain, my lip trembled, so Eli went to try and take over, but I squeezed his arm and shook my head. Gathering myself, I let the tears dry up, straightened my back and looked at Nick, who suddenly seemed concerned. He got to his feet and walked over to me, hands pressing to my arms. "What is it?"

"Carter is dead." I explained what happened, how I got there and what I found. The whole time his face remained blank. When I finished it was then several emotions traveled through his eyes.

"I have to notify Declan." He said finally, walking over to his desk phone.

Eli nodded. "I figured as much, but she wants to be primary or at least part of the case."

Halfway from putting the phone to his ear, Nick shook his head. "Impossible. You know how Declan is about that kind of stuff. Anything concerning his Directors or divisions within the human government is to be investigated by the King's people."

Eli went to open his mouth, but I just shook my head. "We have enough on our plate with the Covert thing to figure out." I sat down in a chair, feeling just plain worn out. It felt like the weight of the world was on my shoulders now. The only person I had left on this earth was now gone. Lucifer and my mother didn't count, they never did and never would.

"Let me call Declan and see what I can do, I know you knew Carter, but the way you are acting makes me wonder if you can handle being the Guardian." He put the phone to his ear. "In the meantime, I think you should rest, because the Director of Illinois is coming tomorrow. Apparently there have been more people disappearing there." Not waiting for a response, he spoke to whoever was on the phone.

Standing up, I felt weak and defeated. He was right about resting. Things will only become more crazy and the more rest I got the better. Maybe I was so tired because of all the power I used up when my emotions became too much for me to handle. Eli put his hand on my back. "Let me take you to dinner, then we can watch a movie here if you want, when we get back."

For a second I debated on saying no, I rather just lay in bed, but when I thought about the last time I actually went out for fun I came up with a blank. My last real date was probably three years ago and even then it had just been a quick lay. So I agreed, hurrying up the stairs after finding some new energy.

Eli had picked out a nice Italian restaurant outside of the city in a smaller town. I chose pizza to eat, not looking for anything fancy. My stomach growled when we entered the place, the smell of food assaulting me instantly.

The hostess gave us a table in a far corner away from the bar patrons. It was a dark secluded area which we both liked. Eli pulled out my seat for me before going to his chair. He removed his jacket, putting it on the back of his seat. When he sat down, our waitress appeared eager to take our orders. You might have wondered why if it weren't for the looks she kept giving Eli. Oh yeah the man was gorgeous, but she could have some respect for his date.

Shit.

Was this a date? My heart began to beat rapidly as Eli gave the girl our orders. My leg began to bounce up and down nervously while he stared at me. "This isn't a date." He said, as if he could read my mind. But he could if he was an Ancient. Right? Gods, I didn't even know.

He reached over touching my arm, since I had my hands clasped down in my lap. "Seriously, you don't need to worry."

Giving me a reassuring smile, he opened his cloth napkin and placed it in his lap. "I know you aren't ready for a relationship."

Normally, I would have agreed to this, but the way he said it almost sounded like a challenge. My body automatically went stiff as the predator in me leaned forward, my nostrils flaring. I knew my eyes were dilated watching him. "Oh really?" I asked softly allowing my thoughts about Carter to slip away for a little while. I could numb it all.

He leaned in, his nose only inches from mine, gave me a lopsided smile. "Really."

Smiling, for the first time since I found Carter, I met him the rest of the way, pressing my lips to his. He seemed shocked by the move, but I relished it, taking full advantage of surprising him. My tongue went into his mouth, touching his. If it weren't for the table, I knew he would be all over me. Smiling again, I bit his lip and pulled back. "Challenge accepted."

Dinner was excellent. We agreed not to talk about anything depressing, so he told me about how there were fourteen Ancients created, each with a mate. When I asked him about his mate, he shrugged and said she took off when she had the chance after they defeated the Demigod. Apparently the Demigod wanted a superior race, but wanted them matched to their required mate. The Demigod tried to make it so they were automatically drawn to their mates, but something went wrong and it never worked out that way.

The Ancients all died when people first found out vampires existed, but by then they all had their children. The Ancients were really an example of what was considered the superior race, because they were too arrogant to realize their lives were at risk. That eventually a vampire hunter would kill them. Eli had gone into hiding in Europe up until he ran into Nick. Then they came to the States looking to change things for vampires, fighting in wars together and whatever else.

When dinner was finished Eli led me back toward his BMW, but on a last minute decision I took him in the other direction leading to the river. Why not try to escape reality for a little while longer? He took my hand into his, smiling down at me before we went under the trees that hid the moon. "What do you think the Director of Illinois is going to want us to do?" I asked.

Eli shrugged his broad shoulders, bending down to pick up a long branch that had fallen from one of the trees. He released my hand, picking off the leaves. "I am guessing he will want to join the investigation." He put the stick to the ground, satisfied with the sturdiness of it, he took my hand back into his. "Not sure how I feel about that, considering he is known for trying to control every situation even if someone is a higher rank." He rolled his eyes. "He has tried to be King before, but Declan is a hard one to beat."

"You can beat him." I said, looking up at him.

Shrugging, he nodded slightly. "I could, but will I? No. I rather avoid trying to manage the vampires. I am fine with assisting Nick."

"What about Michael?" Leaping over a pot hole, I frowned glancing back at it. The town should really fix that. If I were human my ankle probably would have busted in pieces.

He sighed. "Well, he is a problem, of course."

"You think? He will use that when he needs it."

Going alert, Eli froze mid-step, listening. He pulled me in the direction that he heard the noise. When I took a few steps with him it was then the noise reached my ears. We went off the path through the woods, not even tripping up over the fallen trees or branches. There was a section of river that narrowed. He pulled me over with him, leaping a lot farther than I could.

His strength managed to pull me over without stumbling.

The noise sounded like some kind of whimpering. A child? No, it didn't sound like one at all. I went to open my mouth to tell him we were already up on the source, but he already had us coming to a stop, finding a cat confined inside a small animal trap.

Releasing my hand, he bent down to open the latch. The cat shot to the back of the cage, his ears back, fangs out and one paw up ready to attack. His orange coat was matted with blood and mud. Eli opened the latch all the way, leaving the door open so the cat could come out on its own. Finding the chance it was looking for, it bolted out, disappearing into the bushes.

I busted out laughing, throwing my head back. "You-" unable to breathe, I bent over placing my hands on my thighs. "I thought someone was dying. It was a damn cat this whole time?"

He grinned, pulling me up, then wrapped his arms around my waist. "Glad you found that hilarious, but that cat was starving and alone."

Rolling my eyes I nodded. "Sure, I can see that, but you had us running like it was a life and death situation."

"It was!" He said in mock exasperation.

I patted his chest with one hand, giving him an expression a mother would to her child. "Well, at least we know there is someone out there to save all the animals of the world."

Unexpectedly, he leaned forward pressing his lips to mine. All the adrenaline in me surged ahead, making me desperate for someone to touch me. Feeling my urgency, his hands went up my back, one going into my hair pulling my head enough to expose my neck to him. His lips went down it, fangs scraping along the skin, making my whole body shiver with anticipation. I whimpered, wanting him to hurry because I need him inside me.

My hands went to his back, underneath his coat, trying to pull his shirt from his pants. Finding the warmth of his skin, my finger nails dug into his back when he pushed me up against a tree. His lips found mine, pressing and bruising. Hiking me up so I could wrap my legs around him, I felt his length pressing into me causing an involuntary cry. Pulling away from the kiss I moaned, eyes rolling back as pleasure rippled from my core to the rest of my body.

Growling as he ground into me, he squeezed my ass unable to contain the shivers of his body when my lips found his neck. Finding the vein, I ran my tongue over it, enjoying every bit of his need. I wanted him so bad. Grabbing for his pants I tried to unbutton them, but was having a hard time. "Come on!" I hissed. The button flew off, my hand went to my mouth in shock. "Oops!"

He chuckled, letting my feet fall to the ground. Pouting, I looked up at him, but he only smiled, taking my hands and putting them up over my head as he ground himself into me. I panted, writhing. "Please." My eyes rolled back when he let go of my hands to cup my breasts. I nearly sank to the ground from the shocks of desire.

"Oh no you don't. Stand up." He growled, sending more shudders through me from him sounding so commanding. His voice took on a hard edge from his own spiking need. "Pay attention, I want you to feel all of what I do to you."

Whimpering, I only nodded. He stopped, hesitating. "This isn't the best place though, we should-"

"Don't even fucking think about it!" I said, rolling my body into his so he got the hint.

He sucked in air, quickly getting back to work. I laughed, looking up at the crack of light in the trees from the moonlight. My shirt was the first to come off, his lips closing over one nipple, after yanking down my bra. He nibbled as his hands trailed down my stomach finding the top of my pants. Slowly he unbuttoned while I wiggled, eager for him to get inside of me. When he finally got them open, he slid one hand in, pushing a finger inside of me.

"Holy-wow." I moved into his hands before searching for his pants. I pulled the zipper down and pushed for his pants to move out of the way "I can't wait."

When he went to refuse hurrying, I grabbed a hold of his length, smiling in the dark when he hissed. "Fair is fair," I purred into his ear.

He laughed, pushing my pants down before getting to his own. He picked me up from the ground and dove into me causing me to gasp. Slowly he moved as he found my lips with his, diving into my mouth, the bark at my back not even deterring me. He slammed into me hard making me cry out so loud the crickets went silent. When we rode near our climax my head flew back ready for the explosion as it built higher with each thrust. My whole body was starting to burn and shake, unable to contain the mountain it was building. Eli's teeth sank into my neck and I cried out again, the waves coming harder with the combined pleasure as he drew in my blood.

Chapter Eight

Crying, I crawled along the floor trying to find my way out. They would see me, I know it. My body ached all over and for once the need to survive overrode the pain. I let the pain take hold of me for far too long. More tears came, blurring my vision. Couldn't go back, no that would be bad. Anymore of them touching me would send me into the dark place again and I hated that. Freedom was just a few feet away, I could see the door. Soon I would escape and be back home, hopefully losing the memory of my experience.

No the memory probably wouldn't go away. It would never be forgotten. Those faces would haunt my dreams forever, no matter how much I try to escape them. One bite here. One bite there until I was too weak to stay conscious. Sobbing now, I continued to crawl past the door where another slept. They didn't know I could get out of the ropes. I hated waiting for them to become full enough to leave me alone again. I was crying again, tears falling from my face and dropping onto my hands. Why wouldn't they stop? Would they ever?

Someone grabbed me around the waist. I screamed, thrashing around. They found me! Couldn't go back, I would rather die first, but the arms only tightened.

"Blake! Wake up, Blake!"

Blinking, my vision swam, finally coming into focus to see the carpet beneath me. My legs and arms were hanging, someone was holding me. Looking down at their bare feet I tried to move my head so I could see. "Let me go!"

Turning me around in their arms, I looked up to see Eli's concerned face staring into mine. "What the hell are you doing out here?"

My gaze went to his bare chest and my heart began to beat faster. "Dreaming."

"What did you dream?" He asked, walking toward my bedroom as he completely lifted me into his arms.

I just shook my head, wrapping my arms around his neck, pulling him closer to kiss. "Not now, please. Just be with me."

His lips crushed mine as he kicked the door closed and went to the bed to lay me down. When his body covered mine, my hands went to work, eager to find some kind of comfort. Yes, this I could deal with. This is what I wanted. No more nightmares or regret over Carter. I needed Eli and only him. He could help me forget, even for a little while.

*

Eli trailed a finger down my chest to my stomach, smiling when it quivered from his touch. He kissed one erect nipple watching my reaction. I shivered, closing my eyes briefly. "I like being with you," I murmured.

His hand flattened against my stomach as he said, "And I like being with you. I just wish I could stop you from seeing horrible things."

Smiling, I shrugged. "Part of my genetics. I am not sure who it was though. I never dreamed someone's experience like that before." I pictured certain parts of the dream. Her hands on the carpet, manicured nails and silver ring with vines on her ring finger. Married or promise ring?

Before bed all I could think about was Carter, wondering if I should feel bad for having a happy moment with Eli. He comforted and helped me forget everything. As he trailed his fingertips over my arm, my eyes fluttered closed inviting sleep. When he moved to leave, I said, "Stay with me."

*

Waking up to sex is probably one of my number one all-time favorite things. Eli managed to get me three times, but one knock at my door reminded me we had things to do before the Illinois Director showed up. He went to climb to his feet, but I grabbed his hand pulling him back to me. Why not, he was already rearing to go? When he tried to escape I just grabbed his length and he shuddered in my hands saying we needed to be quick. But was it ever quick? It could be, but I couldn't stop wanting or needing him. The desire was always there increasing the more he stayed near me.

Again there was a knock at the door, and I laughed hearing Mitch and Charity going back and forth on who should walk in. Climbing off the bed, I hurried into the bathroom with Eli chasing me. We took a shower, hardly being good but managing. By the time we were finished, Nick was already in the room sitting on the bed with his arms crossed over his chest.

"You do have a job." He glared, looking from me to Eli. "Both of you." When he stood up he smirked. "I say it's lucky that the two of you found each other."

My mouth opened to object to that, but Nick shook his head. "Denying it would only be lying, Blake. And you don't lie to your Director." He looked down at his watch. "The Illinois Director will be here in an hour. We need you dressed and downstairs ready for company."

He left us standing there in shock. Shifting uncomfortably, I wrapped my towel around me tighter before hurrying over to the dresser. He made it sound like the whole relationship was official. Like it was some kind of fate bullshit. Well, I had been in one serious relationship and it wasn't all that it cracked up to be. Sure Eli was here for me through the worst of times and the sex was beyond amazing, but I wasn't ready to take the big step and talk marriage. Forget that shit. Ancients might have fallen for the mate bullshit, but I wasn't. Falling in love instantly was something you found in romance novels. It wasn't meant to be real.

My whole body stiffened when Eli wrapped his arms around my rib cage. "This relationship is whatever you want it to be. It doesn't have to be anything at all." The last part was said softly, so I knew it pained him to think of it like that.

Grabbing silk black panties and a bra I turned around to face him, placing my hands on his well-muscled chest. Gods was it muscled. Did I mention the black tattoo of a dragon he had going from his chest wrapping around his back? It was amazing and the artwork was something I haven't seen before. It made me want to get one. Tracing the dragon head I looked down. "I want a relationship, but nothing official like planning marriage."

He put a finger under my chin forcing my eyes to meet his dark ones. "That is more than I expected. I want to be with you and will wait however long."

Raising an eyebrow, I said, "But that is assuming I will come around to the idea of marriage. We just met Eli. This isn't Ancient times so we-" he cut me off, pressing his lips to mine a smile on them.

"You are putting too much thought into this. Stop worrying, we have bigger fish to fry." Slapping my ass, he turned away leaving me slightly dazed. "Now don't watch me dress, because we both know how easily distracted you are." He shook his head, looking over his shoulder. "I will blame you if Nick comes back up here."

Rolling my eyes I dropped my towel, smiling when his eyes darkened with sudden longing. I slipped my underwear on enjoying his reaction to me as I let the silk slide over my skin, slowly moving. He licked his lips and cleared his throat while blinking several times. "You don't play fair." He hurried out of the room, taking one last lingering look at me before he took off to his own room to hide.

*

When I finally made it downstairs I was attacked. Not literally in a sense of receiving pain, but with questions. Charity and Beth were on me like vultures to road kill. Both were dressed for guard duty and I noticed that on Charity's shirt she had a gold M on her and Beth had a blue one. But before I could ask about that, Charity started grilling me. They were asking way too many personal questions. When Charity asked me about size I was like whoa. "Hold up, chica. I am not sharing that information. A girl has to have her secrets."

Charity sighed theatrically. "Come on! We all have been wondering. Do you know you are the first girl we have ever seen him with?

We gotta know!" She stomped her foot, fist clenched. Yes, I did say stomp.

Smiling, I rolled my eyes. "I will tell you it is the best I ever had." Now that I say that, I gave a warning glare, "Stay away from him."

Beth chuckled. "Believe me, he wouldn't be interested in another female. Men like him are rare."

Nodding agreement, Charity said, "At least until they find their mate."

I groaned. "Not you too. You don't believe in that shit do you?"

Charity nodded. "Hell yeah, I do. Women need stuff like that, so we can believe not all men are raging assholes."

"All of the older vampires already found their mates. Most of them anyway." Beth said, waving a hand. She gestured a lot with her hands when she spoke, it was almost annoying. One day she was going to knock someone out with a flailing hand.

Carter popped into my head when she mentioned the mate thing. He had been so attached to his wife, and when she died people said he grieved a long time. Even now I could tell with him. Well, not now. He was gone now.

Never to find another mate if there was another one. Both girls were watching me and suddenly I was in a giant hug. I wasn't much for the touchy feely shit, but for once it helped.

After a few long seconds of hugging, I pulled away coughing. "Holy crap who is bathing in flowers?"

Busting out laughing, Charity started toward Nick's office pointing at Beth. "Her. The boy toy gave her a gift and well she did a toss in the air thing to get some on her back, and I think half the bottle ended up there."

"Why the hell would you toss it onto your back?" I asked.

Sticking out her tongue, she twisted around to head in the opposite direction. "I have work to do!"

Leading the way to Nick's office, I entered looking around finding Nick trying something from a silver dish. There was a table covered with different foods. The woman at the table was arranging everything carefully. She wore a chef hat and a white apron. One of the people who made the food in the house I guessed.

Nick smiled, waving Charity and I over. "Try this. It is most excellent." He said, gesturing toward a dip. "Crab dip." Smiling, both of us took a cracker and dipped in. When he gasped, we looked up startled. "You use this knife!"

Raising an eyebrow, I shoved the food in my mouth. "For real? You are lucky I don't double dip."

Charity snickered, nodding in agreement, earning a disgusted look from Nick. I walked over to examine the other food carefully, amazed that half the stuff I couldn't identify. What was with vampires and elegant food? I would have just brought in pizza and maybe some finger sandwiches. Nothing that could feed a whole country. As if understanding my exasperated look, the chef nodded mentally agreeing with me. Her almost graying hair stuck out from under her hat.

"You're human." I said.

The woman chuckled. "I believe I am."

Weird. Usually vampires hired other supernatural races, because humans feared a lot of them. Hearing someone talking outside the hall and the argument escalating, I undid the top of my katana strap and walked out toward the lobby.

Kristin was standing out there arguing with Eli, who was dressed in his usual suit and frustration marring his perfect face. When Kristin saw me coming up, her eyes blazed with fury. She wasn't even dressed perfectly, like usual. Her white dress was wrinkled, her lip stick not flawlessly applied and her hair wild as if the humidity went crazy with it.

"You!" She snarled, coming at me with her fingers hooked to tear into me.

Eli went to stop her, but I shook my head at him. Last thing I needed was the Deputy Director trying to save the Guardian. I just stepped aside and she was running past me with not so vampire like speed. She spun around, her fangs out ready to attack again. Then she surprised me by coming at me with the vampire speed, but I already had my katana out. "What is your problem, Kristin?"

She glared, hatred pouring from her eyes. "You are why he is dead. My Carter was burned today, sending him off to the heavens." She sobbed, lip trembling.

I missed the funeral? Why didn't anyone tell me? My own anger mounted, and I glanced over at Eli, who only shook his head, not even knowing himself. "When did they burn him?"

Kristin laughed like a crazy person. Well, she had always been crazy, but this pretty much sealed that deal. "Declan ordered it today because his body had yet to turn to ash! You did this. He tried to get you to go away, cutting off your ties, but no, that didn't help! The Covert came after him anyway, all because of you!"

Eli stepped forward. "That is enough." He growled.

She laughed at him. "Do you think you scare me? My power is triple of yours, I can tell."

I wanted to say something to that, but didn't. If she could sense power levels, she was a whole hell of a lot older than I pegged her to be. Which meant this whole time I underestimated her. "I can't believe they didn't tell me." I whispered, shaking my head in disbelief.

Her laughter filled the lobby. "I do. You are an abomination! You bring bad luck to everyone you fucking meet! This place will go down and all because of you. He tried to be rid of you." She shook her head. "My Carter, gone."

"He wasn't your Carter. I'm sure your shrine scared him long ago." I snarled.

"I don't have a shrine." She snapped back.

"What is going on out here?" Nick asked, coming out into the hall.

Skittering away, Kristin turned into a coward. "Director."

Nick nodded. "What do I owe this visit for, Kristin?"

Hmm, he knew who she was. When she refused to answer or meet his gaze, he walked to her putting a hand under her jaw. "Answer me."

It was then Kristin broke down into tears, hoping to make Nick feel sorry for her. She clutched his shirt, not seeing his bewildered expression. "She killed my Carter."

He pushed her away from him, making her to fall to the floor. "My Guardian did no such thing."

"Guardian? She was working undercover with the SCD until Carter fired her ass!" She hissed, shooting me a glare promising to kill me when she found the chance.

Nick shrugged his shoulders. "If that were the case, Carter wouldn't have had her sign papers stating she was only working for me and not the SCD. If she fails to comply, the result is death."

Kristin's eyes widened. "He was protecting you." She threw back her head laughing hysterically as if she just figured everything out.

"Holy hell, get her out of here. Send her to the basement in one of the cells. The woman is a complete loon." Nick said, shaking his head in disgust. The British in his voice coming out thicker as he became more agitated. He took a deep breath, then turned to look at Eli and me. "Women like that make me want to kill them." He turned on his heel to head back to the office.

My mouth fell open in horror, and Eli looked as shocked until Nick looked over his shoulder, grinned, showing fang. Bastard was trying to spook us. Never would I get used to the idea of him being Jack the Ripper. I did the crazy gesture with my finger to my temple. Eli nodded in agreement, as two guards appeared taking Kristin into custody. She screeched, trying to run the other way, but they snagged her around the waist as her fingers claws on the marble floors. I watched in revulsion as she tried to bite at their legs, her teeth snapping.

"I knew she was crazy, but this is beyond what I imagined. She is the type that would stow away a body in her basement, if it meant keeping her close to it." I pictured Carter in her basement and shuddered.

Eli put his hand on my shoulder. "It will pass." He promised, giving me a reassuring smile.

Nodding, I touched his hand with mine and then went forward. "Come on, Eli, duty calls, none of that in the lobby, sicko!" Shocked, Eli ran after me, but I was already in the doorway of the office.

*

It was almost forty minutes later when one of the guards came into the office to let us know about the Illinois Director arriving. It was two seconds later, probably one of the most gorgeous men I had ever seen came into the office. Seriously. Eli was freaking hot, but this Director was like a god. His beach boy good looks kind of made you think twice on if he was truly serious about being in such a high powered seat. His hair was short, all over the place like Nick kept his, but slightly longer. His blue eyes met mine and he smiled.

"This is the girl I have come to meet."
He all but purred, holding a hand out for mine.

From the corner of my eye I saw Eli
stiffen, his hands clenched. Jealousy? Smiling
back to the Illinois Director I took his hand, but
was surprised when he brought my hand to his
lips and kissed them softly. Shit.

Nick came up beside me and smiled,
holding out his hand to the Director. "Troy, a
pleasure as always."

Smiling up at me, he reluctantly released
my hand to shake Nick's. "Pleasure is mine,
Nick. Shall we get down to business?" He
asked, the political master coming out.

Eli went to the door to shut it, and I took
my place behind Nick's chair when he sat down
at his desk. "What can I do for you?"

Troy took a seat in one of the chairs after
unbuttoning his jacket, crossing a leg over the
other. "I need to borrow your girl here." He
winked at me, but I ignored it.

"I'm afraid she is unavailable. As my
Guardian she must remain by my side.

Annoyance flickered across Troy's face.
"Someone took my Deputy Director's daughter.
I feel it is the Covert."

"Why would you think it was the Covert?" I asked, taking an interest and obviously over stepping my bounds when Nick's jaw clenched.

Pleased that he caught my attention, Troy sat forward. "Because I found a body in my bed. A girl that I think is related to Michael. She was branded."

Double shit. I almost couldn't stand still. When Eli came closer to me, my head turned flashing him a warning. We didn't need public display of affection in front of another Director. "What do you want me to do? You have your own people."

Nick nodded in agreement. "She is correct there."

Troy stood up and began to pace. "I have heard things about you and one in particular is you did contracts for the SCD. Killing contracts." He saw my mouth open to say something, but he held up a finger. "That you are part demon." He started laughing, which almost reminded me of Kristin. "Do you not realize that your girl is one of the most desired Guardians out there? Here Crispin thought he had the best of the best by finding that Samaria warrior, but that is hardly the case at all. No one can compare to Blake."

I rolled my eyes now. "Please. I am not special and I just started!"

He shrugged. "Obviously you do not know your worth. Lucifer's daughter and the only half vampire and half demon there is." Troy paused then. "I guess I should throw the witch in the mix too, since your mother was first that."

How the hell did people know so much about me? Was there a biography out there? A pocket size book that people can cheat out of if they needed to know some fun facts about me? Maybe a special fan club. Get your tickets here! Someone probably had their own shrine of me! One of those creepy hair dolls. Maybe snuck my underwear at some point. Gross. Finding my back bone, I looked at him straight on. "Why do you need me?"

He sighed. "I need you to include our missing in with your case. I want to add one of my guys to help aid the investigation."

"No." Nick shook his head. "We don't need someone trying to control our girl when she is the primary on this investigation."

Troy shrugged. "My man would work under her. She would be completely in charge."

"Fine." I said.

"Wait, you don't even know all the terms." Eli said, stepping forward.

I shrugged. "I set the terms, agreed?"

Smiling, Troy nodded. "I like this girl."

"I'm sure you do." Eli growled, his dark eyes flickering. For about two seconds I saw his power peak out, but the other two vampires didn't notice.

"Let me introduce you to the person who will help." Troy said, straightening his suit. When nothing happened, we all stared at him expectantly. "Me."

Nick shot up from his chair, and Eli stepped forward objecting immediately. I was just plain shocked, staring at him. "You are a Director, what about your people?" Eli asked.

Troy smiled, pleased with the reaction he got. "Temporary stepped down. My Deputy is in charge for the time being."

"And Declan approved?" Nick asked in shock.

"I do not need permission if I am on temporary leave." He replied.

Shaking his head in disbelief, Nick walked over to Troy, grinning. "As long as we have known each other you never cease to amaze me, friend. Come, let's have a drink." When I went to follow Nick shook his head, signaling he would be fine without me.

"I think it would be wise that you brought Blake or myself with you, Director." Eli said, still behind the desk.

Nick rolled his eyes. "I appreciate the care you wish to take, but this is my brother. I hardly need protection from him."

Choking on my own spit, I slapped my chest to clear it. "You are full of fucking surprises!"

Both Nick and Troy laughed. I couldn't help but wonder if there was more to the relationship than they were letting on. Like partner meet partner again. I sighed, "No slashing throats or rolling in blood for fun!" I called out, only to receive a chuckle from both. That sounded almost like admission to me, but chose to ignore it for the moment.

Moving toward the door Eli grabbed my arm, once again concerned for my welfare. Holding up my hand I sighed. "You have to let me do my job, Eli, or this won't work. You can't protect me all the time and I refuse to be barefoot and pregnant."

Watching the idea pass through his head, my mouth fell open as he considered the situation. I jerked away. "Stupid boys." I muttered.

He laughed. "I was only kidding. But not about letting you run off with Troy the Ripper to our Jack." He stopped when I kept going, disappointment flitted across his face.

I turned to look at him. "You coming? This thing won't solve itself!"

Going down to the parking garage area I had every intention of climbing into my car and going somewhere. When I reached it, I threw up my hands in anger realizing I lit the thing up. Buying a car was the least of my concerns, but without wheels how would I get around? Glancing back at Eli, who was catching up just now, I frowned. No, didn't want to let him drive all the time. That would suck. My goal for the moment was to get to Michael's club, so I could interview some of the staff and maybe even the usual customers to see if they knew anything about the raves. Maybe someone would talk. But I had to do this in an official capacity, since it was likely that he would be angry over my sneaking in pretending to be having fun.

One more glance at Eli, I realized bringing him might be a mistake if I were trying to get my way with Michael. But it was hardly fair to play the field if Eli was a relationship I was contemplating on taking seriously. My skin prickled with anger. This was another reason why I stayed out of relationships. When there came a time at possibly advancing somewhere, you always had to consider your partner in bed. Not that I was a slut or anything, but I could pretend and tease without feeling guilty in the back of my mind.

Eli walked to his car, unlocked it with a click of the keypad. His handsome face looked at me questioningly. Gods he was gorgeous. Walking over to him I put both hands on the side of his face, tracing my thumbs over the sharp angles of his cheek bones. Touching my lips to his, I completely melted when he wrapped his arms around me. Sighing as pleasure rippled through my body, one hand moved to his and grabbed the keys. "Allow me, lover."

He grinned, moving toward the passenger side. I was surprised he would even think of letting me drive. Most men were possessive of their vehicles, especially ones as nice as his.

When the engine purred to life I all but moaned, earning a raised eyebrow from Eli. Clearing my throat, I started the car forward, ready to hit the gas once we made it out to the street. The weather was clear, allowing the stars to peek out. Stars and the moon always were a favorite of mine. If there had ever been a point in time escape was needed, my day usually ended with watching the sky from the roof of the apartment building. Granted the landlord had to replace the locks several times because of me, but I always paid extra on rent to make sure the costs were covered. Probably almost a year later he realized it was me doing it, so he just gave me a key, muttered something about respect and not dying by falling off the roof.

It was only fifteen minutes before we arrived to The Beast. Eli didn't even ask about where we were going. He probably already suspected as much. Troy wanted be in on the investigation, but took the first chance he had to escape with his old killing buddy. It was probably a good thing. Dead bodies popping up randomly with guts spewing out was not something I wanted to encounter while investigating missing people.

The Beast was pretty crowded, as usual. Cars were all over the parking lot, so finding a spot was a big hassle. We ended up having to pick a spot way in the way back, but at least Michael's club had adequate lighting and other security measures, like cameras lining the entire area. I allowed Eli to take my hand despite the professionalism issue I had with it. We were going to have to talk about it, so he didn't try it in front of other people. People needed to take me seriously and they won't if they saw hand holding and all that other lovey, lovey crap.

Nearing the front, I slowed down seeing a familiar motorcycle. It was an all-black Ducati with the initials ER in fancy lettering. Seeing me hesitate, Eli gave me a questioning look. Shaking my head, I hurried toward the club doors, only to be stopped by the bouncer again. One look at my weapons and he shook his head, his shiny bald head reflecting the light from the security lights.

"No weapons, Miss." He said, sounding as if he said that several times a night.

Eli stepped forward. "Eli Dexter, we are here on the behalf of the Director."

"No weapons." The bouncer repeated.

Growling, my eyes flashed. The bouncer stepped back in surprise, saying something into his mic. Within seconds the door opened, and Michael with a couple of body guards came through ready for action. I couldn't help but admire how he went to the front of the line when danger appeared.

Michael's gaze swept around until his eyes met mine. He smiled, coming forward smashing me into a hug. "Welcome back, gorgeous."

"I thought I was the only gorgeous in your life." Came a silky female voice behind all the men.

The guards parted exposing the owner of the Ducati. Sharp intake of Eli's breath was the reaction that I expected. Every male did it when they saw Electa Raines. The woman was a spitting image of her mother. Her mother being a long dead movie actress and who would have thought she was actually a werewolf? She was probably the only girl I could possibly be attracted to and that is with my hand on the Bible and sworn in to say that I was completely straight.

Electa's fair skin was smooth, flawless, and promised endless perfection over every part of her curvy body. Her dark eyes showed ever bit of wolf she was. You could tell there was wildness about her just from looking at them. Anytime she acted a certain way by actions or words, you looked into those eyes to see if she was serious or not. Her body was shapely and her upper half not leaving much to the imagination with her corset, which was all black, matching the black leather pants and biker boots. Her plump lips were painted red and her eyeliner was thick, creating cat eyes.

"Blake!" Electa cried out, flinging open her arms to embrace me in a hug.

Grinning, I hugged her back with the same amount of enthusiasm. We had been best friends until she disappeared to work undercover. In her case she was a real assassin, believe it or not. Her mother had dropped her off to a pack in California, so she was raised the way the rest were. Killers, but able to blend into the crowd of humans. Now that the secret of the supernatural world was out to the government, she was all for showing her wild side. The government could barely keep her in check, so they made sure to keep her busy by giving her assignments.

Releasing me, she leered at Eli and growled, touching her index finger to his coat. "And who is this?" She purred, leaning in close to sniff him.

"Hey! He's mine." I nearly snarled.

She laughed, her voice sounding musical. "Well, you finally did settle down."

"Hardly." Eli said, rolling his eyes.

Sending him a dirty look, I saw Electa shaking her head. "She is a hard one to keep roped. You have your work cut out for you."

Michael put an arm around Electa. "If you are through with introductions and walking down memory lane, I would like to take you three back to my office."

Electa led the way, getting her ass slapped by Michael. The guy was a freaking horn dog. He earned a teasing wink from her and I just shook my head. She always was a flirt, but never meant any of it. It was how she got close to a lot of her targets. The werewolves were very sexual creatures and the women used it to their advantage, if they had to.

"Boss, we have a problem." The bouncer said, catching our attention.

We all turned as a car parked in front of the doors. The cops. Swearing, I looked around for more. Why would they be here? Someone had to have told them something was going on. I was worried they now knew about the missing people. I watched as the man climbed out of his black unmarked car. My nose flared taking in the scent of werewolf. At least he was supernatural and part of Michael's pack, or so I thought.

Michael was in front of us in a flash. "What are you doing here, stray?" He growled, his whole body tense, ready to jump. "Ballsy to show live on pack territory, but plain homicidal to come face to face with the alpha."

The guy's gaze went to Michael, but moved away dismissing him. He didn't even acknowledge him. I was almost scared for him, but looking at the guy, he could take care of his own. If the power radiating off of him was any indication, he could take Michael, easily. Only he hadn't and didn't seem to have the intentions to.

His brown hair was streaked with red highlights that were completely natural. I would have thought his hair style was natural, if it weren't for his face looking like he just woke up. When his dark brown eyes met mine he stopped, pulled out his badge. "I am Detective Gideon Jones." He shoved his badge back in his jacket. "I need to ask you questions, Miss Noble."

When his nostrils flared, his eyes darted around, finally landing on Electa. Her eyes widened, her own nostrils flaring. She cleared her throat, running off into the club. Wonder what that was about? Looking back at Gideon I said, "How did you find me here?"

"I followed you." He replied.

Annoyed, I crossed my arms over my chest. "Why not just wait until I get home?"

Something flickered in his dark eyes, but I didn't catch it. "Because I can't. The Director's property is off limits for the locals. We have to go through Federal channels in order to approach you." When he realized I was waiting for more information he sighed. "None of the Feds believe you are involved with murder victims."

Smiling, I flashed my teeth, exposing my fangs. "What makes you think I am part of that?"

He tilted his head somewhat. "I don't, but I know you are investigating them."

Michael growled. "Get out of here before I make dog food out of you. How dare you come on my turf!" he snarled, his teeth snapping like a rabid dog.

Usually another wolf would meet that challenge or at least submit, but Gideon only stared at him. "As part of the police department I am within the law limits."

Sighing, I dropped my arms. "Fine, meet me at the diner up the road in an hour. We can eat dinner, since I am starving." When he went to object, I glared. "You're on my time. You are lucky I am even allowing you to interview me."

He nodded once. "I suspected as a former Federal cop you would at least allow me that." Gideon turned quickly, marching to his car. He gave one long look at the doorway where Electa disappeared into, then got into his car.

Chapter Nine

"I need to question your staff to see if any of them know of these raves. I figure since a lot of the recruiting seems to happen here we may learn something." I said to Michael, after I took a seat in his small office.

Michael shook his head. "Recruiting does not happen here."

Eli sat forward. "How do you know? They passed around a card last time we visited."

Meeting his gaze, Michael flashed teeth when he smiled. I had a mental image of those teeth tearing into an animal, blood everywhere. Shuddering, I rubbed my temples, feeling a headache coming on. When was the last time I even drank blood? I ate regular food, but my last feeding was the second time Eli and I had sex.

Watching me, Michael frowned as he spoke. "How do you know it wasn't just part of the trap for Blake?" He asked.

Realizing that probably was the truth, Eli shrugged. "Either way, they were here. Someone may know something."

I was getting dizzy, my vision swam as I leaned against my hand, and elbow propped up on the arm rest. Suddenly hands were around me, lifting me up. I heard some arguing as I was laid down on the couch.

"When was the last time she fed?" Michael asked. My eyes opened a little as he unbuttoned his shirt to reveal his neck. The vein in his neck moved with the beats of his heart that was now echoing in my ears. Eli growled, realizing what Michael planned on doing. "You're vampire, she needs more nutrients, so I am the only option right now."

"Maybe you should let me do it instead." Electa said, coming into my vision.

Angry now, I sat up, finding strength. My beast was out now, starving, in search for blood. I should have never gotten this far, but my control was gone. Eli paled as he looked at me. Electa jumped back, landing on the desk, crouched in an attack position.

Michael rolled his eyes. "It is her demon. And you call yourselves friend and lover." He tilted his neck in offering. My brain was saying fuck no, but the vampire in me was beyond reason. Like a snake I attacked, my fangs sinking into him.

"Holy shit!" Electa stared, mouth hanging open. "Her demon is fucking freaky for sure, her eyes are red and she is sprouting horns!"

Eli hurried to my side, touching my arm. Michael groaned, feeling my pleasure ripple through him as his arms slid around me, bringing my body over his to straddle him.

"She can't get like this." A new voice in the room said.

It was Lucifer. He came to stand next to Eli. "This is a mild comparison of what can happen if the hunger strikes and her demon falls into the desire for blood." He shook his head, looking at Eli with anger blazing in his eyes. "You need to keep her fed. I should have told you before, but if you love someone you make sure they are fed!"

Pulling my fangs from Michael, I looked over at Lucifer. "It has only been over a day." I said, the hunger curbed, but not all the way.

Shocked, Lucifer thought about this. While he did, my hunger for blood subsided, but my need of a different hunger struck just as fast. I could feel Michael's length pressed against my core. I nearly moaned, but forced my mind clear, as I wiped my mouth with the back of my hand. It came back with a smear of blood.

Michael grinned. "That was wonderful. I never let a vampire feed from me before." He shivered, his hands sliding under my shirt. "I know you want more, I can feel it."

Rolling my eyes, I licked the puncture wounds in his neck to seal them over and he shivered again, growling. "Nice, but not necessary, love. Werewolf healing."

Feeling like an idiot, I climbed off him, avoiding Eli's gaze. Lucifer was still thinking and Electa was staring at me, but was looking at the top of my head. She used her two index fingers and put them to her head to indicate horns. Horror filled me as I went to the mirror to look. Sure enough, two little spikes came through my hair. Speechless, I spun to Lucifer, who was staring at me with fascination. "They will go away." He promised. "Just keep fed, I must do some research on this more frequent hunger of yours." He disappeared.

"Was that Lucifer?" Electa asked, eyes wide.

Michael stood up, brushing off his pants. He nodded. "Yes it was, now get off my desk." He said, shocking her. Usually he flirted and made some comment, but now he was all business, not fazed by the female presence. Sitting down in his chair, he clasped his hands together and looked at me, eyes serious. "I will make a deal with you. Information for something I want from you."

Eli stepped forward. "Absolutely not! Sex is out of the question."

"I never said sex, so sit down before you hurt yourself."

It was then Eli's control nearly snapped. His power leaked out, swirling around the room. Electa's eyes bulged and mine probably did too as the breath was sucked out of us. Michael leaned forward trying to catch his own, while the anger only grew in his eyes. But the power disappeared when Eli started to breathe in shallowly to get control.

Clenching a pencil and breaking it, Michael took in a deep breath, his chest expanding largely. "As I was saying before we were interrupted, a deal. If you promise to feed from me for one month, once a week, I will tell you where the next rave will be."

"You are taking pervert to a whole new level for yourself, Michael." Electa said, shaking her head as she finally climbed down.

Michael ignored her comment while watching me. It wasn't a bad deal, to be honest. He was a powerful werewolf. His blood was coursing through my veins, sending vibrations throughout me. The power wanted an outlet and my demon wanted to give it. I felt like I could do anything. To prove to myself I could, I lifted my hand and thought of fire. A ball of flame sparked to life in my palm and everyone gasped. "Agreed."

*

Eli was pissed. More than pissed. He stomped out of the club, his rage trailing behind him. I could feel the power rubbing along my skin. My own body pulsated with power, poking each corner looking for a way out. The demon liked the fire I made and it wanted more. In fact, it wanted destruction, but I held down firm on my control, trying to keep it in check. Electa was shocked I accepted the offer, but it was worth it when he told me the location of the new rave. It was somewhere that you would least expect. It would be taking place at a local rogue's house. He was pretty famous for his stunt roles for major action actors. Jobs were usually his for a few reasons. One, he was immortal in most cases. Two, he was old enough to have his own ability, which was to shift into different people, including women. If he was part of the Covert keeping track of him would be difficult.

Michael had come by the information when the guy came into the club with a bunch of girls on his arms. He was bragging away about how people were coming to his house for this rave and it would be the best thing yet. He didn't say what would happen there, but coming from a vampire only one thing comes to mind. Obviously, he wasn't that bright he if he was talking about things like that out loud, but Michael said he was a frequent customer, who was often high on human blood laced with some sort of drug. Some vampires didn't learn. Human laced blood was highly addictive and would even affect a vampire brain after a while with constant use.

The rave was to take place the following night after midnight sometime, when people were usually leaving the clubs to get laid. Last I knew, the vampire lived in a really flashy neighborhood. Wishing I had my computer to search through records, I drummed my fingers on the roof of the car. Eli was still avoiding me. He needed to get over what I did.

"Let's go meet the detective. Think you can stop your tantrum long enough for me to do that?" I asked, climbing into the car.

Eli stared at me in disbelief. "How would you feel if some woman wanted that from me?" He demanded, eyes furious.

My mouth opened, but then I closed it. He was right, but the deal was already made. Pissed off at myself I did the only thing I knew how, placed blame on someone else. "We aren't tied down with each other, Eli. Realize that. I can do what I want, when I want."

He sat back, startled by my words. Then his own rage filled his face, all other emotion disappearing. "If that is how you want it."

Wishing I could take it back, I nodded sharply, refusing to back pedal. Climbing back out of the car, I tossed the keys at him. "See you later." Slamming the door, I turned to walk toward the diner and Eli didn't even follow me.

The diner was just ahead and I could see Gideon's car parked outside in front. The lights were bright, reflecting off the hood and the rest of the street in front. Shoving my hands in my pockets, I quickened my pace, anger fueling me.

How dare he act that way? Or did I really blame him? Hell yes, I would be pissed off if he took a female like that. Why was I really mad then? Why did I walk away as if everything was his fault? Because it was. He shouldn't have pursued me. I didn't want a relationship, yet he continued to push at me. If he would have left me alone, I wouldn't have to worry about other people's feelings. All that would matter were my own. How did my life end up so jacked up anyway?

Feeling on the brink of tears, I stopped to take a deep breath. Control. I needed control, or Gideon was going to think I was off my rocker. Which was probably true considering I just accepted an offer where I was sucking the alpha werewolf's blood once a week for a month. But who could deny such power? It rolled through me in waves, encouraging me to use it in ways only my demon would know how. The demon wanted to be released to take on the world. The desire for blood was overwhelming. Not to drink it either, but to spill it. To see the liquid of it gather on the ground in front of me when I slit someone's throat or sank my teeth into them.

Shuddering at the pleasure of the feeling, I moved forward looking through the window to find Gideon was drinking coffee at a table near the far end of the diner. He was looking around and waiting. Bringing the demon in back under control, I pulled open the door, earning looks from the waitress and the cook in the kitchen. There were a few customers, most of them older men who didn't have anything else to do at night besides escape their wives at home. My demon reared its head again, trying to steer me in the direction of a middle aged man whose dark brown hair was graying around the edges. He looked up at me, showing more interest than a married man should.

My demon scratched around inside me, demanding we make him pay for being unfaithful, but I pushed past him toward the table Gideon sat at. His eyes roamed over me once, appreciatively, but looked away gesturing for me to take a seat.

The waitress brought me my own cup and poured coffee into it, then poured more into Gideon's. She was older, probably nearing her retiring age, but she had enough spunk to wink at Gideon before sauntering off away from the table. I raised an eyebrow in question and he grinned forcing the tiredness to disappear and allowing the manly charm to expose itself. "She's nice and deserves some kind of attention." He said, pouring sugar into his cup. I winced, realizing he used more than I would ever dare to.

"That's sweet of you." I said, earning an eye roll from him as a blush crept up his neck to his face. Ballsy detective was shy when it came to women. Interesting.

Pouring in my own sugar and then some cream, I stirred my coffee looking at him, studying every feature. He was awfully cute, which goes without saying when it came to paranormal. They all looked good, just some looked better than others. In a way he reminded me of some country boy forced into the city. He didn't fit in at all, which kind of made me wonder why he was even here.

Taking a sip, I scooted further into the booth, adjusting my katana so it didn't make me uncomfortable. The only way that worked was if I put one leg up on the bench, so I did. He looked over my one leg and smiled. "Where is the boyfriend?" When I didn't say anything he made an "o" with his mouth. "Falling out, I see."

"Something that isn't your business. What did you want to talk about?"

He sat back, ready to get down to business. "It has come to my attention that people, mostly girls, have come up missing. I am not sure why the Feds aren't all over this, but it has me suspicious."

Nodding, I copied him by sitting back in my own bench, then decided to move forward again, 'cause the whole pose looked like I was offering more than I was. Like 'Hey, big boy, want some of this?' "They were. I was. But my boss let me go and now he is dead. So I don't know what is happening with the Feds. I have to work this Guardian job because I signed some paper thinking it was part of my undercover, but guess what?"

"It wasn't."

Shaking my head, I sipped more coffee. "This whole thing is fucked up. I can't give you information, because now I am bound by vampire law and now my Director. I am loyal to only him now."

Gideon blew out an irritated breath. "I keep getting road blocked. By my superiors, the Feds and now you."

"What is your interest in this?" I asked, blowing at my coffee.

He leaned forward, close enough for me to smell the coffee on his breath. "Carter was my friend."

That floored me. Never once had Carter mentioned being friends with a wolf named Gideon. In fact, it sounded kind of false to me. I would know. Or would I? He did let me go without a second thought, protecting or not. So I just waited, gauging Gideon's reactions and sincerity. "How do I know you are telling me the truth?" I asked, voice low and threatening to remind him the truth would be wise.

Gideon's gaze never wavered as he said, "Because I wouldn't know that you are his adopted daughter, now would I? I also wouldn't know that he fired you because Declan threatened to kill you."

I shrugged. "Declan is King, even he is bound by vampire law."

He raised an eyebrow at me, like he was saying, "Really? Are you really thinking he follows the laws?" After that, I just shrugged and nodded at the same time, as if saying yeah he was right, Declan could get around anything if he paid the right people.

"Alright, so what do you want from me, then?" That was the million dollar question.

When he hesitated to answer, I sighed. "Come on. I have places to be, people to see. You know how it goes."

Chuckling, he nodded. "Fine, I want to help you find the killer for Carter. I think it is related to the Covert, which is also probably related to Declan."

Shocked, I sat back, not caring what my posture looked like to the rest of the world. "Why would it be Declan?"

He shrugged. "Why not? Money, power, and the resources. When you get too close he threatens Carter. Then when you seem to think Carter could give a shit less, he kills him thinking you won't care." Shaking his head, he continued, "But you aren't the typical vampire. You care about people, no matter what and despite all that they do to you."

It was making sense to me now. "How do we take care of Declan?"

This time he looked blocked, as if he didn't even have a solution. "He has so many people under him, he doesn't even need to come near the operation. We need proof, which means we need to show he is receiving income from this."

Okay, okay, I could do this. Sure, it would make sense for it to be Declan, but I had one question, "Why is he going after people that matter then?"

He shrugged. "That is for us to find out."

*

Leaving the diner I thought about what Gideon had said. We made arrangements for him to come with me to crash the rave. He said he wouldn't be there in an official capacity, since his department didn't sanction him going after a Federal case. They had jurisdiction, which meant if he was caught he could be fired from his job. After talking to him for a while, I didn't think the job mattered to him as much as some people would think. A werewolf with a background like his could get a job anywhere if he wanted. Why he chose a civilian life was beyond me, but as long as he was offering his professional help, including access to records, I was game with him helping out. Now if only Nick would agree. That would be the hard part.

Walking toward the mansion I heard a motorcycle coming up behind me. I knew it was Electa, but I kept moving forward, not caring for a confrontation and maybe a scolding for being an idiot. When she slowed down she offered me up a helmet and I accepted. When she first started riding motorcycles being a passenger was the only thing that was acceptable. Bikes scared the shit out of me, so riding on the back of one was a big step. Getting beyond that step was another thing. Thanks but no thanks, I rather stick to vehicles that would suffer more damage than I would if there was a crash.

Electa took me straight to the mansion, never saying a single word. The guards expressed interest when they saw me hop off and hand her my helmet. I grinned. "Want to go car shopping with me tomorrow? I burned up my mustang, so I need a replacement."

She flipped up the visor of her helmet and grinned. "Fuck yeah, that would be awesome. I can pick you up around six." She offered. Giving a thumbs up I nodded, waiting only a few minutes to watch her take off down the driveway, despite the speed limit signs urging vehicles to stay at ten mile per hour. The girl never followed directions well.

Grinning, I hurried up the steps, hearing no one when I entered the house. Praying Eli was in his room, I climbed the steps creeping past his room to get to mine, only his door opened just as I made it a foot away. Stiffening, he cleared his throat. When I didn't move he cleared it again. Sighing, my shoulders sagged and I turned around to face him.

It didn't help he was half naked and only in boxers. He did that on purpose. I wasn't one that could avoid temptation when it came to him, so he thought flaunting like a juicy steak would have me foaming from the mouth? Well, he was wrong! Sorta! Spinning around, I hurried to my room, trying to shut the door behind me, but he pushed it open, stalking me as I stumbled back away from him. "I thought we agreed to end this?" I said, trying to make my voice sound angry, but it only came out small and desperate to escape before he touched me.

"I did not agree." He responded, forcing me against the wall where my head hit.

Eli put one arm up around me, bracing himself against the wall as he looked down at me. His scent filled my nose, causing it to do things inside me. I shivered. "You said if that was what I wanted."

"I only agreed to allow you to do what you wanted. I never said anything about ending our relationship." Before I could protest his lips were on mine. Melting against him instantly, I groaned. His tongue forced its way into my mouth, as he lifted me up by my ass forcing my legs around his waist. Gasping when he bit my lip, my eyes flew open meeting his fiery ones.

His hands tore at my shirt, trying to pull it over my head. I tried helping him, but only made it worse by going in the wrong direction. Finally, he growled ripping it off me, literally.

He dropped it to the floor, putting me down, so he could begin on my pants to unbutton them. Pushing them down to the floor, he slid one hand into my panties and dove his fingers in brutally. I hissed in pain, which only encouraged him more. Kissing my neck he moved down to nibble on my collarbone, where I put my head back urging him on, downward. When his lips came to my bra he growled in annoyance. When he tried to pull back I shook my head and unbuttoned it myself, letting it fall open.

Desire sparked even more in his eyes and he took one nipple into his mouth. "Oh gods." I cried out, grinding myself into him. I tried to push him off me so I could take control, he stood fast, biting the nipple. I cried out.

"You are mine." He growled, lifting me to drop my body to the bed. I shook my head refusing to be owned, he tore my panties away kissing my stomach as he went down. "Say it."

Again I shook my head, trying to push back the fear that was almost taking over the need I had for him. His tongue touched my warmth and I flinched. "Say it." He said. When I didn't respond he grabbed my legs pulling me closer. I sobbed, feeling myself climb to the top threatening to spill over, but he stopped. Gasping, I tried to force him back down, but he only climbed over me, his hardness pressing against me through his boxers. "I want you to admit it. Admit this mate bond is real."

"No." I said, meeting his gaze. "It's fairy tales."

Growling again, he tore off his boxers and pressed his tip at my entry. I whimpered, trying to direct him inside me. He smiled. "What do you think it would do to you if I stopped right now?"

My mouth opened in shock. "You wouldn't."

He nodded. "Oh yes, I would. Now, are you mine?"

Digging my nails into his arms, I slammed myself onto him and gasped out, "Yes."

*

What have I done? I just told a man I was his and we don't even know each other. Never even said I love you. That wasn't the process. Good going, Blake, screw up the process! Knowing you, the baby will come before the marriage! Shaking my head, I stared up at the ceiling disgusted with myself. Glancing over at Eli, I watched him sleep. One arm was over my stomach clutching my hip possessively. It felt good. More than good. I wasn't one to believe in how stuff was meant to be and this was fate. But I could readily admit that being with him felt right at the moment. So why not ride it out and see where it took me? That awareness brought cold hard fear to my heart instantly. The idea of feeling trapped wasn't something I liked. Vampires took their marriages seriously, which meant if I had a change of heart, getting rid of him would be difficult. Did I want to be rid of him? No, I didn't, no matter how hard I tried to fight it.

Rolling over I let him pull me into him, tucking my small body into his large one. He lowered his lips to my neck and took a deep breath. When his hand slid down my thigh I found myself backing up into him in offering. Look at you! Already trying to give him what he wants! Run away the demon screamed, there are other ones who you could lay with so you aren't trapped, but the demon faded away when he slid a hand over my hip, so he could put a finger into me. I sighed.

Moaning, I slid a hand up behind his head pulling him to my lips. He smiled. "Even though it is early and you are readily to deny me, I love you."

At the same time he finished that sentence he slid his length into me. "Bastard" I breathed, eyes rolling back into my head. He only chuckled, thrusting into me.

*

Troy was sitting in Nick's office alone, looking at his phone when I came downstairs. My body felt great. Better than great. I enjoyed being with Eli and wanted it more than ever. After the time with him it dawned on me I was fighting a bond that would never go away. Even if I led myself down the path of torture denying the feelings I had there. No matter what, the strings would pull me back to him, even if it was years from then. I probably would never be able to be with anyone else. This was the mate bond the vampire's history had described. Stupid Demigod! I wanted to shake my fist in rage, but happiness inside me overrode that feeling and told me to deal with it. There was no way around it, no matter how much I tried.

Of course the demon inside of me was shaking her head in disgust, "Sucker." As in another sucker for love and boy was I stupid for falling for it. Females were better without males. Didn't I realize that? Sure I did, so why was I falling head over heels for Eli? Because he fixed everything when I thought it was impossible to be fixed. He was better than any man I knew.

"Evening, Blake." Troy said, interrupting my thoughts.

I was just standing in the doorway, off in my own little world and he was probably trying to contact the mother ship. Earth to Blake, wake up! Annoyed with myself, I forced a smile. "Evening."

Setting down his phone on the desk, he started walking around. "What did you learn from Michael?"

Hesitating to answer his question, I looked around for Eli or Nick to come save me. It was up to them what information I would share with Troy. The guy made me uncomfortable. Every time I looked at him he was closer and it was totally creeping me out. Moving in the opposite direction, I went to the door to peek out. Nick was coming down the hallway looking grim as ever.

When I looked back at Troy I nearly squealed in surprise. He was right in my personal space. "Fuck! Do you mind?" I stepped away and made an imaginary circle around me with a finger. "My bubble."

He started laughing, enjoying the idea of making me uncomfortable. "Those days are long behind me, have no fear."

"No fear? I bet you used the insides for Christmas decorations. You had some serious Silence of Lambs going for you back then."

Shrugging, he said, "I am a changed man."

Nick pushed his way past us, not even curious on why we were in the doorway. He went to sit behind his desk, turned toward the book case behind him and clicked a button on a remote he had under some papers. The bookcase moved revealing a TV and the news flickered on. Moving closer, I put my hands on my hips to watch.

A pretty blond stood in front of the camera, a house that someone rich had to of owned behind her. "We are at Alex Henderson's home tonight, where a female victim was found dead from by what looks to be vampire bites. The police would not elaborate anymore other than damage has been done to the body." I groaned loudly. "It is suspected a group called the Covert is running an underground operation, where they started to take victims from the street to sell. Recently they stepped it up by removing political leaders and celebrities from their homes. Are vampires real? Do we need to stock up on garlic? More tonight at ten."

"You have got to be kidding me! Now they are going public? What the hell do they have to gain by doing that?" I asked, turning around only to run right back into Troy. "Dude, seriously, back up."

Nick frowned. "He is a Director you show him respect, Blake."

I looked at him, my eyebrows raised. "When he wanted to work on this case he agreed to all terms. The boss doesn't respect the little people." Turning back to Troy I found him frowning, obviously not liking me calling him a little person. I just shrugged. "I like my personal space. I don't need him trying to memorize my scent, in case he wants to add something nifty to his Ripper MO."

Rolling his eyes, Nick clicked off the TV, so the bookcase could shut again. "That was years ago."

"Still, he is kind of freaky if you ask me. Keep the knives away and I need a new lock on my door." I pretended to whisper by leaning over and putting a hand near my mouth for coverage.

Exasperated, Nick stared at me. "You are only bringing it on yourself."

Troy licked his lips, once again smiling with his fangs showing. "You would be a good addition to my accomplishments."

He stepped forward and I stepped back holding a hand up. Fire leapt up, startling him back. I grinned. "I'll set you on fire, baby."

"Oh cool trick!" Charity skipped into the room. And yes, she really did skip. "Eli told me you gained some new abilities last night. This is pretty fucking awesome." She clapped. "Show me more!"

Eli came into the room with Reed, Chad, and Mitch. He smiled at me, then went to Nick, who explained the situation with the news. Shock went across his face. "Why would anyone know about Alex's daughter? He wouldn't call the police if he found her dead. He would call the King's men or the SCD."

No one answered, because none of us had one. Alex was the name Mitch used to get us into the club. I frowned. "We have to go talk to Alex then." Everyone agreed.

Chapter Ten

Reporters were still all over Alex's property when we called to check on him. We asked him to meet us at Nick's office and he agreed later in the evening, which gave me time to go out with Electa to pick out my car. Eli wanted to go, but I told him we were having a girl's night, so he reluctantly agreed to stay home.

Electa showed up right on time, which she usually always did. Her pet peeve was people who showed up too late. I was the type that usually did, but rarely did when I had to meet her because she wouldn't let it go. When she showed up on her Ducati I raised my eyebrows up at what she chose to wear. A small black dress and biker boots. She flipped up her visor and glared, daring me to ask about it, so I didn't. Probably a date gone wrong, or maybe even troubles with one of her targets.

I slipped on the helmet, then held on for dear life when she shot out of the driveway, hardly slowing down for traffic as she zoomed out onto the main road. The girl took risks, which was one of my favorite things about her. Her life was always unpredictable. Almost like how I wanted to live mine. When I worked for the SCD my assignments didn't take me off a common course. Usually it was always the same thing, like a vampire draining a human and didn't mean to. Or a troubled pixie neighbor that decided a rash was better punishment than a confrontation. It was all just like a small town type policing. I longed to be in a more adventurous type of life. That might be able to happen if the Guardian thing worked out. I was lucky to have as much control as I did have with Nick. Most Directors would have fired me on the spot, but according to Troy I was one of a kind, so finding a job probably wouldn't be so much of a problem.

Which reminded me, Lucifer was due for my lessons. Things had been so busy that we skipped the last one. Or was it two? I couldn't remember. Though he did show up at the club when he knew my demon was coming out of the hole. He warned that it would be a bad thing. Was that the way I would have to live my entire long life? Worried this demon will come free?

The ride soon ended when we arrived at the dealership, where she didn't even let me look. Her hand held onto mine tight, dragging me across the parking lot. "Hey, where are you taking me? All the cars are up front." I frowned realizing she was taking me in the used section. "Look, I want a new car."

She turned to look over her shoulder at me, rolling her eyes. "You will love this. I found it earlier, I asked them to put it away, so I can surprise you."

Now following her willingly, a man came out of a garage that was hidden behind the dealership. He wiped his hands on an already greased up towel and smiled at us. "There she is. The most beautiful gal I have ever seen." He winked and then looked at me. "Oh, this must be the friend. Well, come along then."

Most of his features were hidden behind the grease mask he wore. His hair was shoved under a trucker hat and the rest of him was covered in even more grease, his overalls looking blacker than the blue they used to be. I could only tell that it used to be blue, because of the area between his legs that showed when he walked.

He led us behind the mechanics garage, where I stopped dead, staring in awe at the beauty before me. It was still new, but it was one that I probably would have not picked out for myself. A black Charger. It was all black, the paint sparkling under the light in the parking lot. Pulling the door open, I looked at the black leather seats with a red pin stripe. "It is awesome."

Electa grinned. "I knew you would like it."

Eager to get it on the road, I hurried toward the dealership to get the paperwork done.

*

News vans were outside of the mansion, the reporters waiting for someone to come out. The guards were now further down the steps, ignoring the questions that were tossed at them. Further down the drive was a group of four people with signs protesting. Of course, how could we possibly avoid those guys? Always have something to protest. One sign said "Kill all vampires before they kill us." A lot of words for a single sign. The woman holding it looked fierce wearing her battle gear. No, I was not exaggerating. She wore military clothes, but obviously was too old to actually be serving.

Electa followed close behind my car as I coasted through the people. Reporters waited for me to park. I could almost see them planning ways of trapping me, because they were unsuccessful before with their earlier victim, whoever that was. Smiling, I decided I could probably just stay inside the car.

Opening the passenger side door, Electa still had her helmet on when she peeked inside. "Get out already." She growled, obviously annoyed. Removing her helmet would be a mistake, considering a lot of her job required going unnoticed. Not that it wasn't already hard, considering she was absolutely stunning.

Climbing out I noticed Gideon's car was there in front of all the news vans. Electa was staring in that direction and suddenly spun on one heel to head up the steps toward the house. When I hurried in that direction one male reporter stepped in my way making me lose my balance. Someone grabbed me from behind and I looked to find Troy. He flashed me a grin, making me move away instantly. The guy reporter saw my reaction, but continued with questions like, "Blake, we heard you are investigating several murders and you're a vampire. Have you come across any human victims?" When I didn't answer and kept going he caught up to me. "Is it true Lucifer is your father?"

Stopping, my eyes met his and he stepped back. I noticed the logo of the news company on his shirt. He was part of the one everyone thought reported conspiracies or lies to sell papers. He flashed a smile. "I guess we got that one right. Look at her eyes!" He called out to everyone.

I went to grab for him, but Troy gripped my arm moving me forward. He sighed. "Now you have gone and done it. Gorgeous vampire demon girl will now be the cover girl of that horrible magazine. Don't be surprised if you have some sort of fan club, or Cosmo wants you to feature on their cover."

We entered the lobby and I turned. "You did this." It was a guess, but gauging his pleased expression about the reporters latching onto me like vultures I was probably right.

He closed the door and smiled. "What makes you think that?"

"Oh my gods! What the fuck did you do? Am I not the boss here?" I demanded, poking him in the chest.

Troy raised an eyebrow, seeming amused by my outburst. I wanted to punch it right off his face, but Nick came out of his office deciding to run interference. "Holy hell, I made her mad." Troy chuckled.

Looking down, my whole body was enveloped in fire. Son of a bitch! "I don't want you here. Come near me again you'll be crossing over sooner than you'd like." And to prove I meant what I said I blew at my hand, where a flame danced off to attach itself to his clothes. "Fucking idiot." I grumbled, shaking away the flames as I walked.

"I am on fire, Nicholas!" Troy cried out.

Nick sighed. "I don't know why you provoke the woman."

"She is your Guardian, control her!" Came back his snappy reply.

I didn't hear the rest because my focus went on Eli, who was leaning against the door frame smiling at what I had done. He opened his arms to me and I went into them, immediately feeling the stress fall away into nothing. My nose pressed into his jacket taking in his male scent.

Straightening, I took his hand, so we could go into the office where my team was waiting with Gideon and Electa. Charity sat in Nick's office chair spinning around. She waved to me before she spun around again. Mitch was leaning against the window, his hands shoved into his pockets, his eyes met mine and he nodded once.

Chad was on the floor. Don't ask me why, but he had his legs folded Indian style, just staring at the desk in front of him. Once again he was slick with sweat, probably coming fresh out of the training room.

Reed was playing on his cell phone, not bothering to acknowledge me, but I was starting to accept that it was part of his personality. He shoved his phone into his pocket and came up beside me. "Who is biker chick?"

"My friend, Electa." I replied.

At the announcement of her name, she took off her helmet and shook out her hair. The room went silent watching as if an angel was just born. A miracle. She always had that effect on people and it cracked me up. She sat her helmet on Nick's desk and met Gideon's eyes. Once again there was the recognition, but neither of them said anything to each other. It was driving me nuts, so I made a mental note to ask her about it.

"Well, holy cow!" Reed shook his head. "I have heard of you."

Electa rolled her eyes and perched herself against the desk. "I'm sure."

Nick and Troy entered the room, both stopping to stare at Electa. Was I surprised? Hell no. I might as well be dancing around naked and still people wouldn't see me. "Who is our guest?" Nick asked, taking a seat behind his desk, which forced him to look around Electa.

She hopped off, sending him a sexy smile. "Electa Raines."

His eyes snapped in her direction. "You are a celebrity among our kind." He said, swallowing hard.

Grinning, she nodded. "I would assume as much, since I killed more of you than anyone I know."

"Why is she here?" He demanded. "I have been tolerating your attitude for longer than I should, Blake. I don't need you surprising me daily."

Shrugging, I leaned on the desk. "Want to fire me? Go ahead."

Troy shook his head, standing next to Nick. "No respect. How can you allow someone like that in your house?"

I looked at Troy. "What? Are you the devil on his shoulder? Come on. I think Nick can manage on his own. Unless you have more advice on how to remove a woman's parts for him?"

Flashing a smile, Troy looked at everyone else that just stared. They still didn't know who he was in the past, but obviously someone unhealthy in the head. "I will, only if you are offering yourself up for the experiment."

Stepping forward, I looked at Nick when he stood between us. His gaze met mine and he said, "I can see this won't work."

Hell yeah, he was getting rid of Troy. Fist pump in the air for me. I stuck my tongue out at Troy, who only leaned against Nick's chair as my Director's gaze met mine. "What?" I asked.

"You have to leave." Nick said. "I have put up with your behavior and with reason, but he is right. You are out of control."

Eli's face turned angry. "You can't do that."

Nick raised his eyebrows to the challenge. "Are you challenging me, Deputy?" Saying his title was supposed to remind Eli of his position and lack of authority. But it didn't. An Ancient could do what they wanted. I didn't know what hurt worse. Nick firing me over his stupid ripper buddy, or the fact Eli backed down. My mouth fell open in shock as my body began to shake.

Electa grabbed my arm. "Let's go."

My gaze turned accusingly toward Eli, but his face was wiped of all expression as he watched me turn to leave. Charity chased after us. "I'm coming too!"

"Get back here, Charity!" Nick shouted.

"I can't allow this to happen." Eli said suddenly. I spun around, hope on my face.

The release of power in the room hit bringing us to the floor. Electa grabbed my hand, fear on her face. Never once had I seen fear on my best friend's face. She was a fearless werewolf that always took risks.

Slowly the power receded. I looked up to find Eli standing at the center of the room looking so unlike himself. His hair was wild and his eyes were lit with a fire I never saw before. The Ancient had appeared. Troy tried to run past, but with a flick of his hand Eli sent him against the wall holding him up in the air. "You'll stay there." He growled.

Then his gaze went to Nick who stood up shocked, but refusing to back away. "You cannot be."

Eli smiled, flashing his fangs. "I am and that is my mate." He pointed to me, not even taking his eyes off of Nick. "You choose her over the man that wants to drag you back to hell? Take you back to the days of murdering people?" He stepped forward looking every bit of menacing that he was. He hid himself pretty well. I couldn't help but get completely turned on by this power of his.

"Gods, he is so hot." I murmured, earning a surprised look from Electa. "Doesn't it make you just want to rip his clothes off?" Growling, I licked my lips.

Tugging on my arm made me stop, Electa was trying to hold me back. "Control the demon, Blake." She rolled her eyes, pulling me back toward her.

Gideon crawled over to us. The power must have flung him out of one of the chairs. "This is fucked up." We all nodded in agreement and watched the show.

Nick moved around his desk as Eli came around the opposite direction. "I am claiming my right as King." He said.

"Then you have to tell that to Declan!" Nick said, ready to bolt out the room.

"I just did." Eli looked over toward the door. We all turned to see Declan there. His eyes were wide with fear. "Come join us, Declan." Like a robot Declan moved forward. It was then I realized Eli was controlling him with little effort.

Declan's face looked contorted, as if he was trying to fight the power over him. He plopped down on the chair. Eli smiled. "Glad you could make it. Have a seat, we have lots to discuss." He folded his arms over his chest. "I am taking over the King position, which gives me every reason to convict you of Carter's murder."

"I did not murder him!" Declan said outraged.

Rolling his eyes, Eli sat on the edge of the desk. It was amazing how he went to looking like someone's puppet to the one who knew he was in control. His perfect face showed no fear, but all arrogance of someone dominant. "You may not have, but you know who did."

Stiffening, Declan looked around the room noticing all the people. He finally saw Troy up on the wall. "Why is he up there?"

Eli sighed dramatically. "Seems he wanted to get away, but we can't have that. Now answer me."

"That Ben fellow told me he was wanted over in Europe for a past crime that just came to light. His father had sent him to retrieve him, but unfortunately never learned where Carter lived." He shrugged. "He had all the proper paperwork."

Leaning forward, Eli frowned. "Did you look over the paperwork?" When Declan nodded, he asked, "Entirely?" His hesitation was enough to say no. "So, he had a kill order, but I doubt it was for what he said." He shook his head. "I am thinking this Covert thing is a lot bigger than we suspected, love." He said looking over at me.

Just then Troy fell from the wall. He brushed off his pants looking furious. "This is ridiculous! I would like to file a complaint." He growled.

Eli smiled. "Against your King? Sure you can do that, but guess who gets the final say so?"

Troy became rigid. "I must go now. We will hear of a ceremony then for your seat?"

Nodding, Eli watched him head toward the other side of the office. "Oh, and Troy, consider your position as Illinois Director terminated. I quite like your Deputy Director having control. I don't want to hear about you leaking information to the news either. If you do, plan on staying in prison for a century or two."

Stiffly nodding, Troy exited the room. "I just love making progress."

Getting to my feet, I went over to Declan, meeting his eyes. "Where did Ben go?"

He shrugged. "How the hell should I know? I am not his keeper."

Grabbing the front of his shirt I put my face to his. "You led him to Carter. Explain to me why Carter dismissed me from SCD?"

Hanging there Declan again shrugged. "He also resigned from his position. My only thought is he figured someone was already coming after him."

None of it made sense. "So he didn't do this to me because of you? He said you helped him draw up papers binding me to this job."

"I did, but at his request. It was actually an old form from a past situation. He was acting unusual that night. When I asked him the problem he told me an old associate of his was causing some trouble and he feared they would come after you if he knew there was contact. He thought you would stay away if he pissed you off enough by making it look like he could care less how you led your life." He sighed. "He wanted to distance you from whatever hole he dug himself into."

Eli looked at me trying to read my expression when I released Declan. "This is a mess."

Declan looked at Eli. "May I leave?"

"You may, but please make the announcement of stepping down from your position, or I am required to challenge you. Choice is yours." Eli said looking down at his nails, as if the whole situation bore him.

Standing, Declan nodded. "I will send an email out immediately."

Nick rounded his desk to look at Eli head on. The shock on his face seemed frozen there, almost unable to say anything. "You have been with me for years. This whole time I had an Ancient under my roof?" He shook his head in disbelief. "Why?"

Eli began to pace, frustration now marring his beautiful face. "Do you think I wanted to be King of the vampire race? No, I wanted a regular life. When you were about to toss Blake for her behavior I had to do something earlier than I planned. She already lost her job and now her father. Just because Troy has some sick need to torture a female doesn't mean she deserves losing the Guardian job. There is something going on with you Nick and it needs to stop. The man I went to war with seems to be disappearing. I stayed with you all these years for a reason. I had faith you could be a leader and I could continue to hide in the shadows."

"I guess she can stay then." Nick said, running a hand through his hair.

Eli shook his head. "No, she will be Captain of my task force."

Surprised, I stared at him. "What if I don't want to be?"

It was his turn to be surprised. "Don't you?"

Grinning, I leapt onto him. "Hell yeah! I want to bring in anyone I want, is that cool?"

He nodded, smiling. Placing a kiss to my forehead he let me fall down onto my own two feet. "Of course that is cool. Whoever wishes to join come forward."

"Is he always going to talk like some kind of old century King?" Charity asked, coming toward us. I shrugged my eyes wide. He was talking a little weird, but then who knows what all he held back in order to hide from the rest of the vampires.

The only ones that stayed back were Reed and Chad. They looked at Nick, who was now glaring. "You can't take my people." He snarled. What shocked me was that Electa and Gideon both came forward too. Gideon worked for the police department and Electa never worked under anyone. She was always a freelance type of person.

"Yes, I can. They have every right to seek other means of employment. So if they wish to work for me, they can." Eli said in a way that dared Nick to challenge him on it.

Obviously Nick still saw him as the Deputy Director, but he instantly backed down when he felt a pulse of power. "Good."

Chapter Eleven

Apparently Eli even had temporary headquarters lined up for when he did his announcement. From the outside it looked just like another one of those realty places inside a house. The old sign had been taken down and replaced with one that said "Guardians" in blocked lettering. Underneath in smaller font it read "Services for the supernatural and all those that serve under King Eli Mason." To me it almost looked like he planned this for a while. It would have to be something asked later for sure.

I raised an eye brow over the change in last name and he explained, "It was the name I used before meeting Nick. I prefer it over Dexter."

The house was painted white with red and black trim. The colors were a neat mixture when compared to the others of plain white on the street. The lawn was landscaped with nothing at all, just a lush green grass. We climbed the steps, Eli leading the way. It reminded me that it was something that would have to change now that he was King. One of us would have to lead, just so we could be sure no one attacked him unexpectedly. No doubt he would probably fight me on it.

Inside the house we found a reception desk that was already occupied with a young vampire. He was busy trying to set up the computers at each desk. He hardly seemed to notice us come in, until Eli put a hand on his shoulder causing him to jump. His glasses fell down his face and with one hand he shoved them up. Nerd. That was the first thing that came to mind when I saw him.

Eli smiled, "This is Brian. He will be the one that does a majority of our research, basic office work, and other random things." He patted his shoulder again. "He is human but his girlfriend was one of the victims taken by the Covert. Strangely she was a vampire."

Nodding, Brian said, "Uh, hi."

Charity bounced in after me and gave Brian thumbs up with an over enthusiastic expression on her face. To be honest I think it scared him, because he clutched the keyboard, he was trying to connect to his chest, like a shield as he sank back into his chair.

Electa snorted, shaking her head. When Brian saw her he stared so long he dropped the damn keyboard. Grumbling, Mitch and Gideon walked past. "Leave him alone girls. He is about to piss his pants." Mitch said.

"Hey, no picking on him!" I said calling up to Mitch, but he was already up the hall following the direction Eli went.

As we passed doors I peeked in the first one finding a large bathroom. It was all white and smelled like cleaner. I wrinkled my nose and continued to the next door, which revealed one office space. Inside were a desk and a file cabinet. Nothing special, so I continued forward finding two more offices.

The door Eli went to was third to last. He stood in the middle of the room with his arms out and looked at me. "Well?"

Stepping in, I continued to examine the large room. It had a thick oak desk, far back center of the room, next to a window that looked out into a yard. There was book shelf and a table on the right side of the room. I looked up. "Is this your office or something? Rubbing it in?"

He chuckled, coming forward to put his hands on my arms. "No, this is your office, everyone gets one. They are on the second floor. Mine is in the back here with yours, next to the kitchen."

Confused, I studied his face. This had to take longer planning. "How long have you been organizing this?"

He exhaled, dropping his hands and looking at the others when they all lined up behind me after entering the room. "All of you go pick out an office."

Charity shrieked. "Let me through!" And they all ran, boots thumping on the wood floor. They were like children trying to pick out a room of a new house before their sibling snagged it. Ridiculous. I heard a crash and then a bunch of stomping. Someone probably fell and the others went around them.

"I had plans to leave Nick before you showed up, but when you came into my life everything went rolling a whole lot faster. I called Brian asking him to find us a location with several offices. That was pretty much from the first night I saw you."

Rolling my eyes, I punched him in the chest. "Whatever. That means you knew that night."

He grinned. "You don't believe this mate business do you?"

I shook my head, walking over to the desk running my hands over it. On the floor was a box for a laptop. I picked it up and started to open it. "I don't, mainly because it never happens."

Eli walked over behind me, wrapping his arms around my waist. "It is rare, which would mean something to you. This happened with us for a reason."

Laughing, I laid my head back on his shoulder. "You are so old."

He chuckled. "Don't forget you said that you were mine."

"Pfft, that was in the heat of the moment. I would have said a bunch of other stuff." I said grinning.

*

Upstairs Eli had a room full of weapons for us. Everyone rushed in trying to grab the things they wanted. Gideon glanced over at me, which reminded me we needed to talk about things. Someone who was dedicated to their job didn't just quit at the first offer. He saw me coming, so he turned around examining a katana. When I stopped in front of him I gave him an expectant look. He sighed, setting the katana down. "You have to let me join up."

"Why? Explain to me why I would want a detective on our unit?" I asked, propping my hands on my hips.

Everyone stopped to listen, each holding some kind of weapon in their hands. Electa stepped up behind me waiting for the answer herself. "Like I said, the police department won't allow me to investigate."

"So you should follow orders and investigate cases that you are allowed to have."

Suddenly furious he got two inches from my face. "You said I could help."

Pushing him back with one hand, I shook my head. "This is personal."

When he wouldn't say anything Electa did. "He is looking for his sister. Seems the Covert is on everyone's hit list." She grumbled.

"Sister?" I asked.

He glared at Electa, annoyed she let the cat out of the bag. "I took leave from the PD after they refused to allow me to investigate the disappearances. Once they heard it was the Covert it automatically went to the Federal government. We didn't know what the Covert was until someone from SCD explained it, when they shouldn't have." He rolled his eyes. "Fucking government bullshit. If I would have known about this group I could have found my sister by now." He growled.

Eli came up behind me, I could feel his body heat radiating off of him. Automatically I went to lean in his direction, but stopped myself. "How long has she been missing?"

Running a hand through his hair in agitation he said, "Two years now."

Charity and I looked at each other. The odds of her still being alive were slim. "Tell us about her." I said, just in case the girl was one we already came across.

We all took a seat in some chairs around a table meant for cleaning equipment. He leaned forward, suddenly looking more tired. "Black hair, really tall, and green eyes. She was in high school when she disappeared. A big track star." He smiled. "When I told Michael about her he said he couldn't help. That is why I never joined

the pack. He should have helped as an alpha."
We all nodded in agreement. "Anyway, she
wore jewelry, especially a silver ring."

I froze. My dream? It was her?
Frowning, I looked down at the table drawing
imaginary eights with my finger over and over
again. It had to mean she was still alive. "Where
did she learn how to untie knots?"

He looked up sharply, his eyes boring
into mine. "How do you know about that?"

"Answer the question." Eli said,
watching him.

Gideon drummed his fingers on the
table. "Her boyfriend was in the military. He
knew all sorts of tricks."

"Where is the boyfriend?" I asked,
curious.

He shrugged. "Overseas. Probably thinks
she left him."

Looking at Eli I said, "I had a dream
about her, but I don't know if it already
happened or not. She escaped and was crawling
down a hallway. I woke up right after that."

Hope filled Gideon's expression. "When
did you have the dream?"

"Couple days ago."

We all sat in silence, until Electa patted his hand in an awkward attempt to sooth him. "I am sure she is okay."

Nodding, he said, "Maybe, but don't make me promises." He forced a smile, squeezing her fingers before going back to what he was doing. "So, we go to this rave tonight. How do we breech them?"

Eli looked over at me, signaling I had the floor. Being in charge was going to take some getting used to. I stood and began to pace, since moving helped me think better. "Normally I would suggest we pose to get in, but it seems like they expect a password upon entry or something. I think having that card does something. Kind of like a ticket to enter the house." I shrugged. "The way we will do it is just take the house. Storm in like a bunch of swat people."

Raising his eyebrow, Gideon frowned. "That is your idea? Just busting down the doors, regardless of the guards?"

"Do you forget we have an Ancient?" I asked, pointing at Eli.

Mitch cleared his throat, almost afraid to interrupt. "Do you fail to recall that maybe the

King should stay behind, mainly because he is the King?"

"You're right. We have to do it alone." I said, forgetting Eli was the King now. How could I not remember that big of an important detail?

Eli stood. "I am coming. I will not be left behind just because I took over this position."

"With all due respect, royalty sits on their ass." Electa said, checking the weapons in her boots.

"I am the King, so my decision is final." He said. When they all turned to me he glared. "Don't look at her! She can't decide for me."

Walking up to him, I patted his chest and smiled. "As your Guardian, yes I do. I say you sit behind the lines. We can do it without you."

He growled, but I already walked out of the room.

We went back to my apartment, since all my stuff was still there and obviously the rent was still paid up. Electa offered Charity a place to stay, while Mitch was invited to Gideon's home until he could get on his feet, since leaving the Michigan House.

My apartment smelled like me, but somewhat stale for staying closed up for a few days. I went to my bedroom closet to look for something to wear for the night. What I had on probably would have worked, but I wanted to look awesome, bad ass. Eli came in to sit on the bed and fell back, pouting like a baby. I ignored him as I slid over some hangers. I found a pair of black leather pants and then a short leather top to go with it. "Taking a shower!" I sang, running into the bathroom in hopes to lock the door in time. But he was fast, too fast.

"You are letting that power go to your head, mister." I said, trying to hold the door shut.

Eli only grinned, sliding through, which meant when he got through, the door slammed into place, making me grunt in surprise. Before I could turn around he was on me, his front pressed against my back. I bucked trying to get him off. "Hello, I have to take a shower." My voice muffled by the door.

He leaned close to my ear and said, "You have time to play." His breath making my whole body shiver. He pulled at my shirt, making it go over my head while not allowing me to turn around. What the hell was he doing? He unbuttoned my pants, letting them fall to the floor. I kicked them away the best I could considering my position.

"Do I get to shower?" I asked, laughing.

He answered by running his hands over my hips and moved them over my stomach forcing my rear end into him. I groaned. "Okay, let's move to the bed."

Moving the door open, I hurried over to the bed only in my bra and underwear. He watched me climb up onto the bed and look over my shoulder at him. He growled, hurrying over to me. I laughed, moving forward thinking I could make him chase me, but I was mistaken when he grabbed one leg pulling me back toward him. Within seconds he tore my bra and underwear off. "Hey those cost money you know!"

"I'll buy you more." His tone uncaring to my need to keep my undergarments intact.

"Hey, you aren't even naked!" I whined when he flipped me over onto my stomach. "Stop handling me like I am Jane to your Tarzan."

Eli laughed. "You are my Jane."

"You know what I-"I was cut off when his mouth touched my core. I hissed in shock, nails digging into the bed. "You-"gasp, "Don't play fair. Evil man."

He laughed again, vibrating where his mouth was. I moaned, moving into him. His hands gripped my thighs trying to hold me still, but I couldn't. Finally he just flipped me around, his body over mine. Reaching up I pulled onto his tie, bringing him down to me so we could kiss. He went to my neck, then to my chest, kissing softly. Then when his mouth went to my breast his fangs sank in. I cried out, crashing over the edge promptly. When he pulled away my whole body felt weak. He undressed, watching me watch him.

Sighing, I touched his bare chest when he came back to me. His body warm against mine as he slid into me. I moaned, eyes rolling back. "I love you, Blake. I am so happy you're mine."

Emotions crashing over me as I realized he would be all I had left, my fingers went into his hair and pulled him to my lips. I kissed him fiercely, my tongue touching his. Tears spilled from my eyes and he pulled back wondering if he did something wrong. "I love you, too." He was all I had left, so I had to cherish what we could, even if there was a possibility of us not being together later. Confidence was the key, right?

Chapter Twelve

The house was a pretty large one for a stunt guy to own. It was almost like he had another income for himself, which was entirely possible if he was in fact involved with the kidnapping of the females. Cars were actually parked along the road and on the driveway. One guy stood up front at the door and according to Mitch's report there was one stationed in the back. They took security pretty seriously. That made sense because it was a business, but an illegal one. Any kind of warning to let them escape was better than none, even if a guard or two ended up dead.

Glancing to my side at Electa I smiled. It was nice having my best friend here. I was genuinely surprised she wanted to join my team. When I asked her about it she said it was because this was her dream. Since we knew each other she had a desire to work with me, but she feared I wouldn't want to take on the life of someone who killed people for money. And she didn't want anything to do with the Federal government, unless it was them paying big bucks to kill a terrorist.

Goal for tonight was to go into the house with guns blazing, basically. Because this was a vampire house the King was able to do whatever he wanted. If it had been the humans, according to the law, they would have to have a warrant. Since Eli was the boss man we could do whatever we wanted apart from killing, unless in self-defense. If we were able to capture stunt guy, then we brought him in for questioning. Same thing with Ben, if the illusive bastard showed up. I wanted him dead and so did Eli, but vampire laws existed for a reason. For those of us who thirsted for blood we had to be patient.

The problem was we still didn't know who was in control of the Covert. It seemed like we were trying to find our way through the dark. Not that it had been that long since I started investigating them. Since starting, nothing went the way I thought it would. Ben was supposed to be a coworker and even in a weird way a friend. Carter was the only father I had, if you didn't count Lucifer, my sperm donor. I wasn't even given the choice to attend his funeral. It was then in that moment I promised myself to visit his grave after the ring leader of the Covert was taken down.

Someone showed up at the house, so both Electa and I tensed to see who it was. Neither one of us recognized the person, but they were vampire. Most of the people that entered the home were male. Surprise, surprise, right? They handed the guard a white card, like the one I had when I was attacked. He opened the door for them, where all that could be seen were the lights from inside the house. No shadows passed through the windows or anything. Which meant a lot of the action was taking place somewhere in the house other than the first two floors. That left the basement.

"When are you letting us go?" Mitch asked over the ear piece connection we had.

Something crunched from behind us. Electa and I both spun around with our guns poised, but it was too late. Lights were out.

*

Cold water splashed on my face snapping me awake. Blinking, the first thing I saw was a light, then the light bulb itself. Looking around I realized I was in some kind of basement, most of it dark. Seems there was only enough light to brighten up the immediate area, not the rest of the room. My head swam when a sharp stabbing pain went through it. Someone hit me and Electa knocking me out.

Groaning, I forced my eyes to try focusing. A face appeared in front of me, at first blurry, but then as it began to come clear anger surged through me. "Ben." I hissed.

He grinned. "Glad you remember me." He joked, reaching out to touch my cheek, but I snapped my fangs at him. Laughing, he pulled away. "Sorry about the cold water, but I had to wake you. I rather the girl be awake when I fuck her." He looked at me up and down as if I were a piece of meat. "Damn you look good tonight. Nice leather." He touched the top of my head. "Too bad I left a mark here, though. It should go away soon with your healing."

Moving my head away I glared at him, refusing to say anything for now. He was dressed in a suit, but more expensive than what I had seen him in before. He saw me looking, so he posed, one hand to his chin as he turned sideways. "I look hot, no?"

"Are you running the Covert?" I asked, unable to hold the questions popping into my head.

Ben smiled, walking around behind the chair I was tied to. His hands slid over my shoulders down to cup my breasts. "Would it make you want me?"

Trying to hold back my shudder, I turned to look up at him. "So is that a no?"

He sighed, pulling away from me. "No, I do not run the Covert. I won't tell you who does either." When he started heading away from the light he said, "You might as well give up that tough girl routine, because you won't be found where we are. You're mine, so you should learn to love me."

I heard a door close and everything inside of me began to panic. Where was I? Why not try to disappear from here? Use my demon powers. So I cleared my head thinking about a place I wanted to be, but nothing happened. Fire? I tried fire, but nothing. Panic all over. Why couldn't I use any of my powers? Trying to jerk from my bonds, I had my question answered when I rocked it hard enough to let me fall to the floor. A circle. There was a circle of salt around me. What the fuck?

When someone summons a demon they make a circle to contain the demon, so it doesn't decide to run off and do whatever it wants. I was trapped. Not that I knew this would work on me, but obviously if my powers wouldn't work it did. Swearing, I tried to move but couldn't. My face laid flat on the cold wet surface under me. Eli was probably freaking out. What happened to Electa? Was she dead? Did they take her or leave her behind?

Angry at myself for letting my guard down, I tried scooting again. Finding it useless I looked up. Obviously Ben knew I would come to the raves, so he waited. Why he wanted me was something I didn't understand. Why me? Did he have a long time crush on me? We usually bantered back and forth, but nothing to hint he liked me. I shivered thinking about what would happen after he took me out of the room. Rape me? Would I be in another circle of salt?

"Dear child, what have you gotten yourself into?" Hearing the voice I looked around trying to find Lucifer. "I am over here, but the light doesn't come this far. I can't come into the circle or I will be trapped too."

Sighing, I laid there feeling more helpless than ever. "Can you get Eli here?"

Lucifer must have shifted, because I heard a scuff of his shoe on the concrete. "If you mean make him appear here, no. But I can tell him the location."

Relief flooded me. "Good, get him to come here."

"It may be a while. You don't realize where they brought you." He said, no longer moving. "You are in a basement in Hawaii. He has to travel here, yet."

"Hawaii? How random is that?" I rolled my eyes. So like Ben to be a dumbass. At least he was who I thought he was most of the time. "So, if I want to catch these bastards I need to play along until Eli can get here."

"Pretty much."

"Gee, thanks for the help."

He laughed. "I am helping. I will go get your mate and all will end well."

"Oh, and you can see the future?" I asked, laughing.

"No, but if you are mine and your mother's daughter you always can find a way out of a situation. I will go now."

When I heard nothing else I assumed he was officially gone. The feeling of being alone was overwhelming. The sound of silence was the worst thing possible for a kidnapped victim. At least so I thought. When you hear someone coming you always have hope. Here, there was nothing. No sound you could make out from outside. Just dampness on the floor. Why the hell did I struggle anyway? Now rats could probably crawl all over me. Were there rats in Hawaii? I didn't know and didn't care to find out.

My head was hurting pretty bad, to the point where I wanted to throw up. Finally I did, but not that I could move out of the way, so I was pretty much laying in it. So nasty. The smell was horrible. This was probably the one time I wished Ben would hurry back, so he could at least set me back up right.

I heard a moan from the far side of the room, which did actually sound far. It almost echoed around me. "Hello?" Nothing. Probably passed back out. It could have been Electa, but I wouldn't have been able to tell just from a moan.

When Eli made it here I needed a plan. Hopefully I would get the okay to kill him after we tortured him for information. Did it make me sick to want to hurt him so bad? The dude kidnapped me and then planned to rape me. Was he so horrible in bed that no one wanted to sleep with him? I wondered what the attraction was for vampires. Was it the blood? If it was, then why couldn't they just take it from a human instead of doing it the illegal way?

If it were for the sex, then they had to be desperate. But somehow I doubt it. It had to be for the thrill and the ability to have someone hunt down the perfect girl for you.

My heart leapt when I heard the door open. Within a few steps Ben appeared again. He frowned, looking down at me when he saw that I was on the floor. He sighed, already looking agitated. "Why did you have to do that? Now you smell like vomit." He barked.

"You were the one that hit me in the head, smart one." I said, grateful that I was no longer on the floor.

"Right you are. So I guess it is my fault you are barfing everywhere." He reached into his coat pocket pulling out a bottle of water. "Here, I brought you this. I can't bring you upstairs until I get everything covered in salt. I have one of my men doing it around the house. But I like to be careful, so every room will be done." He grinned. "Then we can get it on."

I held back a groan. Gross. "So I have to stay in this basement for a while longer?"

He nodded. "We could do it down here, but I rather not." He made a face. "It should only be a few minutes more and my men should be done."

"Who is over there on the other side?" I asked, pretending to try and create conversation.

Frowning, he said, "Luther. The bastard won't stay away."

"Probably because you killed Carter."

He stiffened. "So you found out, huh? Pretty pissed off?"

Did I want to ring his neck? Yes, I did. Could I? Nope, because I was trapped here. Even if I could best him in combat, would I be able to cross the salt? If I couldn't, would I be willing to deal with the consequences? Hell yeah! Thinking of a plan, I watched him stand in front of me as he told me how long he had planned to snatch me.

Maybe I would allow him to initiate things upstairs, then when he would relax enough for me, I could catch him off guard. That sounded good. That would be the plan. "Since you started the SCD, I planned on trying to take you. But then mom-"he cut himself off. "No, can't tell you that."

He tilted his head in a way that made it look like he was listening to something. Flashing me a smile, he told me he would be back. When he disappeared I tried to call out to Luther, but didn't get any answer. Sighing out of frustration, I wanted to stomp my feet like a three year old desperate to get a candy fix.

Please hurry, Eli. I thought. If anyone could help me it would be him. Worry for Electa nibbled at me when I remembered how we both were attacked from behind. How did Ben get both of us at once? That was something I needed to find out, not that he killed her. Then I would be seriously pissed. Wasn't sure I could keep him alive then. The monster would have to be put down literally, only not animal friendly.

Ben returned, moving toward the back of me, he untied the part of the rope that kept me bound to the chair. Then he did the same with my legs, but made sure it was completely off them so I could walk. Helping me up, he led me through the dark, where I could see a small light peeking through a crack of a door. When he opened the door there was a set of stairs leading to yet another door. Both were made of steel, looking like they were new additions.

Climbing the steps I nearly fell flat on my face. He grumbled in agitation trying to keep me upright. When he got the top door open, it revealed a huge kitchen that probably could have held one of those cooking shows you see on TV. Things were done in white and yellow, like it had a woman's touch. Was it even his house?

"Mom is gone for a few days, so we are good to go with playing." He said, almost too excited.

Again, I hid a shudder that crept up all over my body. My skin crawled, like it was trying to find the cleanest place possible, but finding no escape. There was salt all over the place, around the walls of the kitchen. The windows were littered with it.

Leaving the kitchen, he moved me the opposite way of what looked to be the living room and probably the front exit. The steps led straight up to a wall, where we had to round the corner. There were four doors, three of them bedrooms and the final one a bathroom. Not a huge house, but comfortable I suppose. Not something I expected from royalty over in Europe.

Ben took me to the far bedroom, it was decorated with nothing but posters of women in suggestive poses. He kicked the door closed while I studied my exits, only finding the one window and the door we just came through.

Moving around, I spun around noticing he had a butt load of locks on his doors. Geez.

Smiling, Ben turned around to face me, his hands getting grabby. He frowned, shaking his head. "Your moving will not do. I have to tie you to the bed." He nodded toward the contraption he called a bed. The thing looked like a death trap to me with all the chains and straps. He even had one of those swings hanging from the ceiling. I seriously hoped he didn't plan on making me use that.

Forcing a smile, I held up my hands. "I can't do much with my hands like this." I pointed out.

Looking at his eyes I could tell he was debating on letting me loose. He was eager for full cooperation, but he knew some girls were tricky and I was probably one of them. He smiled, "Let's make a deal. If you stay a week with me then I will let you go."

Pretending to believe him my eyes went wide with hope. "Really? You will let me go?"

He hesitated, then finally nodded. "I will. I just have wanted you for so long and girls are so horrible these days." He made a disgusted face as he went to my hands to untie them. Tossing the rope to the dresser he went to the doors to lock them. "Not that I don't trust you, but sometimes people walk in and to be honest, no one needs to see Little Ben but you."

I really wanted to throw up then thinking about how Little Ben would be too close for comfort. Stretching out my fingers, I watched him toss his jacket onto the chair, next to this small desk covered in comic books. He started to work on his tie while watching me.

This was becoming too much. I didn't know if I had it in me to even kiss him. Even though he was really good looking, the idea of him being a creep was a total turn off, but I had to clear my head, get him to trust me. There was no way in hell I would drop my pants for him though.

Slowly he came to me, unexpectedly nervous. His hands began to shake when he touched my arms. It took all of my strength not to shrivel back from him. He closed his eyes and leaned forward. Totally felt like high school. "Are you a virgin, Ben?" I blurted out.

Flames lit in his eyes when he pulled back sharply. "No!" He said defensively.

"I didn't mean anything by it, I was just wondering." I said, trying to seem sincere.

He calmed down after a few minutes, realizing that it probably was just an innocent question, so he shook his head. "No, but no girl has ever been like you. Who knows, maybe you will end up liking me too." He shrugged, suddenly very shy as he sat down on the bed hands clasped together.

Sitting down next to him, I forced a hand to touch his leg in comfort. I pictured it squealing, like it might shrivel up and die from being near him. Gods, it felt nasty being near him knowing what kind of person he was like. "People are assholes these days. It's not you, just them."

He looked up with a smile. "You always did know what to say, even if it was to be funny and insulting." It was then he chose to lean over and I flinched. Ben didn't even notice. His lips touched my cheek, then went down to my neck. I shuddered, but he mistook that for being turned on. His hands went to my breasts, groping too hard. Suddenly it was as if he changed into someone else. He slammed me back into the mattress, the sweet Ben disappearing and now introducing the evil one. He climbed on top of me, straddling. "It is a lot better when you girls fight."

It was all a show. He pretended to be innocent, but he really just planned to catch me off guard. Ben's hands went around my neck, cutting off my air. I tried to push him off, but his strength seemed to come out of nowhere. When he saw the fear come into my eyes he grinned. "Killing that Gideon werewolf really paid off in the strength department. I knew you would be a tough one, but this is way too fucking easy."

Gideon was dead? How and when did he kill him? Dread rippled through me. Ben was a lot more dangerous than I gave him credit for. Though, he did have years of experience on SCD and an uncle, who was basically a European version of a mobster.

My shirt tore open and Ben looked down at me appreciatively. My heart pounded as I tried to buck him off. He only laughed, riding me out like I was some rodeo horse. Leaning forward he smelled my neck, holding my hands over my head. He shuddered, excitement filling his face and his eyes going wild. How could I not have seen the crazy person inside of him? He couldn't have been that good in hiding. Usually, those who couldn't think normally gave off a stench. A stench of rot from the brain, basically signaling their mind was going slowly and would eventually have nothing left given time. And there was no such stench coming from him. Which meant what? That he knew exactly what he was doing?

Anger began to replace the fear. Anger at myself for believing his innocent boy routine. Anger because I was in this situation, if only I had used my brain in the first place. As it built inside of me, I could feel myself nearing an explosion. Not that I could do anything with my demon powers restricted. I screamed with my eyes closed, expecting him to laugh, but he only screamed back in response. The pressure on my hands disappeared, so I opened my eyes finding him on the floor unconscious from hitting his head on the desk. Somehow I managed to get him off me. Odd considering the demon powers were bound from the salt.

Scrambling to my feet, I was going to take the chance when I had one. Who knew when the guards would be upstairs trying to break through the door. Stopping for a few seconds, I strained to hear any noises. My vampire hearing picked up some laughing. "He either has to pay for it or kidnap one of those bitches."

Okay, so I had to assume that the screaming was normal, even his. Moving around, I looked for some weapons, finding nothing but a damn baseball bat with a signature on it. Rolling my eyes I snatched it, looking around some more. Maybe a cell phone. That would help. I searched his jacket not finding one. Then looked over at him. He was breathing normally. Did I take a chance? This shouldn't have been up for debate! If he wakes up knock the fucker back out! My mind scolded me.

Moving toward him, I bent down to pat his pockets, not liking the idea of having to shove my hands down into them. He groaned causing me to freeze mid pat. My inner child screamed no don't wake up, but my demon was like yeah let him! Sure the demon would be all for it despite the binding of the powers. Shows who's in control of this relationship. Rolling my eyes, I felt a cell phone in his front pocket. Watching his face for any signs of waking up, I slipped two fingers into the pocket hoping to just grab it that way, but it slipped down further into his pocket. Shit! I winced thinking about what might be happy down there. Last thing I wanted was to touch that. I would rather chew my arm off trying to escape a bear trap than that.

Taking a deep breath, I closed my eyes briefly trying to get control. Reopening my eyes, I slipped my hand down inside his pocket while biting down on my lip, trying to get it quickly. My fingers found it and slowly I pulled it up, prepared to dance like a Leprechaun around a pot of gold. Only when I finally palmed the thing, the bastard opened his eyes. He looked confused for a minute and I was frozen in panic. Quickly instincts kicked in. I stood up with the bat and swung it like a golf club smashing into his skull. A combination of a splat and crunch filled my panicked silence. His eyes closed again.

Hurrying, I grabbed the rope he had for my hands and rolled him over to his stomach, trying to avoid the blood that now covered the floor. If he were human he would probably have been dead, but I wasn't that lucky. He would heal soon, so I had to tie him up. I made sure to tie him up good, then searched around for something to shove in his mouth. Spotting a dirty sock I grinned. Snatching it up I shoved it into his mouth, hoping he liked the taste when he woke. Then I grabbed his tie to do his legs. I could totally win one of those rodeo cow tying things. Doing the football sign for touchdown, I grabbed the bat wiping the blood off on his suit.

If I were to make a phone call the vampires downstairs would probably hear me. Who knew if I could escape the room, since it was surrounded with salt? He did get me over the lines without a problem. Still, his little guards could have closed the circles after he brought me up. Deciding to test the barriers I looked out the window that gave a nice view of the beach. No one was outside. Sliding up the window, I thanked the gods it didn't make much noise. I would have to hurry before they began to suspect anything. My guess was that Ben wasn't a quiet lover, so they were probably already curious. Maybe even sneaking up to see if they could get a cheap thrill.

Finding the salt on the window I held my breath, praying I could get past the barrier. Touching the edge of the salt to force a break, my breath went out of me in relief. Strangely I was unable to use my powers inside a circle, but I could still escape. How fucked up was that? Not taking any more time to think about it, I put a leg out the window and ducked out. It was ungodly hot, so humid my lungs were acting as if they had to wade through water in order to take in air.

Searching my surroundings I still found no guards. My hearing picked up two of them inside the house, wondering if they should head up the stairs to see if Ben was still working on me. I crept along the roof trying to find a spot to disappear. Teleport. Ah, yeah, forgot about that. Closing my eyes I pictured being at Eli's office, but nothing happened. Frowning, I ran a frustrated hand through my hair and froze. It was dry and gritty. Smelling my fingers I swore. The bastard covered me in salt water. That moment I wanted to go back and strangle the fucker. Turning around, the demon nearly had me convinced. No… escape! The vampire did her own eye roll. You would think I had multiple personalities here.

Moving over the roof, I went toward the side of the house where there was a shed next to it. The guards were now heading up the stairs. I had to hurry. Moving a little faster I looked over the edge still finding no one. Leaping over to the shed roof I nearly screamed when I over estimated my jump. Falling straight to the ground my legs almost snapped from the potency of the jump. They screamed in agony, refusing to bend the way my body was forcing them to go. If I had been human my legs would sure as heck broke.

Lying in the grass to get control of my breathing, I heard the guys knocking on the door of the room. Move! My brain screamed. Slowly getting to my feet I grabbed the bat that managed to fall a few feet away from me. Good thing my hands managed to hold onto the cell phone. Knowing the luck I seemed to have the thing probably would have busted in a million pieces, but at the moment, fate was on my side.

I had to hurry. Vampires would be able to find my scent. Spotting a neighbors car I snuck over, glancing around for any unsuspecting eyes. No one was around, but anyone could be looking through the windows. The car was a black BMW, exactly like Eli's. Just thinking about him made my heart squeeze with grief. I missed him and I wasn't out of danger, yet. What if we never saw each other again? A sob escaped me at that thought, but I pressed on, glad the driver side window was down. Not that it mattered, because the door was unlocked. My escape would be perfect if there were a key in the ignition. Glancing over with some kind of hope I made a dirty face. Yeah, right, did I really expect the key to be there?

Annoyed I may have to hot wire the car, I went to the wheel wells searching for a hidey key. Nothing found. Peeking under the bumper I saw a black box. With a short inner celebration I grabbed the box and took out the key. Hearing the front door of my escaped prison open and close, I raced to the driver side slipping inside. The key turned in the ignition and the car purred to life. Backing out with the grace of a stunt driver, I slammed the car into drive and hit the gas. The tires squealed giving away my position, but at that moment caring wasn't at the top of my list. Three men appeared at the end of the prison driveway. Ben looked pissed, blood covering the side of his face. He lifted his arm revealing a gun. Shit! Ducking, I heard the shot go off, the bullet flying into the glass of the driver side window as I passed them. Burning pain hit my leg and automatically my hand went to the area that was hurt. Relieved to know it was only a graze from the bullet, I looked from the corner of my eye spotting a hole in the seat next to me to confirm I was okay.

Couple more shots went off breaking the back window of the car. I swerved around the corner relief going through me at my escape. It wouldn't be long before they would come after me in their own cars, if they weren't already. Hitting the gas, I lit up the screen of Ben's cell phone. Putting in Eli's number, I shook my head over barely remembering it. The phone rang several times, but on the fourth ring someone picked up.

"Hello?" The voice was wary, but it was Eli.

"Eli!"

"Blake?" Surprise combined with relief filled his voice. "I am almost there. Just stay put."

I wanted to cry. The female in me was thinking she was saved, but the vampire tapped her on the shoulder pointing at the hummer that appeared behind us. "Shit." Gathering my wits I said, "Look, I escaped, but I need you to meet me somewhere. They are following me, so I have to let you go. Meet me at the Bishop Museum."

"Okay, I should be there in an hour."

Shocked, I asked, "Really? That is fast."

He chuckled. "Private jet."

Oh, well, that explained it. Glancing back up in the rearview mirror I saw the Hummer getting closer, they were going to ram me from behind. "Gotta go, love you!" I braced for the impact as the phone fell to the floor. The car lurched forward threatening to spin, but I took control with little effort. I practiced this shit in the SCD. Grinning like a fool, I went around a corner faster than the average motorist would have liked. The tires squealed as I went around, getting the attention of some people on the sidewalks. When I spotted the Viper police officer I swore, glancing back in the rearview mirror again. The Hummer was coming up to make another attempt. I could have sworn I saw Ben's crazy eyes before he slammed into me again. The car spun sideways, but I reacted fast enough to correct it. The Viper pulled out, lights on, but that didn't stop Ben. Oh no, he came at me again, slamming me forward in my seat. Swearing, I went around another corner, speeding through a red light, barely missing a younger couple, who dove off to avoid the oncoming traffic.

Rounding another corner I nearly rammed a car. Last minute swerve, the BMW leapt onto the sidewalk taking out a trash bin that luckily hadn't been cemented in. People screamed, dodging out of my way, staring in shock as two more cars came after me. The police siren wailed and soon more joined. Fuck! That was all we needed. The Vampire King, wait… Eli was King now. Laughing hysterically, I wiped back a tear before I turned the car onto another main road at a high speed. Cars swerved trying to avoid me. I hit one, but kept going, knowing it was a love tap compared to what Ben would do to me when he caught up again.

Never once in my life did I think someone from my old job would be chasing me end my life. I was laughing so hard it was difficult to concentrate, because my eyes watered so badly. At some point I needed to either escape them fully by car or jump out to do it by foot. By foot would probably be best, considering people would see a bashed up BMW a lot faster than a beat up older car.

The Hummer was still behind me, but further back. At some point they had been held up. The Viper along with some other cruisers were now behind Ben their lights flashing. Hitting the gas I dodged around a few cars, once again going through a red light. The car skidded around a corner as I took it too fast, but I managed. Taking a side street, I easily avoided the old lady walking a dog. Even though I zoomed past, it barely fazed her. Probably not good for her to be out in public if that was the case.

Hitting another side road where families lived, I swore at my bad choice of direction. Hopefully no one got hurt, because then I wouldn't be able to forgive myself for it. The museum was about a mile away by foot. So taking another side road I slammed on the brakes, leaping out of the car with the cell phone. Leaving the bat behind to avoid any unwanted attention, I raced through a couple of houses relieved the Hummer wasn't anywhere around. They were close though, because the sirens were nearing. Leaping a fence of someone's backyard I earned a shocked look from a family playing in their swimming pool, frozen mid action to stare at me with wide-eyed expressions. I grinned and waved. "Nice backyard!" I said, waving one final time before I leapt the back fence into someone else's yard.

Something growled and a big dog bounded out of the house at me from his doggie door. Big doggie door. The Rottweiler looked vicious. Kicking in my vampire speed I hurried toward the fence, feeling the hot breath of the dog on the back of my legs when he tried to take a chunk of me. "Holy shit!" I sang, leaping over. He crashed against the chain linked fence as his paws grabbed through the holes. Seriously, he was climbing it? I squealed like a girl, hurrying through another yard. Leaping over their back fence I ran into the road, nearly running into a parked car. Nice. Who runs into a parked car?

Barely out of breath, I looked around trying to take in my surroundings. The sound of traffic was to my right, which was the way I wanted. The sirens were now on the road that I abandoned the car at. There were more houses on the street I chose. Kids were playing in their yards. But most of them stopped to stare at the weird looking lady. Sure my hair was clumped and I probably had dried white spots all over me, but… yeah they had an excuse to stare. Let's not forget the torn shirt. Shaking my head in disgust, I tied both sides into a knot, like a homemade halter top.

Running again, I went straight toward the main street, but taking a detour down one right before it. Zooming past a few more houses, I heard someone shout. Looking behind me, some kid held up a phone for me. Slowing down I patted my pockets. Sure enough I had dropped it. "Keep it!" I shouted. The boy grinned as he turned around to play with the buttons on it.

The Bishop Museum was off of the Likelike Highway, so I was bound to run into it eventually, I thought. Passing more people and more cars, I finally spotted a parking lot that was filled to capacity. In front of me was a large building that was a gorgeous part of Hawaiian history. The only reason why I knew its location was because Carter took me to it once when we had a "family vacation." It was only me and him at the time, so we spent nearly two weeks in the wonderful state. It was where I received my first kiss. Of course, Carter caught me doing it, only blaming the demon in my blood for encouraging me to press my luck with humans. At the time vampires were still in hiding, so he was mostly relieved he got me before I ended up draining the boy of blood. I had only been thirteen, so you could imagine how that would have looked. Vampires at that age didn't know a whole lot about glamouring someone so they wouldn't remember the incident. My first successful incident was on another family vacation in London. I had several victims then.

Slowing down, I went toward the entrance of the building. The gray stone outside loomed over me as I looked up. People were staring at me, giving a reminder that I was covered in salt. But what could I do about that? Wash up, of course. This would take some work so I could get inside. It was rare that I would have to charm a human into ignoring me, since my job always consisted of doing things legally. Charming a human to gain entry into a facility was very illegal.

My eyes focused on the person accepting tickets into the place. They opened their mouth to say something to me, but only smiled after a couple of seconds delay. In my head I instructed the older woman to say, Welcome to Bishop Museum, enjoy your visit.

"Welcome to Bishop Museum, enjoy your visit!" Okay, she said that more enthusiastically than I wanted, but I hurried through searching for the bathroom. Women's bathrooms were always full. Picking out a woman in the crowd with a black Hawaii hat and two tank tops on, I instructed her to meet me in the bathroom. She wore those tank tops where you could put two on. One was longer and a different color from the one on top. In my head I was telling her to act like my best friend and to go into one of the stalls with me.

Relief filled me when the handicap one was unoccupied. We went inside and she robotically took off the hat handing it to me. I put it on, shoving my clumped up hair underneath. Pulling off my shirt, I shoved it into the trash bin next to the toilet. She handed me the yellow tank top, then stood waiting for me to give her more instructions. Her pale face was blank and something I never liked to see on someone's face. It took little power for a vampire to do that to a human. That was why it was illegal. Putting her back in friend mode, we both left the stall laughing.

I allowed her to come to the sinks with me, so she could fix her short blond hair after having a bad case of hat hair. She washed her hands, then waved to me as if we ran into each other by accident. I couldn't ignore the stares from women trying to figure out why two grown women went into the same stall with each other. Or was it just me, because I felt stranger over it? When I looked around no one stared like I thought. Okay, it was just me then.

Looking in the mirror, I threw water on my face to get the dried salt off. I should have felt that at Ben's, because it was dried on, causing my skin to be stiff. Though at the time I feared rape and death, so I guess that was understandable. Checking out my face in the mirror once more, I wiped down my arms, then tossed the paper towels into the trash bin before leaving the bathroom.

People were all over the place. Some were guided, but some not. Kids ran around with parents chasing after them. Was that allowed in a museum? I pictured one of the dinosaurs falling over killing people. That was kind of morbid. Shaking the image from my head, I went to look around, wondering if Ben would think to check here. Maybe. Depending. I really didn't even know what Ben would do, since I never even knew him in the first place. Frowning, I looked down at some brochures. We worked together for a while, and in a way it saddened me we wouldn't be joking around like we used to.

Suddenly a thought hit me. Luther. I left him there! What a greedy bitch I was. Swearing, I got a glare from a mother, who covered her kid's ears. Rolling my eyes, I said, "Please, I bet you let him watch worse things on TV."

The mother went to object to that, but I already walked away, trying to form a plan. Ben would probably go back and leave if he couldn't find me. He possibly already figured on me calling Eli, so he wouldn't search for long. Angry with myself, I looked around for someone who had a phone. These days everyone used their phones. Sure enough, it didn't take long for me to find a teen boy texting on his. When I approached he looked up. Thinking I could just pile on the sweetness instead of charming him, he glared. Okay, so I was not hot with a hat and an ugly yellow tank top. Frowning, I took over his young brain making him happily offer up his cell phone. Quickly I dialed Eli and he answered the second ring.

"I am about ten minutes away." He said, sounding flustered. "The traffic is horrible. Some accidents on the main roads."

"Oh, yeah, there are some." I said.

He laughed. "I guess you had a part in that."

"Sure, some part." I grinned. "Anyway, wanted to let you know I am leaving."

"What? No, stay there, I am almost there!"

Tapping my foot impatiently, I said, "Look, Luther was trapped in the basement with me. I have to go get him."

Eli growled. "You can't go alone, just wait for me."

"Fine, but if you aren't here in two minutes I am leaving." I hung up, handing the phone over to the boy, who went back to texting as if I never approached him.

Moving toward the exit I hurried through the crowd of people, earning annoyed looks as I went. Out front I hid behind a tree, spotting Ben and his goons storming up the parking lot. Ben's expression was furious. He looked around trying to find me. Spotting the entrance, he and his men went inside. He was really nuts if he would take me out in front of a crowd. The sirens were no more, so I had to assume he charmed all of them into leaving him alone. The bad part of charming was even the bad guys had the ability. Even though you charmed them to do something and they wouldn't remember, they could make them remember.

Getting impatient, I hurried out from behind the tree and down the sidewalk. There was no time to wait for Eli. I had to get to Luther and eventually Ben would realize I went back for him. The sun was uncomfortably hot. Despite the myth of vampires burning in the sun it did cause damage. The sun always caused damage, no matter what you were. The body was in constant need to repair itself. That meant soon I would need blood. I already did, considering the last time I fed was... I couldn't remember that.

Hurrying down the sidewalk my gaze swept the area, trying to not attract attention. Soon they would follow my scent out here, so I needed to hurry. Speeding down the street I crashed into something hard, grunting as I fell to the ground. Looking up I met Eli's gaze as he looked down, almost angry. "You were going to go back? He wants to rape and kill you."

Rolling my eyes, I wiped the palms of my hands off on my pants. "You going to lecture me or help me up?" I demanded with a glare.

Realizing what he was doing, he took my hand that I held up. His expression went blank, as he searched around before saying anything else. My heart fluttered taking him in. He wore a plain white t-shirt that was tight over his chest and blue jeans that were slightly faded. He looked powerful, even in regular clothing. Sensing my eyes on him he turned, putting a hand to the back of my head and gave me a brutal kiss. I met him back with the same amount of fierceness. I moaned, pulling closer to him, barely realizing my leg coming up around his hip.

"Kids are here!" Someone yelled.

Coming out of my hormone induced coma, I pulled away noticing a woman across the street shielding her son's eyes. The look of horror on her face had me looking down, finding I already had Eli's pants undone. "Shit."

He grinned, buttoning back up. "Come along. If we are to save Luther, we must go now before Ben realizes you aren't here anymore."

Chapter Thirteen

We made it back to Ben's house with the aid of Eli's rental car. We parked down the street in someone's vacation home driveway. Moving down the road we hurried, worried Ben would be back. The house was eerily silent when we approached. No one was inside, so we rushed through. I felt my powers dampen immediately when I stepped inside. Though it didn't worry me since Eli was next to me, but it still felt uncomfortable, since something of mine was held back. Almost like missing a limb.

Now that I didn't fear immediate death I looked around the house, admiring the living room as we passed. The couch and sofa were white leather, the walls maroon, and the carpet tan. The colors were kind of neat and bold. Not something I would have braved, since I lacked a synchronization bone in my body. Looking up at the pictures on the fireplace mantle I froze. Hurrying over with Eli objecting, I snatched a picture off and stared. He came up behind me, frowning.

Born vampires stopped aging at twenty-five in human years. So humans wouldn't be able to believe a mother and son if they looked the same age. Now that the supernatural were out to the humans it was easier to comprehend. Looking down at the picture I felt rage. Tears pricked my eyes as I began to tremble. Eli came around, questions in his eyes, waiting for me to explain what was wrong. In the picture was Ben as he was now and a woman who looked like his sister, but I knew that wasn't the case at all. The woman in the picture was Fiona, Carter's wife. The one he thought was dead.

"This is Carter's wife, Fiona." I said, shaking with rage. The frame broke, so Eli took it from my hands before I cut myself with the glass. "I don't understand."

Eli studied the picture, something passed through his eyes that looked like shock to worry. "I thought she was dead." He said.

"You and me both." I said, counting back the years for Ben's age. "Ben is Carter's son." Horror filled me that a wife and son would kill their own husband and father. Confusion filled me then, unable to understand how this whole thing turned even more complicated. And Carter never knew until the end. That was why he decided to let me go before Fiona would realize my importance. Sure vampires were known to easily detach themselves from emotions and the rest of the world, but Ben knew how much I meant. Only Carter didn't know Ben was his son. He was betrayed by one of his own. Someone who should have respected him as his superior.

Grabbing my shoulders Eli looked into my eyes, black meeting my brown ones. "Focus. This is a lot worse than I thought. Let's get Luther and get the hell out of here."

Hurrying through the living room, I followed him toward the basement door. He turned to me. "Stay up here." When I went to object his eyes flared. "Someone needs to be up here in case Ben returns."

"Don't you think I should get Luther then? You are stronger than me." I pointed out.

Frowning, he was obviously torn about leaving me exposed to harm. Finally he nodded, so I went past him, jogging down the steps to the next door. Turing the knob, I opened it enough to feel for a light switch.

Flicking it on I went forward, grateful the whole basement lit up this time. Nothing was down there besides chains, which gave me a sickening thought of what really happened here. A smell I hadn't notice before filled the basement. Blood and rot. Panic set in as I went around the foundation poles searching for Luther.

After getting past half of a wall, I found him lying on his side on the floor. His arms hung from chains, the cuffs cutting into his skin, because he could no longer hold himself up. He was covered in blood, wounds not healing, which only meant he ran out of blood in his own body to repair. His heartbeat was there, but faint. Looking around for a way to get the cuffs off, I found a single key on the wall. Easy.

Snatching it off the wall I hurried to his side, not thinking about the consequences of getting near a hungry vampire. A starving one at that. He groaned, eyes flickering open. "Blake?"

I flashed him a reassuring smile. "In the flesh!" I slipped the key into the cuffs letting them fall against the wall as I helped him straighten up. His eyes seemed to focus in and out. When his fangs came out I almost leapt back, but stayed where I was, trying not to trigger the hunter in him.

"Hungry. Get out of here." He groaned, eyes rolling back into his head.

Getting into a balanced position, I hoisted his body over my shoulder thanking my vampire strength. All of a sudden his fangs sank into me, making me cry out alarmed and in pain. He drew hard on my blood and I collapsed to my knees, unable to handle the amount of blood he was taking from me at such a high rate. Feet pounded on the steps. Eli appeared trying to read the situation. Realizing Luther had his fangs in me, he came over swinging his arm. Luther went flying, hitting the wall. He slumped over, but only for a second, then came flying at us, rage in his eyes. Suddenly he froze when Eli looked at him.

Turning back to me, Eli gaped at my wound, which probably looked like hamburger, because he tore Luther's fangs out of me. "Can you walk?" He asked, annoyance in his face. He was obviously angry about letting me come down here, but there was little choice and I should have suspected Luther would try to eat me.

Nodding, I got to my feet, closing my eyes briefly to get a hold of my dizziness. Opening them up, I watched as Eli put Luther on his shoulder and started to lead the way out. We got up the stairs hearing car doors outside of the house. I followed, ready to attack with no weapons. All I had was my vampire strength, but Eli wasn't worried as he went to the front door.

"Hey! We can't go that way!" I hissed.

He ignored me, opening the door revealing the Hummer in the driveway and three men. Ben was shocked to see Eli standing there. He went to run, but Eli gestured with his hand, dropping Ben in front of us frozen. All but his head. The other two goons went to run, realizing he was an Ancient. The 'holy shit' expression on their faces was obvious. With another gesture from Eli, they were both forced into positions next to Ben.

Eli motioned for me to come next to him. He glared at the men in front of him. "Where is your mother, Ben?"

Ben sneered. "Like I would tell you."

Raising an eyebrow, only a father would give a child for doing something he wasn't supposed to, Eli reached for Ben's neck taking him in a hold that made him gasp for air. All this with Luther still on his shoulder and two other men under his power. "Tell me or I will snap your fucking neck." He snarled.

Even I stepped back in fear when I saw the monster come out in Eli. His power flowed out of him like a dam breaking. It nearly choked me, forcing me to my knees, making me bow to the stronger vampire in front of me. He was demanding obedience from Ben, but not focusing it on him. My whole body trembled, the stones in the driveway cut into my palms, as I tried to breathe through the heat wave of his power.

Ben tried to breathe, his eyes bulging. When Eli dropped him to the ground, Ben started coughing, holding a hand to his throat. He looked up at Eli and smiled. "She is far from here, ready to defeat you. Should have seen her surprise when she learned you were alive."

Abruptly there was a crack and Ben fell to the ground in front of us. Eli then turned to the other two vampires. Another crack, but only one fell to the ground, leaving one beefy guy. His hair was shaved low to his head, fear in his gray eyes as he visibly shook, despite Eli's hold on him. "Go to Fiona and tell her I am coming for her."

Eli knew Fiona? Jealousy reared its ugly head in me as I thought about that. Past lovers? Carter's wife? Frowning, I watched as the last vampire ran down the street, afraid he would die if he stayed in Eli's sight. Eli began to walk down the road as I watched Ben and the guard turn to ash.

Catching up, I got up beside Eli, who seemed to be in his own world. I was pissed off not knowing about him and Fiona. But then why would he even tell me? Vampires had a history with people romantically and not with their long lives. Yet, here I was fuming because he slept with another female. My demon girl wanted to make an example of his boy parts. Quietly I watched him dump Luther into the trunk of the car, not caring about anyone who may be watching. He slammed the trunk shut and looked at me. He saw my expression. "What is wrong?"

I might have taken that for concern, but his voice was flat with zero emotion in it. Hurt? Hell yeah, I was. I just found out about a female from his past and suddenly nothing about me matters. Not that it was for sure the case, but I was feeling sort of vulnerable. Usually the Eli I knew would come over to comfort me. But this was the powerful Eli that didn't show emotion. This was the man he tried to hide from me. "You knew Fiona?"

He heaved a sigh, running a hand through his hair, not caring to get into the conversation. "Yes."

Just yes? I almost flipped out. Short answers wouldn't work with me! "Just yes?" I asked, repeating my thoughts.

Eli motioned to the car. "Get in."

"Yes, my King." I said, earning a cold stare from him with my response.

Was I acting childish? Yeah, probably, but I was hurt, hungry, and pissed off. The whole time I was kidnapped all I thought about was getting back to him, but then I find out someone may have held his heart at one point. Plopping down in the passenger seat, I closed the door and crossed my arms over my chest staring forward. "So, what number of lover is she?" I asked when he started driving.

He gave me a sideways glance. "I haven't had many lovers."

I rolled my eyes then. Every man said that and that wasn't what his SCD file said! "That is what they all say."

"What do you want me to say? I can't help the Demigod figured she would be a good match for me! We have a past and I can't do anything about it." He growled, his hands curling around the steering wheel.

"She is an Ancient?" I asked, bewildered. When he nodded I went nuts. "So not only do I have to compete with a beautiful woman, but an Ancient at that? Why the fuck didn't you just tell me that when we were at the house? You weren't even going to say anything, were you?"

Eli's surprise didn't register in my brain. "There is no competing."

"Yeah, right. The Demigod paired you together. How can you refuse a bond that has been there since day one?" I asked shrilly. Okay, insane stalker girl was totally coming out. "Maybe you guys should just make amends and hook back up? Gods know that would solve all our problems."

Finally emotion appeared in Eli's face, but it wasn't what I wanted to see. I said something mean and even though it wasn't on purpose it hurt him. "You regret us?"

Refusing to apologize I sat back, eyes forward on the road, bringing an awkward silence. I loved Eli. I came to that realization, but refused to acknowledge it earlier. In our short time together our future was molded into stone. There was no way I would get over this man, even if he chose to dump me off somewhere. My heart was gone and totally in his hands now. Knowing he was probably going to break it with his first chosen was probably one of the most painful things I was going through. Never mind the physical pain I endured in my lifetime. This was the worst pain possible. A broken heart that probably would never mend. The kind of broken heart that deserved only death in the end to be rid of the pain. How dramatic, right?

When I didn't answer right away he took my hand into his, the power rolling off of him onto me. "No, I don't regret it." I said finally. I visibly could see him relax at that admission. "But how do I know you won't as soon as you see her? The Demigod paired you together. And if what you say about fate and all that bullshit is true, how can you refuse it?"

Eli squeezed my hand as he stopped for a light. "Because the Demigod wasn't about the love. He was about power. He wanted a powerful race, which was about breeding and only creating more powerful. Someone like that doesn't consider things like love. To him that is small and unimportant." He exhaled noisily, realizing he would have to go into more detail. "Something not mentioned in our history is his wife. She was a Demigod, a result of a goddess of love and war. She realized the flaw in her husband's plans, but felt the idea of him creating a race was irresponsible, so she put her own magic into it. She gave us the option to find love in a true mate."

He saw my skepticism on this. This sounded all like fairytale stuff. Things you learned in school that wasn't true. Then again to anyone else vampires and werewolves didn't exist for a long time, yet they did. People were forced to believe then, but why didn't I want to believe Eli on this? Because after a while just like humans, vampires began to lose their belief in their creators. Like humans in God lost belief, because all they had to go by was words in a book. All we had to go by were a race created and also words in a book. Yet here was the real thing that was created by the Demigod himself. One of the first vampires on Earth was telling me the story and even I doubted him.

It was all more complicated than I cared to deal with at that moment. Life as a vampire was at risk because of Fiona. But why did I think she was the one risking our race? Just because she was related to Ben? Maybe it was because Carter told me of his past. About how he and Fiona had been into some bad things I didn't need to know about. When his wife died he was a changed man then. Those were pieces, but I couldn't figure out how to put them together. I turned toward him, dropping his hand. At the moment I didn't feel like being close to him. Everything just felt wrong. "Why are we going after Fiona?"

Eli frowned. "You don't know why?"

"I know she is part of this, but not sure exactly how. Why is she involved? Why did she lie to Carter?"

I watched as he went onto the highway heading toward the airport. "Fiona was born sadistic. Her and the one of the males named Hedrick used to kill humans just for sport. Now I know that vampires did that for a while, a long many years after that, so that isn't surprising. The ones that did are somehow from their lines, either born or bitten. I guess it mixes as vampires breed, but that is where it started, anyhow." He hit the gas passing an old man in the fast lane. "I and a couple of other Ancients tried to control them, but eventually they went off on their own killing spree."

"They were mates?" I asked.

He shook his head. "No, but they shared something in common, so they decided to take their own path away from us. Over the centuries we would hear about town massacres or a serial killer and we knew it was them. But even when we tried to track them down, it became years of endless searching. They were good at hiding. It had always been a rule with them to only take those that didn't matter, until there was a break in their usual ways and then a massacre would happen. Blood lust. She was crazy and to be honest, I am shocked she even has a surviving child."

"Had." I corrected.

Moving his head a little to the side he nodded. "Right, had." His lips pressed into a thin line before he continued. "Hedrick died eventually when a vampire hunter spotted him on the streets stalking a prostitute. By then they all knew their ways-"

"We call it M.O. in the cop world. Modus Operandi." I explained.

Smiling, he nodded. "Right, M.O. Anyway, when he died Fiona went crazy and decided to hunt the vampire hunters. Eventually she grew bored as their numbers began to dwindle. Back then they were an organization. Not sure if they even exist anymore to be honest. I kind of wondered if there were some gifted ones in there, but the only ones I ever came across were fully human. We can usually smell if one is psychic or uses some kind of witch power. I heard rumors that some were werecats even. They are supposed to be the most gentlest of the supernatural world."

"Okay, going off track here." I said to him, raising an eyebrow.

Grimacing after realizing I was right, he focused more on our topic. "When she met Carter they were probably the worst of our kind in history, period. I bet no other vampire can ever compare."

"Not even Nick?" I asked, remembering the whole Jack Ripper thing. I didn't think it could get worse than that, but you never knew.

Shaking his head he said, "Not even Nick. They did some pretty horrible things. Nothing like mutilation, but they did kill tons of people while they were in the middle of blood lust."

I shuddered. Blood lust was when a vampire lost control. Basically, they developed an addiction for blood, consumed with the power when they came across a gifted one. When they got someone with a supernatural power it was like a high. Kind of like what I got when I took Michael's blood. Just thinking about his blood had my heart pounding in earnest. Man, I wanted some more. Licking my bottom lip I looked around out the window, embarrassed that Eli just got me thinking about another man. The man's blood not his boy parts. Sheesh.

"So, how does this sex and blood slavery thing fit in with Fiona?" I asked.

He sighed, then gripped the steering wheel. "Because she used to do it with Carter. Before she died," he did a one handed quote gesture, "they had a business over in Europe where they stole victims off the streets to sell as slaves to other vampires. It wasn't that they couldn't get their own back then, but it was sort of a luxury, like collecting cars."

My mouth fell open. "What? Like collecting cars? They collected people?"

Nodding, he continued, "They collected them from other countries as they would collect horses. It was really big back then and the laws were different, of course."

Staring at him, I couldn't believe he could say it like it was just saying, "Yes, I would love some sugar in my tea." Most people would say something like that in horror. Like oh my gods, I can't believe my ancestors did that. Like slavery in the African American way.

"Anyway, I never thought it would have been her, considering we all thought she died many years ago when another vampire hunter came around. Carter was at a local church trying to snag a nun."

"A nun?" If Carter were alive, we would have a major talk about his past. At least he learned his lesson.

Straightening in my seat I decided I learned enough. So we were going after Fiona, who looked to be in charge of the Covert. Questions spiraled around in my head, trying to figure out why she would even go public. She ran the Covert for survival. Why did she fake her death? Why suddenly go after important girls? Why kill Carter? The whole thing didn't make sense. I had to figure it out and get justice for Carter. Why did she leave the bodies in Nick and Troy's rooms? For attention? Bring attention to killers that were similar?

*

It was a long plane ride. When the car stopped in front of the house Eli said was our temporary home, I hit the ground running, letting him take care of Luther. I wanted a shower and a long night of sleep before we tried to figure out where Fiona was. My only goal at the moment was to wash Ben off me with scalding hot water.

The house was a large one, but average if you compared it to a vampire's usual home. It had an iron gate going around the grounds, however small it was. I didn't take too much time to admire the brand new white sizing or the heavy dark wooden door with a giant dragon head knocker on it. That would have to go.

When the door opened I stopped, trying to see who it was, tense for a fight. Screaming, I ran up the steps pulling Electa in a hug that had her falling over in surprise. We toppled to the floor, the wind knocked out of both of us. She started laughing, squeezing me a lot tighter than a human could probably handle.

"Wow, this is almost as good as mud wrestling on pay-per-view," said Mitch, appearing from down the hall.

I looked up and smiled. "Haha, when did you develop a sense of humor?"

He grinned, opening his arms for a hug. "When you disappeared, because it's the way to cope around the depressed ones."

Leaping up, I went to hug him in a less aggressive way. "Where is Gideon?" I asked, hoping that Ben was lying about taking his blood.

Electa climbed to her feet, looking beautiful as ever in just a pair of jeans and a plain black t-shirt. "Upstairs in his bed. He lost a lot of blood when Ben attacked him."

It was better than dead, but the news was still depressing. If it was taking him this long to recuperate then Ben nearly drained him. That moment I was glad Ben was dead. He couldn't hurt either one of us anymore. But that left Fiona, who would now see me as a target, since we killed her son. Not only that, Eli sent one of the guards to deliver a threat. Thinking of Eli, I looked behind me, where he was coming up the walkway carrying Luther. The man was still out, but that was because Eli had his powers keeping him that way.

Mitch raised a questioning eyebrow. "This is Luther. He was one of the guys we worked with in SCD. Ben had him in the basement, where I was for a while."

"So you were part of the SCD as an agent?" Mitch asked.

Nodding, I closed the door behind us. We all followed Eli into one of the spare bedrooms on the first floor where he laid Luther on top of the bed that could probably fit five of us. The colors were meant for a female, though, so when Luther woke up I'd have to poke fun.

Different shades of pink and flowers all over everything. It almost made me dizzy just looking at the pattern. Whoever designed it needed an update on their interior decorating skills.

"Then that explains why they called Nick looking for you." Mitch said, coming up next to me. "They are investigating Carter's murder and apparently they want to question you."

Annoyed it took this long to contact me, I nodded. "Took them long enough."

Eli put an arm around me. "No one notified them about his death. They were just starting to wonder why he wasn't coming to work."

Shaking my head, I looked down at Luther. He was pale and covered in blood. Some of it mine. His eyes began to move, which I then assumed Eli had released his hold on him. Looking over at Mitch I said, "Could you get him some bagged blood? He was starving pretty badly when we found him."

"He looks fine to me." Electa said, looking closer.

I gave a halfhearted laugh. "That is because he took a chunk out of me."

Her eyes went wide, then she nodded in understanding. Crossing her arms over her chest she leaned against the wall. "We have to find the Covert leader." She said. "This kidnapping and killing business is bullshit."

We all nodded in agreement, watching as Luther slowly came to. His eyes blinked open, slowly at first, then when he became lucid enough, he looked from Electa's face to mine and Eli's. When Mitch entered he looked at the bagged blood, his fangs sliding out. Mitch held one out and Luther snatched it, slapping it to his fangs. His eyes rolled back at the relief of finally getting more blood. It was usually really uncomfortable if your body was craving it. More like your veins were on fire and nothing would put it out besides the blood.

After his third bag he was sitting up, ignoring everyone staring at him. If it had been me, I would have yelled for people to leave me alone, but not him. Luther always took things in stride, never trying to keep attention, but didn't even care if it was on him or not. He tossed the final empty bag into the trash next to the bed and sighed happily. "That was good, thanks."

Eli nodded. "I am-"

Luther cut him off. "Eli, Deputy Director for Nick."

"He was anyway," I said. "But he is now the vampire King. Declan has stepped down so now we serve Eli, one of the Ancients."

Luther stiffened, immediately getting to his feet with vampire speed. He teetered, nearly losing his balance from moving too fast, but Mitch was at his side offering support. When Luther got his focus he went down to one knee and bowed his head. "My King."

Never would I get used to that. Of course, I probably wouldn't do the same thing, unless it was to piss Eli off. So I watched as he recovered from the sudden obedience from Luther. He better get used to it, because a lot of vampires, including the older ones, were all about showing respect. To top it off, Eli was an Ancient. I stiffened and he sensed it. When he gave me a curious look I said, "If Fiona is an Ancient, then she can attempt to take the throne from you."

"Right, but I doubt that is her goal, considering she would have taken the position long ago if she wanted it." Eli said, looking back at Luther, who had yet to move. He seemed perplexed, not sure of what to do. "You may rise." He finally said, with what seemed like a long internal debate.

Luther rose, looking down at his clothing. "I apologize for my appearance, my Lord." As if it was his entire fault! Seriously, some of these vampires needed to stop dwelling on things they couldn't control.

Eli waved it off. "We just rescued you from Ben. Least of my concerns, but if you wish to clean up," he looked at Mitch, "he will get you to a room, where you can do that and use some clothes from one of us."

Nodding, Luther followed Mitch, who led the way out, leaving me alone with Eli and Electa. They both stood in silence, which drove me nuts. Pulling away from Eli, I smiled at Electa before deciding I would escape the awkwardness. "So glad you are okay! I am going to shower."

Understanding filled her eyes as she nodded and smiled. "Glad you are back, I missed you something fierce. Next asshole that decides to take my best friend, I will gut him myself. There won't be a quick death." She hugged me once more before leaving the room.

I turned to follow deciding Electa could be creepy when she made her threats, but Eli grabbed my arm, his eyes questioning. "Did he?" When I shook my head relief filled his face. He thought Ben had taken advantage of me. "Good, I was afraid the entire time."

That explained his problem back at Ben's house. He was trying to not think about what might have happened, because it would have been too distracting. He needed to make sure he took care of the problems before allowing himself to be exposed to the possibility. Here it sounded like he was the victim and not me. If it had happened, I wouldn't be standing there talking. Probably be on some kind of rampage hunting through the woods with pieces of Ben on my fangs, like some kind of wild animal. The mental picture was disturbing, so I pushed it from my thoughts before any other insane images appeared.

He pulled me into an embrace, his face burying into my neck. I smiled, pushing him away. "I don't know how you can get close to me covered in whatever shit I am covered in."

Shrugging, he kissed me on the lips and smiled. "Let me show you the room." He took my hand, heading up the steps that were nearly right in front of the front door. They creaked beneath our feet as we went up to the landing. When we made it, he took me down the hallway. The first door was the one Luther was in. He had just gone into his personal shower and Mitch was up the hall entering his own room, which was the next one. The third door was closed so that had to be Electa's.

Next came another door, where Gideon was asleep on his bed looking pale as ever. My heart clenched in despair. All of it was my fault, because I didn't realize the obvious. Ben was going to use the rave locations in order to find me. It had me wondering if Michael was involved, since he was the one that disclosed the location to me. I dragged my friends into my horrible mess when I should have been investigating alone from the start. That's what I do, and that's what I should have kept doing. I was such an asshole.

There were only two more doors left, one was a bathroom with a full tub in it and then finally what I assumed was our room. He opened the door, where there were already suitcases lined up against the walls. I raised my eyebrows up at him. "Assuming much, aren't you?" I asked.

He shrugged. "If you would rather your own room, I can take one downstairs."

Shaking my head in response, I went to the bathroom to shower. Closing the door I leaned up against it, shutting my eyes briefly. I was free from Ben. If he had been able to rape me, I didn't know what kind of state I would have been in. Probably nowhere near Eli. The last thing on my mind would be being with him. It was almost too much when I thought about it, but I missed him. However, I would never admit that to him. Selfish I know, considering he went through his own emotional rollercoaster when I came up missing. Sure it was hardly fair of me to be so distant, but that was my way. Emotionally distant was a vampire trait, but it was my trait all in its own from.

Moving away from the door I went to the shower turning it mostly hot since every muscle in my body was knotted up from stress. I tore off the clothes shoving them in the trash, never wanting to see them again. The memory would never fade but at least I could get rid of most of the evidence. I looked in the mirror horrified by my hair. It was in clumps with different shades of white and gray from the salt. Hopefully the water and soap would be enough to bring back the amazing curls that I hated just days before. That feeling would probably last a whole five seconds before I would be ripping out my flat iron to make them go away.

Stepping into the shower I put my head back, allowing the spray to cover my face. Instantly my body began to relax, enjoying the light pounding of the water on my skin. As the salt dissolved I could feel my demon power unbind, filling every one of my limbs. Never realizing how much I missed it until then, I stood completely still as every nerve in my body hummed with power. Opening my eyes I looked around, finding all my shampoos and soaps in the shower with me. Smiling briefly over how Eli thought about the little things, I grabbed the shampoo putting some in my hand, then rubbing it into my hair. I nearly moaned from my own scalp massage. I could totally be one of those people who rubbed bodies. But knowing the demon, she would think it was a demon sex buffet. So that job probably wouldn't work in my case.

Finishing up with the shampoo I went to the conditioner. After squeezing a good amount on my palm I rubbed it through my hair. Yelping in surprise when the curtain pulled back I went flat against the shower wall, a completely unnatural reaction for me. Eli stopped unsure if he should go back out. When he went to turn I grabbed his arm pulling him against me. I needed normal. I needed him. He stayed stiff unsure of what to do, until he understood my eagerness to be with him. I pressed him against the shower, my lips covering his in earnest. His arms went around me as he devoured me with matched impatience to be near me.

He turned hard almost instantly, it rubbed along my abdomen as my lips trailed from his mouth to his strong jaw. Eli tilted his head up, allowing me access to his neck, a move not only intended for lovemaking, but to show he trusted me. He knew that I had to feel in control again, so he stayed against the shower letting me devour him. My fangs scraped along his skin when I licked and sucked his neck. He groaned, hands lightly going down my sides. I shivered, pressing myself against him more. I was hungry, but I could hold out longer.

After my experience with Ben I had to know I was in control. Needed to know. My lips made a trail down his chest to one of his nipples. He hissed when I nipped one. Growling in a way only a predator would, I went down putting my lips over him. His fingers went into my hair as I did my best to make him mine. I needed him to beg. When he did my body hummed with pleasure. Moving up I kissed him hard, my tongue touching his, his hands grabbing my ass, as he slid me over him.

It wasn't long before the waves of pleasure filling me reached a toppling point. When I fell over the edge he quickly followed, only this time I sank my fangs into his neck completely shocking him. He shuddered beneath me as his own orgasm exploded from the two different intense feelings that enhanced each other with their combination.

Both of us stood very still, afraid to move away from the other. Licking his wound I made, I smiled. "You taste good."

He chuckled, eyes meeting mine. "I missed you." He kissed me softly, expression suddenly becoming serious when he pulled away. "I didn't know what to do when you disappeared. I wanted to rip apart that rave demanding someone to tell me what happened to you. When Lucifer showed up to tell me..." he trailed off, suddenly looking like a frightened boy. "Never leave me. Promise me."

I laughed. "As long as no one tries to kidnap me again I think I can make good on that." Kissing him before I slid off, I bent over to pick up my bottle of body soap. He took it from me offering to wash my back for me. This kind of life I could handle. If I had to experience anymore like what I did with Ben, I didn't know if I could actually come back from that. Even though it didn't go as far as it could have, it scared me to death to come so close.

If Eli hadn't been there for me, I wasn't sure what I would have done then. Carter was gone, but I did have Electa. Even though we knew each other for a long time, she was also an emotionally distant person, but with reason. Her life had been a lot worse than mine, but you kind of expect that from an assassin, right? They always seem to have a childhood memory that made them want to kill without a single regret. She never had regrets, but there had probably been at least one that was the driving force behind her ability to kill without a single emotion. The woman was probably the only person in the world I knew that would kill just for the sport of it. Thinking of her reminded me we needed to talk about what Gideon was to her.

Chapter Fourteen

Brian was sitting at the desk when we arrived at the office the next evening. He barely glanced up when we came inside, but Eli stopped at his desk and Brian grabbed a pen and notepad waiting for instructions. He was so eager to please Eli, it made me smile. That was exactly the kind of thing Eli needed. Someone who was willing to put all of their effort into making him into a successful king.

"I need you to look for any business or homes owned by Fiona Forrester. Also check to see if Ben has any properties. Even search with Carter's last name for Fiona." He said, motioning me and the others to move forward. Obviously he wanted some privacy with Brian. It kind of annoyed me, but then again what right did I have when he was the King? I may be his lover, but that didn't mean I had a right to know about everything. So I kept telling myself, but I totally did not feel that way.

We went to Eli's office that was way more elegant than ours. His computer was already set up and it looked like he had been there for at least a year and not a few days. To me that seemed odd, but I decided to just let it go, since he did explain to me there had been some prior knowledge to setting up the office.

We all chose a seat and that included Gideon and Luther. We told Luther he could go if he wanted, but he asked Eli if he were looking for anyone else to join his Guardians, and he said he would be pleased to have Luther on the team. SCD was out of yet another agent. Wonder how they would feel about that? I took Eli's seat, despite the fact he would need it when he came in. It was then I realized we were missing a person. "Where is Charity?"

Mitch shifted uncomfortably wanting to say something, but hadn't decided if he were allowed to or not. Watching him, I sat forward grabbing a pen to tap impatiently. "Well, I know you have something to say."

"Nick asked her to come back, offering the Guardian position." He finally answered, looking relieved to say something, but suddenly froze when Eli entered, like he had just been caught. What the hell was his deal?

Electa tsked. "Mitch let the cat out of the bag about Charity."

Shooting her a hateful glare, Mitch sat straight waiting to be reprimanded. When Eli said nothing he relaxed a little. Eli smiled, touching my shoulder. "It is okay, I meant to mention it last night, but with everything that happened I completely forgot."

Charity leaving wasn't a pleasing message. I liked her a lot and figured we would be good friends. At least I wasn't surprised when she showed up following Nick twenty minutes later. He tried to look commanding, but I had a hard time picturing it when I saw him pretty vulnerable next to Eli. He put his hands behind his back, looking at Eli, who now sat behind the desk with me perched on top of one end. "My King." He said, obviously having a problem saying it when his jaw muscle twitched, and the way he said it sounded like it was with teeth clenched.

Eli crossed one leg over his knee and clasped his hands together. "What can I do for you, Nick?"

The role reversal was hard for me to adjust to. I always pictured Nick as the one in charge, mainly because that was what I had been used to. He had been in charge since before I was born, so it would have to always be that way right? My mind kept trying to rebel against it, but the change was still there. Charity was now behind Nick, prepared to challenge anyone that dared to harm him. She barely acknowledged me when I tried to catch her gaze. A robot. She was like a damn robot. It took every bit of control I had to not go up and shake her.

Annoyed, I looked down at my nails frowning when I realized one of them was chipped. Uncool, that was for sure. "Am I boring you, Blake?" Nick asked me.

Looking up, I frowned holding up my middle finger. He stared at me exasperated, then looked to Eli to punish me. "I chipped my nail." I huffed.

Out of nowhere Charity busted out laughing, unable to keep her professionalism. She received a glare from Nick when he turned around to look at her. "Dude, I totally missed you."

"Me too, man!" I went over and hugged her. "I was afraid he brainwashed you or something."

Charity shook her head. "No, he said I had to be professional, so I took that meant acting like a robot and karate chopping the bad guys. Benefits are good, plus he offered me higher pay than Eli. Who has the bigger wang and all." She rolled her eyes, referring to how Nick thought he needed a better Guardian than Eli.

"Charity!" Nick snarled.

Eli only smiled, shaking his head in amusement. He was used to dealing with me so I doubt anyone could really do anything to surprise him. He wouldn't be a good mate for me if that was the case. No, not mate, I mean, boyfriend. Anyone that could deal with me was someone that I could be around for a little while. Stick up butt type guys were the ones I could hardly tolerate. Nick was supposed to be a tolerable one, but he had a hard time adjusting to the idea of Eli being King. Someone he considered lower than him surpassed him in one day, so I could only imagine how much that irritated him.

After a few minutes of silence and Charity making faces behind Nick, we all waited for the reason for their arrival. Finally Nick accepted a chair that was offered by Gideon. He was still kind of pale, but you could tell his strength was almost back. Following Mitch's example, he took a standing post on the side of the room, legs spread and hands behind his back. Luther still looked a little dazed, so he remained seated, barely sparing a glance at Nick.

Not that anyone was judging him, but he looked around seeming to realize his error for not actually acting like a Guardian. No one said anything when he stood up next to the other men. Electa just shrugged and sat sideways in her chair kicking her feet like a four year old. I would have never expected anything different. My best friend had always been really carefree. You took what she gave and nothing more. If you tried for more, you only got a rebellious teenager and eventually a runaway. She ran at the sign of authority, but was willing to make an effort for me. That made me happier than she probably realized.

"I came here to let you know I received the email this morning about Fiona. Had I known you were looking for her, I could have sent you to her current residence here in Michigan." Nick said.

We all stiffened. Why hadn't we thought about asking Nick? The Director would know all the vampires in his state. What made me unhappy was the idea he knew Fiona was alive when the rest of us had no clue, including Carter. "Why didn't you tell Carter she was alive?" I asked, standing up, fists clenched at my side.

His chin went up in defiance. "It was her request to not let anyone know. As you know, some vampires wish to stay out of trouble, so after notifying the designated Director they are allowed privacy." He shrugged. "We accommodate if it means less trouble."

It made sense, but it still infuriated me. "This whole time the Covert leader was in Michigan. Where?" I demanded.

You could tell he was going to refuse to answer me, so Eli leaned forward with his elbows on the desk. "Where is her location?"

Nick pulled out a paper from a pocket inside of his jacket and set it on the desk for Eli to look at. I leaned over his shoulder to read. She actually had three locations, two of them were in the Upper Peninsula. The other one was in Jackson, which was only about forty five minutes away. My immediate reaction was to go to her home and capture her, but that was what got me caught in the first place by Ben. This required real planning, so I needed to do it the right way before someone got killed. Every one of my teammates held an importance in my life, so losing one would be like a piece of me gone.

Eli stood handing the paper to Mitch, who went to take it to Brian to get whatever information he could on the addresses. "Thanks for bringing this to our attention, Nick." He looked over at me, because I was dancing around in place. "I know we ended things on bad terms, but I hope you can still consider me a friend after a while."

Looking somewhat appalled, Nick shrugged. "It was bound to happen, though I wish you would have told me sooner about your," he hesitated, "condition."

I started laughing, pressing one palm to the desk as I leaned in, unable to hold myself still. "Condition? Why are you calling it that? He is a fucking Ancient!"

Eli gaped at me over my language, but didn't say anything. "Well, we will get past it. If you find any other information out, please let me know as soon as possible."

Nick stood, holding out a hand to Eli. "I will and if you need any of my guard let me know."

After he left, Eli asked the rest of the team to leave, so he could speak to me in private. Electa raised her eyebrows up and down at me as she left, making me snicker in response. When the door closed Eli came up to me, put his hands on my arms and became serious. "We have to go about this carefully. We will get blue prints of her homes before jumping in. I will send Mitch and Gideon to see where she currently resides, then we will go from there."

He expected me to object, which was why he wanted us to talk alone. For me to argue in front of him would make him seem weak if he were to give in to me. Finally I sighed, nodding. Eli didn't know if he should believe me or not, because he stared studying my expression for what seemed like hours. Eventually he pulled me into a hug. My arms just hung there as if I wasn't happy. I waited for a reaction, expecting him to panic. When he pulled back with alarm I grinned, pulling him into my own hug. He was easy to play with.

"We need a bigger team, Eli. It just can't be the few of us. We need at least four more people and we can then use SCD or Nick's people for backup." I said when he pulled away to pace his office. Did I mention he was freaking hot?

The suit he wore today was one of a rich man. The way it fit his body made me think he had it specially made. Which it probably was. The blackness was blacker than I had ever seen of a suit. He wore a royal blue button up shirt underneath with no tie, making him appear like he was ready to hit the clubs. My heart began to beat faster when I thought about removing those clothes from him. He smelled good. My demon clawed her way up the path eager to get access to whatever deliciousness he had to offer. She wanted some Eli. My vampire nodded her head in agreement to this fact. We wanted Eli.

He stopped, his eyes going wide once he realized what I was thinking. "Oh, no. Not right now." He laughed, not meaning a single bit of it.

Moving swiftly, I was on him like a lion on a gazelle. "Too bad."

*

We ordered in dinner while Eli made some phone calls to some old pals he knew. He didn't actually call them that. With my best Eli impersonation he called them, "Warriors I fought next to a millennia ago." So when I said old pals he shook his head immediately, feeling it lacked the reaction he desired. When I insisted he call them that he walked out of the room, deciding not to argue with me over something so lame.

Electa sat in a chair with her feet up on the table. Apparently there was a meeting room, but none of us knew about it until Eli kicked us out of his office. Now we were in a large room with several bookcases filled to the max. There was a table on one wall with several computers that I assumed would eventually be used with whatever extra guards we ended up with. On another wall was a dry erase board, where several brand spanking new markers sat, still in their package. On the table Brian had thrown some notepads and pens in whatever direction they felt the need to land. After that he disappeared for a few minutes when the front door buzzed.

Mitch and Gideon had already left when we decided to hold a meeting. Later on they would have to be briefed, but there was no way in hell I would just sit around to hear news on what they found out. In the meantime, we could go over the blueprints and other information Brian seemed to have available at his fingertips. The man was a wiz. He had a full folder with information on Fiona's current life, not even getting to her past yet.

After a couple of long minutes, Brian returned with two boxes of pizza. The smelled filled my nose, causing my stomach to rumble with anticipation. Scrambling forward, Electa and I both raced to get the first slice. Luther just rolled his eyes watching us. He was always a patient man. Plus, he knew what I was like, so he learned to let the pigs go first to save himself a hand.

Electa snarled when my hand reached in for the first slice of Hawaiian pizza. I yelped, pulling back in time before her teeth could bite off a finger. Luther busted out laughing, slapping his knee. "Don't you know anything about canines?" He asked me.

I stuck my tongue out at him, going for a slice when Electa began to pick off pieces from hers. Sitting back in my chair, I took a bite of the pizza, moaning like I was getting the best sex ever. Luther's mouth dropped open as he watched me. "This pizza is fantastic." My mouth full.

Luther leaned forward to read the name on the box. When I raised a questioning eyebrow he said, "Just checking, so we know to order it every time. You looked like you were about to have an orgasm just from taking a bite out of it."

Electa snorted. "She always does when it comes to Emo's Pizza." She shook her head, shoving the food in her mouth like it was her last dinner. "They are fabulous. Eat some, Luther. Don't make me force feed you." She threatened.

He grinned, shocking me. It was the first time I ever seen Luther truly laid back. When we worked for the SCD he was always acting as if his underwear were too tight. Now he seemed…normal. He probably would take that as an insult if I told him that, but it was the truth. Maybe this was what he needed. For the first time in my life I felt like I was in the right spot. My best friend at my side and my man leading the way. What else did I need?

Pulling the folder to me I opened it to examine what Brian found. He came in after grabbing some paper plates from the kitchen, frowning when he realized it was a wasted effort, but Luther took one to make him feel needed. Brian forced a smile, then took a seat to grab his own piece. "Anyone need napkins?" He asked. When he saw Electa licking her palm he shrugged, throwing them on the table. "Guess not."

I snickered, grabbing another piece of pizza. "Don't worry, Brian. It just shows we are more like family than you thought. Things we do will annoy the piss out of you."

Realizing I just called him part of our family he smiled broadly, like I just made his day. The man was probably used to being kept on the outside of things. To finally be included was the first time he had been accepted. He grabbed his own pizza, taking off the pineapple with his nose bunched up as if he was disgusted. I opened the other pizza box finding it was the same thing. "Why are they the same?"

Brian sighed, looking at the office door. "King's orders."

It was my favorite kind of pizza. It warmed my heart knowing Eli ordered the toppings to my specifications. "I will make sure next time he gets what everyone wants."

Electa gave me thumbs up, since her mouth was full. We then all leaned forward to examine the information. First was a short biography on Fiona with her picture. She was super model gorgeous and every bit of a Victorian queen. You could tell she was from another time by the look on her face. If it wasn't that, you could tell she was a coldhearted killer just from her eyes alone.

The date of her birth was left blank. I was surprised no one bothered to make sure that information was filled in. Though with some vampires they tended to forget the date they were born as years passed. Immortals lose time faster, since they have so much of it.

Flipping to the next page I found some extra pictures of her. Some older, some not. There was no information on Ben, which was a little surprising, she kept him a secret this whole time. Then there was a little history on how she became a famous artist. So that was the cover she hid under. The name Felicia Osborne was her second identity. Good to know. The other stuff was information on her homes. The one in Jackson was a horse farm of Thoroughbreds. She had it since 1962 when she purchased her first horse. It was a huge ass farm too, housing nearly four hundred horses. The house itself had fourteen bedrooms and seven bathrooms, sitting on five hundred acres. The notes even mentioned several people approaching her to purchase the property. Lucky for them she didn't kill them for being annoying. We all knew she would be one for that kind of thing, flicking them off one by one like flies.

The smallest place was the farthest up in the Upper Peninsula. It was just a small sized cottage that sat on the edge of the lake. At least the paper said small sized, but the footage showed nearly over three thousand feet. It was on twenty acres, where a hunter usually leased it so he could hunt the land. Common thing for Michigan. Those who wanted to have their own area to hunt usually leased the land from some owner who wanted a few extra bucks. It seemed like she didn't stay there often enough. What I found amazing was how well they kept tabs on her. It was probably for the sake of her past to avoid any repeats but a whole lot of good that did, considering she had been the leader of the Covert for so many damn years.

Annoyed now, I flipped the next page, passing on the other information to Electa and Luther. Her other house was a possibility, too. It was in the middle of fifteen acres with over six thousand square feet. Why someone needed such a big house was beyond me, but hey, maybe she needed more room for her torture chamber. Frowning, I looked over the blue prints, admiring the work Brian collected. He was good at research, but I couldn't help but wonder where the hell he got his amazing hacking skills.

Passing the rest of the information over, I smiled at him. "You are good at this stuff. Have anything to add?" I asked, catching him off guard.

He swallowed his pizza, nearly choking on it. Luther reached behind him to a small table, where he poured water from a pitcher into a glass. Brian swallowed it, attempting to clear his throat several times. He passed Luther a grateful glance and sat back in his seat. "Well, my advice is to go for the place in Jackson. Someone like her wants to be close to the action. To be honest, I am surprised she doesn't have something closer." His leg began to bounce, unable to hold still for a few seconds. "But the Thoroughbred farm is a good cover. No one would suspect her as being someone in charge of an organization like the Covert. She wants to look like another citizen."

I pulled the Thoroughbred farm blue print toward me, examining it. According to the information on the security page, it had top of the line security. She had cameras all over the place. Guards everywhere too, which those were all expected. Our problem was getting past all of her juicy security. Then it hit me. "I could teleport in."

Luther sat forward, suddenly serious. "You could, but what if she is prepared for you, then traps you with another circle?"

Good point. I stuck my tongue out at him, earning an eye roll for a reaction. I sighed, tapping my chin with one finger. "Obviously we can't go in guns blazing." I said.

Brian grinned suddenly, like a kid in school with candy and knew everyone else had none. I eyed him suspiciously. "What are you holding back?" He revealed a folded paper. He totally planned that. "Dork!"

Electa snatched it from him, stealing his glory. She dropped her pizza and slid it over to me. I glanced down, then looked at Brian. "A secret tunnel, for real?"

He nodded eagerly. "Oh yeah. She uses this tunnel to bring in the victims. This is how she does her business. The big money comes through here. Anyone that wants a girl will contact her and then this is how she gets them into the area to pick one out. This is how they are stored and transported." He explained, tracing a finger down a path on the paper that could only be a tunnel.

At the end of a tunnel was another building a whole five miles away. One that looked to be an abandoned warehouse in an abandoned town. "A fucking ghost town. A real ghost town. I never knew they existed, but they totally do!" I said, sliding the paper over to Luther and Electa.

They both looked at the paper and sat back, identical expressions of amazement on their faces. "Holy shit." Electa said, looking back down at the paper. A spark of excitement lit her face.

"That is pretty clever if you ask me." Luther said, thinking out loud.

The meeting room door opened and Eli walked in looking exhausted, carrying bags of blood for everyone. I liked my meals warm, but right now there was no time to actually go hunt. Going to see Michael probably would piss Eli off, so alternative method it was!

Eli no longer wore his jacket, his shirt unbuttoned more and his sleeves pulled up to his elbows. "Well, looks like we have the four guys we need. Took some convincing, but we have our team." He looked at our faces, suddenly realizing what was up.

I stood up and thrust the paper at him. "Look what your brilliant researcher found!"

*

The only thing we were waiting on was confirmation from Mitch and Gideon. No word yet, two hours into their little mission. It had me wondering why. When Eli sent a text Mitch replied back with "checking security." We really needed codes or something, in case one of us loses our phone. Not that some random stranger says, "Hmm, I found a phone. What does it say?" If I saw a phone I would totally snoop! Knowing our luck, the people who would find it would run screaming to the police station.

Mitch was a very thorough guard so I was glad when he wanted to be part of my team. Gideon, I still had to get to know, but his heart seemed in the right place. At least I hoped. We hadn't talked much, but with the kidnapping and us just not having a moment, it was pretty hard to accomplish. However, I was determined to corner Electa when I had a chance. As soon as the guys left the room to go and Electa about to follow, I used my vampire speed to block the doorway, my arms and legs spread out as if we were in elementary school.

Raising her eyebrows she looked at me, the wolf peeking out wondering if there was a challenge involved. When I only grinned she put a hand on her hip and glared before yawning wide, letting me know she was totally bored with whatever idea I had.

"So, tell me about Gideon."

She froze, her mouth hanging open, not expecting that one thing to come out of my mouth. Usually I mind my own business, but she should have known I would have seen all the signs of awkwardness. Even Gideon was keeping his distance and well, two healthy sexual wolves like them didn't do that. Now it was Blake's own personal intervention time to get information. I could tell Electa was gauging her success rate for getting past me. She could probably make it past with bulldozing me, but then again, I would be able to teleport to trap her again.

I grinned. "Just admit you are stuck telling me. Out with it."

When her shoulders relaxed I dropped my hands and straightened. She motioned for me to shut the door, so I did, skipping over to the table for some juicy boy gossip. Electa always had strange adventures and for one of them to be with wolfboy was kind of exciting.

Finally, after a too long hesitation she said, "Seems he is my mate, I sensed it right away."

My whole body froze, not expecting it. What was with the damn mate thing anyway? I knew it was a more popular thing with wolves though. Every wolf always became mated, no matter what. So, for her to find Gideon was supposed to be good news. From her blank expression I wasn't sure if I should offer up a cake or prepare a coffin. So in a nervous voice I was like, "Yay, greaaaat." And gave her a little awkward tap on the arm.

She just rolled her eyes at me. "It is good news, but I am not ready to settle down yet." And then the panic set in. She got to her feet, pacing the meeting room like a trapped wolf. Shit. I saw this before. Usually it ended up with someone hurt. Electa trapped was bloodshed waiting to happen.

Looking around, I tried to find some kind of shield. I could probably hide under the table, but she might snag one of my legs. Chewing my bottom lip, I looked up startled when she said my name with her hands on her hips. "Are you looking for an escape route?" She asked sharply.

"No..."

"You are!"

Shaking my head, I started to slide under the table. "You know, escape smape..." I hurried underneath, crawling like a runaway infant. "No offense, but when you start pacing I know the wolf comes out."

Her laughter filled the room and suddenly her face appeared under the table, startling me. Her wolf was out! I was so right! Her brown eyes glowed and nostrils flared taking in my scent. "You aren't even scared. Stop screwing around and come out."

"Or what, you will blow my table down?"

Again she laughed, it echoing this time. "Maybe, now come on."

Finally I crawled out, taking my seat back and propped my feet up on the table. I did an elegant wave with my hand to tell her to continue. She rolled her eyes, taking up her pacing again. "He confronted me about it, but I told him I need distance for now. So that is what he is doing. But the wolf is going crazy. She wants out to be with her mate, but I am like fuck no man." She shook her head in disgust, spinning around to face me, then slapped her palms down on the table surprising me. "Love is so overrated."

Thinking about Eli, I kind of almost agreed. Despite my willingness to love him and do the dirty with him, the girl in me was still afraid this was all some fairytale conspiracy. Sure, we all dreamed it while playing princess and dragons as kids, but now we were grown up. Being with a man meant being tied down and wasting precious time that could be used for the fun stuff. Not that we didn't have a lot of it being immortals, but the fact still remained. We could be doing better things with our time than trying to cater to a man, who probably wouldn't want us ten years down the road. Plus, men were high maintenance. The stress!

Somehow I didn't think that was the case with Eli or Gideon. The creatures we were had the magic. We knew who our soul mate would be. Carter hadn't been so lucky and the idea was depressing, since he died by the hands of the woman he thought was his true love. But even he didn't know what a mate bond felt like. I did. I was completely drawn to Eli. I knew he was in his office, nervous about the next few days. His nervousness echoed in my own stomach, forcing it to flop like it wanted to expel its contents.

"Well, I don't know much about Gideon, but he must check out if Eli has allowed him on the team." I tapped my chin with a finger thoughtfully. "Only issue I have is his name. We have to change his name."

Her eyebrows met in the middle with confusion. "Change it?"

"Yeah, don't like his name. Other than that, I put my stamp of approval on him."

She rolled her eyes. "I like his name and thanks for the approval. I know I can go on now that you made your final decision." The last part she said with sarcasm before looking out the window.

I shrugged, even though she couldn't see me. "Hey best friend approvals are important, you know?"

Electa snorted. "Sure, if she wants to steal him down the road sometime."

"Uh, no. Usually the friend tries to keep you away from him."

"Yeah, okay. But let's stop talking about this, because honestly, the heart to heart is totally freaking me out." We both laughed, totally agreeing on that. Still, we knew we had each other and that was important. Neither one of us likes to spill our guts out onto the floor, but we did it if it meant keeping each other sane.

Standing up, I stretched, suddenly buckling with pain when the vision slammed into my head. I nearly screamed from the force of it, which only meant it would be a big one. A hand was touching me, so I thought it was Electa offering me comfort, only the voice didn't go with the body. "Ride this one out. I knew the bitch was going to do it." Lucifer growled.

"Your fault!" I screamed, barely hearing the door of the meeting room open.

Lucifer laughed, but not the least bit amused. "I know, love, it is my fault and I apologize." When his fingers went through my hair actual comfort came over me.

Dropping to my knees, I let Eli come next to me to take my hand. Abruptly he started to cry out in pain, and then the vision went full force, like molten lava pouring through my veins, threatening to take out every nerve ending. Trying to breathe through it, I followed the images that flickered through. I was looking through Fiona's eyes as she killed. Blood was all over her hands and the thrill of the life pouring from their mutilated bodies brought my demon pleasure. It was exhilarating and addictive, the high of it flowing through my entire body, insisting on causing more blood to splatter so my demon could lick it off my hands. She swung what looked like a sword at her next victim, who barely had any time to react.

The girl held up her hands, her mouth open for a scream that I couldn't hear. The horror on her face would be one I would remember. I shouted no, but of course I wasn't there to get her to stop killing. Then I saw the ring on the girl's finger and my heart nearly leapt out of my chest. Gideon's sister. I screamed as if it would help stop the horror that was about to happen, but the sword came down as the girl struggled against the chains that held her to a wall. Then with the grace of water putting a fire, the images disappeared, along with the pain.

My head pounded hard, brain screeching like an animal in pain or was that me? Pulling my knees to my chest I curled into the fetal position, feeling hands all over my body as people tried to comfort me. I could hear Eli's low soothing words next to my ear as his warmth laid closer to me. Slowly the pain receded the more he ran his hands over me, like he knew some kind of healing spell. That didn't stop my body from going into protection mode. I passed out.

Chapter Fifteen

Shooting up from the couch, I groaned immediately, regretting it when my head swam and my vision blinked in and out. Eli was by my side, concern written all over his handsome face. He sat down next to me on a couch that I didn't even know was in the house. The room wasn't one I recognized, but it looked like a regular living room. There was a TV, a coffee table, and a black leather couch. Magazines lay on the table with some coasters for drinks. My head swiveled taking in the new surroundings, spotting the mini fridge on a table with a coffee machine. A break room? Interesting.

Up on the wall were pictures of him with pin holes in his face. Darts sat off to the side on a nearby table. I raised an eyebrow and he rolled his eyes. "Electa says since I am the boss they have to hate me now."

Grinning, I turned on the couch, allowing my feet to hit the ground. He had taken off my boots and set them on the floor next to the couch. I rubbed my eyes trying to get focused again. "How long have I been out?"

Eli put a hand on my thigh, making tingles shoot up to the rest of my body. I shivered, watching a slow smile appear on his face. "Two hours. Gideon and Mitch are back, going over what they saw right now. We can fill you in as soon as you are able to get up without any problems. I'll go grab you some blood."

Gideon. I stood up heading for the door of the room, ready to tell him what I saw in the vision. How Fiona managed to connect to me that was both irritating and puzzling. She knew about my visions and she was strong enough to force me to have them. It made sense, considering she was an Ancient, but it still pissed me off! The bitch would pay for all the pain she caused. We needed a plan and a good one. I went to reach for the handle, but the door wouldn't budge. Eli. Spinning around, I glared at him. "Open the door!"

Shaking his head, he got to his feet still looking worried. I was sick of people being concerned for me. I survived this long without someone looking out for me. He hovered and it was really annoying. When he got close enough

I punched him in the arm. His mouth fell open. "Ow!"

"Glad it hurt, now open the door!" I stomped one foot while clenching both my fists.

Amused, he smiled. "You are cute when you are mad."

"Catch me if you can!" I sang before thinking about the meeting room to disappear.

Silence met me when I opened my eyes to find everyone on my team staring with their mouths open. I waved, then sat down in an empty chair, crossing my arms, while watching the door. After two seconds, Eli busted in, like the room was on fire and someone needed saving. His gaze focused on me and instantly relief flooded his face. All I could do was roll my eyes. Seriously, people needed to lighten up. I teleported from the other room without a problem. I impressed myself. People should know I am fabulous.

"What are you doing out of your room?" Luther asked suddenly.

I raised an eyebrow in challenge. "Am I not in charge here?"

Luther sat back, but Electa shook her head disapprovingly. "You didn't see what we did when you had that vision. We thought you were dying, even though Lucifer said the Fiona bitch was making a direct vision contact."

As if hearing his name, Lucifer's elegant self appeared in a chair at the end of the table. He was eating… a bowl of cereal? I leaned forward glancing in it with a frown. Lucky Charms. Never in this lifetime did I think I would see a demon eating freaking Lucky Charms. Slurping his milk out of the bowl, he ignored the rest of us around him. Sighing like he filled a long hunger, he tossed the bowl in the air. Everyone flinched, expecting it to break against the wall, but it disappeared like everything else of his. "That Leprechaun knows how to make some cereal." He said, rubbing his stomach. He was dressed in another suit, but this one making him look like an old time gangster. He put his feet on the table, revealing gangster shoes.

"You know the Leprechaun is actually just a mascot right? That the food was made in a factory of some sort?" Mitch asked, making it sound like he was approaching a confused person who just escaped a mental hospital.

Lucifer nodded. "Of course." Then his eyes focused on me. "I need to help you build shields. Had I known another Ancient existed I would have made you do it right away, but someone having such skills is pretty rare." He said, folding his hands over his stomach.

Eli sat next to me, taking my hand into his. "Well, good, how do I do it?" I asked.

"You think of a wall or something impenetrable. After a while it will become such a habit you will hardly realize they are up." Lucifer explained. "Now do it and see if I can force a vision on you."

Jumping up, Eli shook his head, looking every bit of a King that he was. Fury blazed in his eyes as he looked at Lucifer, who just returned a look that made you think he was just bird watching. "She just woke up after being forced one. She needs to rest."

Sighing dramatically, Lucifer sat up. "You are overprotective. I think I know what my daughter can do." He said, daring Eli to challenge him.

"You think you know, but you haven't been around until this last week." Eli pointed out, accepting the challenge.

Lucifer leapt to his feet, his eyes turning a glowing red, which I never saw before. He was never mad. Usually he took things in stride, ignoring those he thought weren't worth his effort. But he was different this time when Eli felt he needed to shelter me, so I spoke up. "Hello, I am here you know? I don't need people to talk as if I am not. I want to know how to do it."

When Eli looked as if he would press the issue I held his gaze, showing him I was going to do it, despite what he thought. "Even if I order you to not do it right now?" He asked.

Holy shit. Did he just say that to me? Staring at him in shock I heard Electa whistle her 'Oh Shit' tune. Anger slammed into me, heat prickling my skin. Lucifer looked amused at my response, fully knowing Eli was in big trouble. "If you ordered me to, then I guess I would have to comply, wouldn't I?"

Defeated, Eli sat down looking away. "Continue." It was a big blow to his King position. I was defying the King, but no one said anything about it. Suddenly I felt horrible for the way I acted. I couldn't challenge him in front of others, or vampires would think he lacked the ability to control the race. He didn't need that. We all didn't need that. Sighing, I sat down. "We can do it after this meeting and probably lunch." I said to Lucifer, who looked a little surprised I had given up so easily, but it didn't take long before understanding came over him.

Mitch leaned forward with a pen in his hand, eyes looking me over. "Tell us about the vision."

It had me hesitating because of Gideon being in the room. If I mentioned his sister's death, he would go charging in, not caring what we all thought was best for the mission. So I just explained the part of how she showed me her killing people, and I felt how much she wanted to see the blood splatter on the floor, while enjoying the fear on their face when they knew death was coming. It was not something I wanted to see again. Killing someone for killing and harming others I had no problem doing myself. But killing innocents was something that would haunt me forever, so that was never an option. The way she allowed me to see the vision gave me a front row view, as if I did it all myself. My stomach twisted in knots, threatening to get sick if I couldn't control my sudden panicked emotions. What if she did get through my shields when I managed to have them up? She was an Ancient, after all. Lucifer was convinced I was strong enough, but was I really?

Despite my effort to keep his sister out of it, Gideon's face was paler than before. He didn't say anything though, just continued to listen to Mitch, who went over the security of the Jackson location. Apparently guards were all over the house. We told them about how a tunnel went underneath to a warehouse in a ghost town and they were pretty surprised. It explained how she could keep up with the business without showing signs of being back in business.

It wasn't long before we had a plan. We were going to enter her home during the hours most vampires would be out at the warehouse, selecting a slave. Eli said anyone else who was there would be arrested as well, since the whole business was illegal in vampire and human laws.

My vision had come around midnight, and I figured that's when the majority of the activity began at the farm. Vampires would probably show up at her home to do their shopping. Just thinking of it as shopping caused me to shudder in disgust. How anyone of my kind could be cruel enough to think of it as a sport or a collection just made me feel so much shame. Many vampires became sadistic over time, or just thought of themselves better than humans. It happened, just like it happened in the human world. We all had our killers in different forms, which would otherwise seem normal to us on the outside.

The mission would take place the following night. Our other recruits were due to arrive and be briefed. According to Eli, they were well trained warriors. Men he would vouch for in a heartbeat. He told me they were surprised to hear he was an Ancient that took the King position. When he invited them to be on the Guardian all seemed hesitant because of their experiences with Declan. At one point in time they served with him and punishments always came with near death experiences. Once I was told about him stabbing a stake in a warrior's chest, so close to his heart that he actually faded in and out of consciousness for several hours at a time. It was a year's worth of torture.

First to show up was a man named Tyler Hawkins. He was a short vampire, but every bit of warrior. His muscles rippled beneath his red shirt as he moved, but it was obvious he was putting on some kind of show. Even Electa was caught drooling over the package he had. The man was beefy! He was nice enough to me and didn't even flinch when Eli told him I was his superior. A lot of the old vampires still looked down at the idea of a woman in control.

Second was an old friend and fellow warrior to Eli. When they saw each other it was like being inside a frat house. They crashed into each other with such force both Electa and I flinched, expecting one to come away wounded. She decided to be part of the greeting squad after seeing Tyler. If Eli had more hot friends, she could totally live being around so many men.

Eli slapped his friend on the back with a boyish grin on his face. "Blake and Electa meet Andy Fear."

Raising matching eyebrows, Electa and I turned to each other. I grinned, putting out a hand. "Nice name Andy."

Andy shook my hand firmly, with a brilliant smile of his own in place. His dark hair was really nice. I stared at it, debating if Eli would be offended if I felt his friend's hair, but I stayed back. Damn, I just wanted to… Next thing I knew, I was next to him touching his hair with one finger. His blue eyes sparked when he saw my interest. "She is as lovely as you said." He told Eli when he looked over at him.

Beaming, Eli nodded. "She is, even though she is a little odd."

Stepping forward, Electa offered a hand, stealing the attention from me. Andy's mouth practically fell open, as if he just then realized the actress look alike was suddenly in front of him. "You don't smell vampire." She said, raising an eyebrow. "In fact, I don't think I have smelled your kind before, ever."

Taking on a serious expression, Andy took her hand into his. "You have a good nose, wolf."

Flashing him a smile, she sauntered off to go do something else. She came for the viewing, nothing else, not that I expected anything else. When a wolf found her mate she didn't really care about being with another man. Sure it didn't hurt to look and they could thoroughly enjoy the eye candy, but their hormones only raged for the one they were meant to be with. As sappy as that sounded. Mental gag, here.

"So what is he, if not vampire?" I asked.

Eli frowned. "He will have to tell you that, since I took an oath of never to reveal what he is."

Debating on if he was serious, I went from him to Andy. Standing rigid, Andy dared me to challenge it. So I did. "I want to know."

Shrugging, Eli walked away without another word, leaving the two of us alone. Was that his lousy attempt to escape answering me or was he trying to give us some privacy? Either way, it pissed me off. I didn't know this guy and he expected me to get answers from him. My eyes blazed, catching Andy off guard when he saw them. "You aren't fully vampire."

"Ding ding ding! You get a prize." I said, startling him with my sarcasm. "Now out with it because I refuse to work with you if you don't tell me what you are."

Andy smiled, tilting his head sideways. "You are a feisty one. How Eli managed to land you is beyond me." When I went to open my mouth to say something snappish he interrupted me. "I didn't mean anything rude by that. Can we talk somewhere private?"

Nodding, I led him to my office that I had yet to use. He looked around, realizing that it was unused too. I gestured to a chair, telling him to take a seat while I went to sit on the edge of my desk that was currently not organized. Brian had just been dumping materials instead of figuring out places for them. The room smelled of fresh paint, so it was then I realized it was no longer white like the first time I saw it. The walls were a navy blue with a cream trim. The windows now had long navy blue curtains that just hung there without being tied off to the side.

Facing Andy, I crossed my arms over my chest, trying to take on the look of a tough guy, but it was somewhat difficult to accomplish when I was in toe socks and not my boots. You know the socks that have individual slots for each toe? Yeah, I had those on. He looked somewhat tickled when he glanced down at them, but I just quirked an eyebrow, waiting for an answer to my question.

He sighed. "I suppose you need to know, if I am to serve under you." The way he said it made it sound like it left a bad taste in his mouth. The guy didn't seem too keen on authority, but neither was I, so I let it pass as he worked through whatever issue he had to reveal himself. "If I tell you this, it must be a secret. No one can know what I am."

I shrugged, nodding slightly, signaling that I would agree. His lips twitched at that. Then he adjusted in the cushiony chair before starting off with his story. "I am what they call a Traveler." When I only stared at him he sighed. "It is an angel that is allowed by God to explore the Earth, so they can find their own purpose. I have been doing it since before the Ancients came to exist."

Okay, so I wasn't expecting to hear that from him. Maybe a troll or say a gremlin, but not a damn angel. Were they even allowed to fight or kill people? This was too much for me to handle, so I started to pace around the room, arms still crossed. "Why would you travel the Earth this long?" I asked finally.

He only shrugged in response, not giving me anything more than that. It wasn't my place to ask and he didn't have to give me an answer. Now if it were Eli asking, or it concerned the Guardians he would have to. I smiled. "Fine, whatever. You are free to go."

Smiling, he got up, bowed, and then left the room before I could snap something smart at him for bowing. Life was getting more and more interesting. Who would have thought angels roamed the Earth as humans, trying to seek some kind of purpose in life? They were like us, not knowing what they were meant to do. They thought there were bigger things for them than having to serve God. As wrong as that sounded, I guess angels had feelings too.

*

The other two guys were identical twin vampires. Yes, I said twin vampires. Both with long blond hair that was tied back in a simple ponytail. If I had a choice, I would cut those off. I hated guys with long hair. It was a serious turn off, but then again, what did my opinion matter when I had Eli? My demon decided Eli could be put off to the side for a while for some side action. My vampire just said men were not needed period, because they caused more drama than anything. My female said we needed Eli. Eventually my vampire would agree because of the mate thing, but she was still independent. But all three of my personalities needed to get along so we could take down Fiona. The bitch had to die and there was no way around it. I wanted to take her down personally for Carter. She ruined everything for me. My life may have gotten a slight improvement with Eli in the picture. There was no way for her to escape me now. I had her number.

Chapter Sixteen

I was nervous. My body thrummed with anticipation of the mission. Something big was going down and I was a part of it. The sky was clear, stars dotted it with bright glows. The moon was full, which left Electa and Gideon really antsy and hormonal. For the first time since their meeting, they actually touched and did some creepy mating thing that you only saw in cartoons. Like a flutter of the eyelashes and little giggles. Yes, I was seriously shocked to hear Electa giggle like a school girl getting heart candy from her boy crush. Not something the public should see, because it was seriously harmful to the mind. Mine at least.

Fiona's property was a lot larger than I pictured by the paper. Never been up close, I guess that would happen. Her property was lined with a tall stone wall with security lights that lit up forty feet from their sides. There was a main gate where two vampires stood guard waiting for action, but expecting none at all. Their hands sat on the hilts of their swords, eyes forward. Every once in a while we would hear one speak asking what they would want for dinner at break, or if they wanted some blood, because they had some to spare.

I took blood before leaving from Michael. Eli was really not pleased to hear about it, but even he agreed that I could not back out of an arrangement already made. He stayed in the room, despite my feelings of it being uncomfortable. Michael, of course, had no problems trying to get me closer with an audience nearby. His blood thrummed through me, making every part of my body feel powerful and limitless. Just three more weeks of sampling him. In a way it was kind of depressing, but I didn't let Eli know that. He would be angry and probably kill Michael before thinking about it. The King simply did not need to make war with the werewolves.

Creeping through the woods, we looked for an opening. According to Brian, there was a gap in the cameras, where we could enter if done at the right time. A specific time. This was when the guard inside the walls wasn't around. The cameras on the wall did not move, so that was easy. We were positive there were more cameras on the actual house, but they were too far away to catch any images of someone jumping over.

We had sent Gideon out to do that work. Usually, according to Brian's notes, the guard circled to that spot every forty five minutes. It was now going on forty minutes, so he should be on his way.

I looked over at angel boy, who was hunkered down on his stomach looking around to make sure no one got close. Since we had our conversation, I had been wondering what type of powers he had as an angel, but even that had to be a mystery to me. It was total bullshit, considering as the boss of our unit I needed to know. Eli promised we would have the conversation after I came back safely from the mission. Despite all of us arguing, he was attending as well. Only unlike with Ben, he had to take care on his entry, since Fiona was another Ancient. When did a King ever go into the front of the line to attack someone? Never. He wouldn't listen, so we all had to worry for his safety. It was our job, even though he insisted we treat him as another member. It was an argument we had before leaving and probably will every time we had to go out to do something. This was why he didn't want to be

King. People tried to restrict him for safety reasons. Treating him like he was the President pissed him off to the point of blowing a hole in his office wall. At the time, all of us stood shocked, unable to think of anything to say. Finally gathering my scattered thoughts, I pointed out that it would be hard to explain this to the guy who had to fix it. He was not pleased with my response to his outburst.

So he was further down the wall with Electa and the twins. Mitch was at the warehouse location with his group awaiting orders for when we arrived. I paired myself up with angel boy and Gideon, thinking we could accomplish more if we didn't need to worry about Eli.

Finally Gideon gave us a signal to move forward, the guard was gone. We crept forward and I leapt up easily to the top, holding onto the edge just enough to keep my balance. Gideon was already down the other side, so I went down, barely making a noise when I touched ground.

Quickly after me was Andy, who flew up and landed over. Both Gideon and I just stared in awe as he did it so effortlessly and well... beautifully. At that second I could have sworn angels were singing. Andy just rolled his eyes when I gave him a questioning look, flapping my arms like wings. Gideon just stared at me with a "what the fuck?" look on his face.

We hurried down the line of the wall, barely making a sound. Like shadows from a distance, we moved with stealth. My breath came quietly, if slightly faster. Behind me Andy was even quieter, which had me look behind myself several times to see if he was still there. Gideon was louder than I would like, but still no one would have heard him if he was across the yard.

In the distance, back where we started, the others followed. We would stay on the grounds, taking different accesses of the house to make sure that Fiona wasn't inside. We weren't sure on where the tunnel entry was from the house, but Brian expected it would be either in a basement or somewhere on the ground floor, where it opened up to a tunnel. The guy was smart, I had to agree with him on that. In my experience, they were always in the basement. Most of the houses in Michigan had what they called a Michigan basement, which was an unfinished basement that everyone was usually afraid to go into. It was seriously creepy. Most of the time they were flooded and reeked like stale water.

Somehow I doubted that Fiona had a Michigan basement. She probably had something more finished and fancier. We all agreed on that one. According to the floor plans, the door that led to a lower floor was in the kitchen so we assumed the tunnel entry was there.

The house was actually a mansion. Almost every window was lit up, but there was no movement to show someone was inside. That didn't mean anything, of course. "We're right behind you." Came Eli's voice over the ear pieces we all shared. He bought some really high tech shit. The pieces couldn't even be seen in your ear, they were so small.

"Kind of figured when you were supposed to follow over the wall." I grumbled.

Someone laughed and I only could picture Electa, since it sounded pretty girly to me. This whole moon high thing was disturbing, so I ignored her for the moment. "No, I mean we are right up behind you."

Turning around, I spotted Eli leading his group, only now it just looked like a long line of people trying to get inside the house. It took all the power I had to not rip into him. What the hell was he doing? He needed to serve as backup, not come up right behind me, like we are going out to eat. "Yes, entry for a party of six."

Sighing, I shook my head showing my disapproval, then turned back into the direction of the house. We didn't have time to mess around, in case someone saw us. Our next steps were to gain entry and take down anyone that was inside the house. That would take place on the west side of the house, where a camera's view did not fully take in. I think that had a lot to do with the fact her security person wasn't as thorough as he should have been. If it had been my house, there would have been additional cameras despite the extra work involved. For such a booming business, certain things needed to be covered at the fullest extent. But luck was on our side, because now we had ways in without causing too much of a warning.

As we rounded the house things were suddenly in motion. A guard came around, one that we hadn't known about. He seemed just as surprised to see us. When his arm moved to reveal his sword I already had mine out and was in action. His steel hit mine, forcing my arm to vibrate. His face was filled with rage and shock combined, but he fought easily and with experience.

Moving swiftly, he spun, nearly having to back bend to stop my straight down slice at his body. He was good, but not that good. I was better. His face began to turn red with exertion.

I grinned and kicked him in the back so hard he fell forward onto his knees. My katana hissed along his blade and then sliced into his back. He cried out, but I was already moving, taking his head. Just as fast as I took that he turned into ash. The screaming would be a problem. Guards would hear it and be on their way.

"Crap on toast." I hissed, moving fast now.

Everyone hurried after me. With my covered elbow I smashed a window, jumping in. The alarms went off, but no one said anything. The screaming guard gave us away already. Vampire hearing would have heard that a mile away. All of us climbed in with little effort. With my signal we separated, taking rooms to make sure that Fiona or anyone else wasn't in them.

Electa hurried up the steps, followed by Gideon and Luther to check upstairs. The house was fucking huge. The downstairs opened up to a huge lobby living room type area. The marble was a tan color. The only carpet was a brightly colored piece, where the couch and sofa set. A fireplace was lit and wine glasses set on the glass coffee table in the center. She had company. Probably a buyer, which meant they would be at the warehouse and not at the mansion.

Moving downstairs, again Electa in front, she whispered it was clear, so we started moving forward again checking the rooms. Not even the help was around. That was probably to keep them from seeing the buyer to keep the transactions private. Now that I thought about it, we never even had ideas of who the buyers would be, besides Ben. They were pretty discreet, and that would explain why the Covert had a successful business. Declan had ignored the problem for far too long. Now things were so fucked up, more lives would be lost, and not just the usual victims.

After searching the rest of the upstairs, we found the basement door in the kitchen, like we figured. The lights were on downstairs, so first I crept down, giving the rest of my people the signal to hold back. Slowly, I moved peeking to see if anyone was there, but there wasn't a soul in sight. So I gave another signal, allowing them to follow me again.

Making it downstairs, we came to an area that was completely finished. There was nothing but carpet on the floor, but the walls were done nicely in burgundy and gold. There were wall lamps lit up with real oil. I walked around trying to find an entry point. Then I saw the cracks of a door that from a distance would look like another part of the wall. There wasn't a door handle, so I stood there trying to figure it out.

Eli came up next to me, looking like a spy. He stared at the door I was at and moved his hand toward himself. The door flew off the hinges, leaving me with my mouth open. "Shh!" I hissed.

He rolled his eyes. "Seriously? In three seconds this place will be filled with her guards. And she probably has been alerted already." He frowned. "I don't know if we should even go in."

"We really don't have any options." I said back to him.

Feet stomped upstairs and Andy cleared his throat. "If we are going, we should go now before they get down here."

All of us were downstairs in the basement trapped now. If we went up, we would face the vampire guards. If we went into the tunnel, we would run into whatever waited. It would probably be Fiona, but I would take six on one any day. That was if she didn't have them waiting. Inhaling, I motioned them to follow, Eli right behind me.

The tunnel was lit up from lamps on the walls, showing it wasn't anything fancy. They dug just enough to fit one person down at a time. It would be a long trek, but that was okay, as long as we found her eventually. Behind me Gideon closed the door, this side had a knob. The curious part of me wondered how to get in. There was probably some kind of switch, like moving one of the lamps on the walls. Or maybe "Open says me" would have worked. Thinking about that, I walked through the tunnel making sure I took in all the dark areas, not that I ran into a monster of some sort. AKA Fiona.

Someone behind me stumbled, but I continued, figuring if there was a sprained ankle they would say something. When it came to supernatural that was a rare occurrence anyway. Amazingly, no one was following us. I took that as two possibilities. One, this whole thing was a setup. Which it could have been, since she was the one that sent me the crazy ass vision. Two, they didn't know about the secret tunnel. That was possible, considering Fiona would only want so many people knowing about her Covert.

Trying to contact Mitch was proving to be a problem underground. There was some serious interference, so we couldn't let him know how close we were. It could be an issue if something bad went down inside and he wouldn't know if it was something he should come in on. Unless his vampire hearing could tell we were inside the building.

When we neared the end there was complete silence. The closer we got the bigger the feeling that this was another trap got. I didn't know how else to capture her though and neither did Eli. We had to go in basically with guns blazing, not something I wanted. We should have attacked the warehouse first. That would have been the better move, but Fiona probably suspected that, so we took the second option. We ruined our element of surprise when the guard gave us away. Dumb bastard.

Before I could look out the opening, Luther squeezed through the front, ignoring the protest of Eli when he tried to get by. "Let me go first. I owe this much to you."

"Luther, get back there before I ring your neck." I hissed.

Expecting him to follow orders and not run out in front of me, I shrieked in shock. He stormed out, accepting any punishment that came out. Only nothing did. He stood out in the opening waiting and looking. He turned his gaze on me and shrugged. Then without warning, his head slid off his neck, falling to the ground with his body following. No!

Trying to grab me, Eli cried out my name when I ran out, my katana ready. I spotted Fiona several feet away looking surprised that I came out charging. Obviously she thought everyone was a killer like her and I sent someone else to do my dirty work. My team followed, each moving in a way to make sure they took in their surroundings.

Fiona was alone and she was all ours. Unless she had a surprise and vampires would pop out of thin air. My demon was clapping for joy inside thinking, "Yay blood for meeeee!" And my vampire was the more logical of the two with her "We're fucked." Only she would be depressing enough to see that, even though Fiona was only one vampire. How many regular vampires made up one Ancient? She could take down an army of vampires if she wanted to.

She was godlike in her appearance. Her picture didn't do her justice, because in front of me was someone that would outdo Jennifer Lopez on a good day. Her long brown hair was done up in a professional style with long twisted tendrils coming down. Her piercing blue eyes were cold, fearless, but excited with the possibilities of tonight. This was a woman that did not fear death. She went at it in a full run, thinking that even though she might die, she would at least get that one last high from the blood spilt.

Her movement was elegant and floaty as if she was walking on air. Her eyes watched me carefully, already knowing my next move. At least that was how it felt. I watched her, ready to move when she did, but Eli had to step forward, drawing the attention away from me. "Fiona." He said.

At first she seemed surprised, but then it changed into delight. She would enjoy spilling his blood. I didn't have to hear her say it to know it from the expression on her flawless face. "Hello, Eli, fancy seeing you here." Her gaze went to me as she kept her sword up, prepared to take me on if I dared to move.

Eli shrugged. "I am King now, so you must obey me."

She laughed, throwing her head back, mouth open. When she looked back at him her eyes were no longer cold, but there was something there, love? No. "You were always so commanding. I would have stayed back then, allow you to have your way with me, just to feel what it was like to be controlled. Maybe even loved." She shrugged. "Carter gave me those things, but he kept talking about stopping our business. That maybe those people deserved to live, but he didn't understand that we were meant to rule and enjoy their blood. We rule as the Ancients. Don't you see, my love?"

Her mentioning of Carter only made me angrier, so I stepped forward, her head snapping into my direction. She figured calling Eli "my love" would win him over. Maybe to some love sick lonely fool, but Eli was mine and soon she would realize that when I took her head.

"And this is your true mate. The one who killed my son!" She growled.

"No offense lady, but your son was fucked up. Who thought someone like him would need to kidnap a woman in order to get laid? Kind of pathetic if you ask me." I said in disgust.

She screamed angrily, coming at me with the sword held high, like she wanted to slice me in half. I moved quickly before she could come down on me. Her sword hit the concrete of the warehouse floor, sparks flying from the impact. I grinned, pissing her off more as she charged me again. My katana met her sword, both of our strengths pressed against each other. I kicked out with my leg right into her kidney. She fell to her knees, but dodged my attempt to bring down my blade on her.

Swiftly she was on her feet, a smirk on her face. "I haven't had this much fun in a long time."

Rolling my eyes, I waited for her move. She spun, her hair and white dress she wore swiveled with her. Only I didn't move in time, so the blade sliced my leg. I cried out, falling to one knee, but dove to the side when she came for a second attempt.

Rapidly she was flying across the room we were in, slamming against the wall. Dust blew around everywhere from the impact. It was then I realized Eli used his powers on her. She leapt down unfazed. "Hardly playing fair, Eli. Want to use power? So be it!" She snarled, casting her hand in my direction. I was airborne, then floundering around like a bug in water. I slammed into the wall, seeing stars. My body slid down, the pain excruciating.

Electa came over to my aid to check me. I heard Fiona laughing at how I was so powerless to her. Anger rose in me, but Electa held me down as she checked my head. "You're bleeding." She said.

"I don't care. That bitch is mine!" Immediately I was on my feet running. Fiona saw me coming, she threw out her hand catching Eli off guard, so he went flying. Then she came at me with her sword. I pictured myself behind her, then I was swinging the blade down. But she had already spun around trying to find me, so my sword went through her shoulder cutting down. Her arm fell as she let out an ear pitching scream.

Grinning, I kicked her arm away. She glared at me, her fangs out and spit flying from her lips as she spoke, "You will pay for that! Not only for the death of my son, but from daring to invade my home!"

Dodging back when she tried to hit me with the sword, I winked. "Whatever makes you feel better. You wanted this. You sent me that vision." I said.

She smiled. "Like that, did you? So Mr. Gideon knows what happened to his sister?"

Shit. She knew who his sister was.

Gideon came forward. "What of my sister?"

"She is dead. I killed her!" Fiona snarled. And when hatred appeared on Gideon's face, pleasure filled hers.

With a roar Gideon came at her, his sword raised, but Fiona was already anticipating that. She swung before I could intercept, slicing across his chest. His whole body seemed to have stopped in mid-motion and then crumble. Electa cried out, horror on her face as she ran to his side to check him. Anger roared inside of me as fire prickled against my skin. Fiona threw her head back laughing her eyes lit up. Eli stepped forward, but I put a hand up to stop him. He debated, I could tell by the expression on his face, but decided against it, so he stepped back, allowing me to stay in control.

Proceeding on Fiona I swung my katana, which she met without a single hesitation, already expecting the advance. Suddenly pain seared my brain as a forced vision was coming on me. She got past the shields that Lucifer helped me create. Fear went down my spine, like a dead man's fingers. My knees buckled and my eyes were wide as I watched her lift her sword up to take my head. She smiled a smile of a sociopath as her hand came down. I heard Eli crying out, but at the last second I smiled, flicking my hand. Surprise flickered on her face before her body went flying. She held on to the sword with her one hand as she slammed into the wall, dust flying everywhere as the rock beneath went to pieces.

Creating a ball of fire in my hands, I went toward her, watching as she tried to focus her gaze on me. I blew at the ball of fire, watching it swim through the air until it found her, as if it had a mind of its own. It went up her legs covering her entire body and she screamed, high pitched, making it feel like needles were being forced through my ear drums.

Abruptly her burning body came flying off the wall toward me. She crashed into me, forcing me to the ground, flaming body turning into an unrecognizable corpse. Her sword arm tried to come down on me, but it was weakening dramatically, pieces of skin burning and flying off in crumbling ash. Kicking her off with my feet, she landed a few yards away. I snagged my katana off the floor, where I managed to drop it at some point. Her mouth gaped open, the jaw slowly becoming unhinged as the fire licked along the now showing bones. It was a slow death, slower than a normal fire would have done. Torture from a demon. Me. With one fast swing I took off her head, watching as the flaming skull fell from her shoulders and finally into a pile of crisp.

Chapter Seventeen

Gideon survived, but barely. Electa had dragged him off to the side, trying to keep him awake until one of the twin vampires was able to get the first aid kit out. Werewolves healed, but the silver in the sword was harmful, so we had to care for it as if it were a mortal wound. I think that was the incident that truly brought Electa and Gideon together, because she took care of him afterwards too. Finally the distant girl I knew most of my life was letting someone get close to her.

When the last of Fiona's body turned to a pile of ash, we looked around the warehouse not finding a single guard. It was almost as if she wanted this to end her life. You know how sometimes a crazy person could have one single

normal thought floating around inside
somewhere, fully aware of how their life wasn't
normal and knew the only way out was to end
it? Eli and I figured somewhere inside her mind
she was aware enough to want to die. Her life
had been full of killing and torture, not caring
about those she hurt. She killed people she
loved. That I loved. Carter would always be in
my heart. We had visited his grave a few days
after the death of Fiona. We even buried her
next to him, because somewhere she loved him.
Ben had eventually been added in a neighboring
plot. It was hard to believe Carter had been
involved with the Covert at one point in life. I
was disappointed, but at least he ended that life
and started a brand new one.

The warehouse had close to forty people
that were malnourished. Some of them on the
brink of death, but with care and some time
spent in the hospital they would make it. In
some rooms the victims were already dead from
not eating for weeks. Some completely drained
of their blood. They hung from their chains with
wounds so infected the smell was filling the
warehouse, nearly making us all throw up from
the stench alone. Seeing the actual festering
wounds made the vampire twins run from the
room to throw up in a corner. I thought they
were warriors?

We had come to the victims of Fiona's when she was forcing the vision on me. Some were headless, blessed with a quick death. Others bled out slowly, suffering the entire time, maybe dying seconds before we arrived, since some of the bodies were even warm. Gideon's sister was still alive when we found her. She would heal thanks to her werewolf blood, but Fiona had apparently ended the vision before I could be sure that Gideon's sister had died. She just wanted to temp me. Why she kept Gideon's sister for nearly two years was a mystery to us all.

I never did find Lucy. There was no evidence of where she was at. Eli took my hand, trying to offer silent support. Someone had her, but we wouldn't know who unless Fiona kept some kind of paperwork. We didn't believe she was dead, since making money was the main reason for the business. Victims that never were chosen died from lack of food and water. She at no time bothered feeding them. She allowed her own guards to abuse them until they were chosen by someone.

Fiona had told her guards to stay away from the warehouse if we came. That explained why no one chased us down the tunnel. She wanted to die like we thought. According to Mitch, the guards were kept outside, only doing enough guarding to make sure a man and a girl escaped. I had asked what the girl looked like and by the description I realized it had been Lucy. Fiona made the last move. Even after her death, she won. Lucy was gone and probably experiencing a life no one would want to endure. I was determined to find her.

*

We had returned home after that. No one spoke. Well, not really. Just enough to make sure wounds were taken care of. The only people who really did anything was me, Eli and Gideon. After Ben died, Fiona just gave up, even if she really didn't see that. We eliminated an Ancient. I knew somewhere inside Eli was mourning her loss. The Demigod made them mates, after all. A bit of information that he left out. We would definitely have a talk about secrets and part of me wondering if I could truly forgive him for not actually talking to me about it.

It wasn't over yet. We had to find Lucy, so I would make it my life's mission to find her. Someone had her and they were ballsy enough to take her despite the blood line. Who would dare take Carter's niece? Was it a request? I thought so. Someone else had been out to get him. After learning more things about his past, he probably had more enemies than I could imagine. Now that he was dead, you would think everyone would just end the wars, but that didn't seem to be the case with Lucy still missing.

Like we thought, Fiona kept records on the victims she sold to vampires. Eli said we would be going through every one of them and visiting their homes to see if they were there. Some were human and probably already dead. I wasn't sure if vampire laws had expiration dates on crimes committed, like some of the human ones, but Eli didn't seem to act as if he would be held back to handing out punishments. He was quiet and reserved, which only had me fearing that he was a bomb waiting to explode. Not something you wanted to see in your King, let alone the one you loved.

I laid in bed after taking a shower. It had been a week since Fiona died. Eli sat next to me, examining any wounds that might have been left. Despite my vampire healing, I felt like someone ran me over with an eighteen wheeler a hundred times over, but I didn't bother to refuse Eli when he started to kiss my neck, seeking comfort from me, though he may have been unaware of it.

"Saved us all, Blake." He said softly, his breath tickling my ear when he spoke.

Rolling over to my stomach, I did a half shrug. "She wanted to die, I just helped a little."

He chuckled. "How considerate of you."

Smiling into the pillow, I shuddered as his lips lightly trailed down my shoulder to my side. "I am a helpful kind of gal."

"Well, I could use a little help myself, you know?" He said suggestively.

"Oh, and what can I do to help the Vampire King?" I asked, not even bothering to look at him. I had a sneaky suspicion it was a bad question to ask. He had something up his sleeve, waiting to pounce on me, and well the girl in me was debating on escaping out the nearest window. Eli was all about long term and I wasn't ready for that. Sure I loved him and I could readily admit that now, but was I ready to marry someone for eternity? Forever? Maybe I was overthinking it. In ways nothing would be different, since we would be together for our entire lives anyway. It was like a dog that thought he had freedom in his yard, but there was that damn invisible fence preventing him from crossing the lines. If you love someone enough, you take the leap. It was all about the risk. Love was risk, right?

Shivering when his fingers lightly went down my back, his lips touched my ear. "You know what I want to ask, don't you?"

I debated on lying, trying to pretend that I was clueless. Maybe even act like the word marriage was a foreign language to me. I could pull that off. Maybe. Might piss him off. So with those thoughts, I rolled over onto my back, allowing him to look over me, fire in his eyes as he did. "Do you love me?" He asked.

Now, was that the question or just the start of how to trap me? Complications. Complications I rather avoid. My life was supposed to be simple, yet, here this man came tromping through, messing everything up. And they say women are high maintenance. I would like someone to prove that theory!

"Of course."

"Let's get a house and share a room with me." He said.

Surprised, I just stared at him for a while, unsure on how to respond. It only confused him and eventually made him panic when I delayed answering. He sucked in a breath, prepared to make his case, but I put a finger to his lips, relieved it wasn't the giant M word. "What about the kids?" I asked.

Confused for a couple of seconds, he suddenly flashed a smile. "Oh, everyone will be coming, but the way I have it planned will make it like two houses. Guardians on one side and our home on the other. I want big headquarters, so we can increase the number of the Guardians. We need a lot of organization, because Declan slacked off in everything, so things are far from orderly." He said, longwinded. "This weekend is when everything becomes truly official and I need you by my side, Blake. If you leave me, I won't be the same man. You are what keeps me happy, so stay here and command your Guardians."

Smiling, I lifted my head to kiss him softly. "Of course, but I have to lay some ground rules here. I mean, I don't pick up dirty clothes off the floor, and well, you know how the lid staying up in the bathroom pisses a woman off? Well, it makes me extremely mad because once I did fall in the toilet." He started laughing before touching my neck with his lips and pressing my hands back into the pillow with his. "Oh, and I suck at cooking."

"We will have a chef, love." He said.

Even though Lucifer used the endearment, hearing Eli use it warmed my heart. I ran my fingers through his gorgeous hair, admiring the model good looks of his. He was perfection and I wanted him bad.

Rolling him over onto his back, I surprised him. I straddled him, trying to contain a shudder from feeling his length pressed against me. "I sometimes don't shower for two days." I said, rubbing myself against him as both our eyes rolled back.

He groaned before saying, "Well, then I think I have to rescind my offer, because a smelly woman is hardly appropriate for a mighty Vampire King."

Laughing, I shoved him back with the palm of my hand when he tried to reach up for me. "I will have to agree with you there. So I guess frequent showers will be in order, but I think I might need some help."

Eli pretended to think this over for a while, until I punched him in the arm. Then he looked at me with a sudden serious expression on his face and said, "Agreed."

Printed in Germany
by Amazon Distribution
GmbH, Leipzig